Child of Mars

This book is a work of fiction. Names, characters, places, and incidents either are products of the author's imagination or are used fictitiously. Any resemblance to actual events, locales, or persons, living or dead, is entirely coincidental.

ISBN: 978-0-9953013-5-1 paperback

For Lisa, Nathan, Brendan and Nicholas

Claim your free ebook of short science fiction stories by going to http://prudenauthor.com

Contents

Child of Mars

Book 3 in the Mars Ascendant Series

D.M. Pruden

CHAPTER 1

Bettani crept down the darkened corridor, a second pair of soft-soled boots tight in her grip. Silently, she counted her steps in the darkness. She had rehearsed for days the exact number required to arrive at the subject's unmarked door.

Her name is Adrianna, she thought.

That was the name embedded in the tiny ID chip now in her pocket. She did not, in fact, believe subject 647 ever possessed an actual name.

It was supposed to take place during the sleep cycle. Up until the lights failed, as Carlos promised they would, she had tossed on her bed, worried she was undergoing an elaborate loyalty test. It was possible that the whole thing was a trap. Her heart pounded as she imagined entering Adrianna's room, to be greeted by the director, delighted to uncover another traitor.

Upon taking her final counted footstep, Bettani groped for the door handle. The latch released, and she realized that Carlos had succeeded in overriding the backup lockdown protocol. With great caution, she eased the door open and peered uselessly into the blackness. After a moment her ears guided her to the bedside. She awoke Adrianna and covered the child's mouth to silence her startled questions.

"Shhh. It's Bettani. I'm here to take you somewhere. Put on these boots."

She listened to the girl fumble with the unfamiliar footwear. A small voice whispered, "Where are we going?"

"The power is out. I need to get you to safety."

Following her instructions, she pulled the hypo-spray containing the programmed chip from her pocket. In the darkness, she located the small wrist and traced the arm up to her neck.

"This won't hurt," she said, comforting herself with the words more than the child. If Adrianna winced when the hypo was applied, Bettani couldn't tell.

Adrianna's small hand found hers, and they slowly made their way toward the door, momentarily fumbling to locate it. With her confidence growing, she guided them back the way she'd come. On reaching the corridor access, the hallway was illuminated in dull red emergency lighting.

Damn, that was faster than we wanted.

No longer hindered by the darkness, she ran down the next passage, pulling Adrianna along. It would take another fifty seconds for the AI to reboot and ten seconds after that for it to determine the girl's cell was empty. Though the new chip she'd injected would scramble the subdermal tracking device in the girl, its effect wouldn't last. Her heart pounded as she rushed them through the disabled security doorways leading to the hangar deck.

Upon opening the last door, the imposing figure of a well-muscled man with long dark hair and a grey-flecked beard blocked her way. Bettani released the child's hand and threw her arms around Carlos's neck.

"You made it," she said before kissing him.

Their reunion was interrupted by the security klaxon sounding through the facility. Concern clouded his handsome features. "They recovered faster than expected."

"Are we too late?" she asked fearfully.

He glanced down the corridor. "Perhaps not," he said. He pulled from his satchel two disks, each the size of a large coin, and handed them to her. "Do you remember what I told you about these?"

She nodded. "Yes, they're explosives, but what are they for?"

"They will disable the locking mechanism of the access

doors. I would set them, but I need to get the aircraft prepped or we'll never get away."

She pushed Adrianna toward him. "You go. I'll set these and join you."

He hesitated for a brief moment, like he wanted to tell her something, but seemed to change his mind and kissed her. Carlos took the child by the hand. She struggled against him until Bettani told her, "Everything is okay. You can go with him. He's here to help. I won't be long."

Offering no further resistance, the girl followed him to the awaiting ship. Bettani advanced to the door down the corridor but only got halfway there when it swung open and three armed security guards burst through. She watched them in stunned silence as they levelled their weapons at her and without any hesitation opened fire.

Pain ripped through her body as the projectiles tore through her torso and limbs. She collapsed to the floor, her breath bubbling with foaming blood. Helpless, she peered through the open doorway to the hangar at her lover standing in the hatchway of the flyer, watching. The last thing Bettani saw was a disappointed look cross his face as he reached into his pocket and produced a small device. Moments later, as the guards approached her dying body, the small disks still in her hand exploded.

CHAPTER 2

The distant rumble caught my attention before I noticed the faint vibrations. It was just a minor tremor. Most of the activity of Olympus Mons amounted to small mars-quakes with little damage done and even less notice by the locals. The unpredictable eruptions from the reactivated volcano rarely produced more than another belch of water vapour, sulphur, and carbon dioxide into the planet's maturing atmosphere. An occasional pyroclastic flow would cascade down the flanks of the massive mountain, but any of the communities that once lay in the path of such things had long since relocated. From where I stood, the uneasy volcano seemed to be little more than a smoking mound along the horizon, with only the irregular shaking of the ground a reminder of its distant, blessed fury.

Only a decade before, it had lain extinct, a poignant memorial to what this planet had once been. That was until the mythical Mother of Mars miraculously sent a spaceship crashing into the mountain. Even this long after the event, the most brilliant minds had yet to unravel how the miracle had been accomplished. None were privy as I was to the details of the technology long declared a state secret.

So Mons and a hundred other volcanoes now belched their pillowy plumes of gas, and the planet became more habitable with each passing day. The still toxic atmosphere was now thick enough that I no longer required a pressure suit to venture outside. I glanced down at the pebble-strewn ground under my boots to see the hardy, newly introduced plant life had not suffered beneath the treads of our vehicle.

"They're everywhere," I muttered to myself.

"What did you say?" Dylan's voice in my headset roused me from my thoughts.

"Lichens are all over the place. Nothing was here six months ago."

His footsteps crunched as he rounded our transport. He stopped and surveyed me. With his silly grin partly obstructed by his breathing mask, his handsome features were unmistakable. He had not aged a day over the last decade.

"Now you're a botanist?"

"Don't be an ass. I was just noting how fast things have changed since our last visit."

"What doesn't change is the demand for your services, Mel. They are squawking over the comm, wondering where you are. People are lined up out the door."

"The clinic is overbooked again?"

"What did you expect? You're the only doctor they see on a regular basis."

"I'm the only doctor they ever see. Nobody else wants to leave their cozy life on Olympia. I'm fighting a losing battle down here, Dylan."

"You're doing what is necessary."

"What's necessary is for the fucking government to care. They need to supply the med-tech these people require. I'm restricted to twentieth century medicine down here. I'm one step beyond being a witch doctor."

He stood in silence, staring at me. The part of his face I could see behind his mask showed he was struggling to contain something he thought funny.

"And don't you dare say anything about me being a witch already, asshole."

"I would never dream of saying that."

His forced seriousness collapsed, and we both shared a laugh at my expense.

Regaining his composure, he said, "In all seriousness, we need to get a move on or we'll fall further behind schedule. We are two days late because of that damned broken tread. This machine is getting past its best-before date." He rested a hand on the hull of the transport that served as our mobile home.

"I'm entitled to grouse occasionally."

He grasped my shoulders and pointed me toward the airlock of the domed settlement we were camped before.

"Complain while you walk. Your patients are waiting, and I need to get parts for the vehicle."

We trudged along in silence for ten metres or so.

"It isn't right," I said. "Mars is basically terraforming itself. The government should free up money to entice more physicians to work in these settlements. Even to set up permanent practices."

"Our illustrious dictator has other ambitions. None of his puppet administration gives a shit about anyone poor or stupid enough to live on the surface. To them we're all a bunch of dirty terraformers who are no longer necessary."

"His dislike for the planet hasn't stopped him from building his brand new capital. The rumour is that it will have city-wide gravity generators. The pampered elite are not going to expose themselves to any of the health problems of living under Martian gravity."

"Melanie Destin, you sound like one of the rebels. You need to be careful."

I rolled my eyes. "I only spout my subversive thoughts to you. To everyone else I am 'Doctor Corrine Ross: Have stethoscope, will travel.'" I emphasized my comment with air quotes.

"That's more like it. Mundi may think we're dead, but I don't want to risk doing anything that would lead him to believe otherwise."

We stopped at the massive airlock door and signalled our arrival.

"Just once I want to stand in the central plaza of one of

these settlements and shout at the top of my lungs, 'I am the Mother of Mars, come to liberate you from your oppression.'"

"What will that accomplish?"

"Hell, I don't know. Maybe push people to act."

"Talus Varr's rebellion has nothing to show for the past seven years except the ruins of the communities that joined him. Nobody else wants to expose themselves to Mundi's retaliation." He grasped me by my shoulders. "Melanie Destin died when that ship crashed into the planet ten years ago. Let's keep it that way, okay?"

I disengaged from his grasp as the door began to open. "Don't worry. I don't intend to paint a fucking target on my back. Boring old Corrine Ross will go work in the clinic and perform medieval medicine like she always does."

CHAPTER 3

Sixteen hours on my feet was about six more than I wanted to spend, but I was finally finished and had just seen the last patient out the door.

"It was good of you to stay, Doctor Ross. I realize you didn't need to see more than those with an appointment."

I returned the smile of the clinic administrator.

"It will be six weeks before my return, and some of these patients couldn't wait. It was the least I could do."

"Still, I'm sorry we've caused you to fall further behind in your schedule."

"My husband is resourceful. We'll make up the time. I'm sure he can find a shorter route to our next stop."

"Well, please relate my gratitude to him."

When I stepped out of the medical centre, I realized how late it was. Dylan had long ago become accustomed to my desire to accommodate everyone who needed treatment. Even though I had most of the clinic administrators along our route trained to take appointments, there were always last-minute patients who showed up without one. In another life I would have turned them away. I shook my head, still ashamed of who I was in those days. Despite the hardship of our fugitive lifestyle, I liked to think I was now a more compassionate person. Maybe I would live long enough to redeem what was left of my soul.

My stomach rumbling, I set off. Dylan and I had a standing arrangement that we would meet for our meal at the local tavern when I was finished my work. Believing he had been waiting for me for some time, I took a shortcut down a darkened alley. Though perfectly safe to do so in most settlements on Mars, my early life on Terra had trained me to expect otherwise from such places. I traversed the dark corridor, alert to every sound and movement.

From behind, a scuffing noise demanded my attention. A search told me I was alone, but my imagination tried to persuade me that something moved in the shadows of a doorway. Not waiting to learn the truth, I hurried to the end of the lane and out into the central square. There were still a few people about, and I released my held breath and reduced my pace. At the door to the tavern, I glanced back at the empty street. I decided that my imaginings were the result of hunger and fatigue and gave no further thought to strange sounds in the dark.

The place was half full, and a quick survey revealed that Dylan was not present. I put my order in at the bar and took a seat in a quiet corner.

When we began our life in exile together, Dylan and I had learned to be cautious, even a bit paranoid. It was a small price to pay to ensure that the eyes of Regis Mundi never fell on us. Though it was an unwelcome return to the ways of my youth, I adjusted and caution once more became second nature.

Most of the people in the establishment were passingly familiar to me. Over years of visits, I'd treated most of the population at least once. The buzz of quiet conversations was comforting, and I relaxed further. I chuckled, embarrassed by my earlier moment of panic.

The creak of the door heralded the entry of a man and the exit of my reacquired calm. There was something about him that demanded my attention, and I caught myself following his every movement as he placed his order and sat on the other side of the room. He did not look about but scrutinized something pulled from his pocket. Realizing I was staring, I averted my gaze and reviewed the other patrons, confirming that I had indeed met or seen each of them before. The man at the table across the room stood out because he was a stranger, and my senses went into overdrive at that realization.

The fact that he appeared mesmerized by the contents of his cup told me everything necessary to conclude he meant no good. Anyone else would have glanced about the room, but this man had already spied the person he searched for and now tried to mask his interest with feigned preoccupation.

The server brought my food, and I picked at it while keeping an eye on the stranger. Whether he was looking for me or it was merely my imagination, I decided I had to get out of there and back to our camp. When the same waiter approached the man's table with his meal, I took advantage of the distraction and slipped away from my table. The path to the front door was too exposed, so I wove between the tables to the back of the establishment in the direction of the restrooms and the service entrance.

The door to the alleyway had barely swung shut when I broke into a run, determined to put distance between me and the tavern. Ducking into alleys and hurrying along familiar streets, I circuitously made my way toward the airlock. After half an hour of evasion techniques, I found myself crouching in a doorway in an alcove a short walk from my objective. A brief moment of panic was relieved when, searching my satchel, I located my breathing mask, which would allow me to leave the dome. Clutching it, I rose to my feet and looked up to see a shadowed figure enter the lane ahead of me.

Backlit by the lights of the main street and blocking the only exit from the alcove, he advanced with a measured gait. As he approached, my adjusting eyes confirmed him as the man in the tavern.

"Who are you? What do you want with me?"

He halted two paces from me, triumph etched on his face. "It really is you. You're Melanie Destin."

"You're confusing me with someone else."

A flicker of doubt crossed his face as he examined me some

more. "No, you're her. A little older and thinner than your picture, but you're the Mother of Mars."

"Look, even if I were, what would you want with me?"

"Want? Do you realize what finding you is worth to me? You're still alive and here in front of me. I didn't think the rumours were true."

"Yeah, well, you're mistaken. This happens to me a lot. I guess I do look something like her, but trust me, buddy, you're going to feel awfully foolish when you find out how wrong you are."

"Well, that's a risk worth taking, given the reward on your head."

He advanced, and I assumed the defensive posture Dylan had taught me. He stopped and laughed. "Come on, none of that. I don't want to hurt you, but you're going to come with me."

I raised my arm in a fighting stance, and when he moved in, I kneed him in the groin. He doubled over in pain and collapsed to the ground.

Without a second thought I leapt over him and fled out of the alcove and down the street, searching for a place to hide. Hearing his curses grow louder behind me, I ducked around a corner and ran into something solid. Knocked down and stunned, I looked up into the face of Dylan. He reached down and helped me to my feet, but before he could ask me anything, the man followed me into the alley.

"Hey, hands off. She's mine."

Dylan glanced at me, his left eyebrow raised. Shaking his head, he pushed me protectively behind him and confronted the stranger.

"Walk away, friend. There's no need for anyone to get hurt here."

The man sneered and pulled a menacing knife from his belt. "You slink away and I won't cut you up."

Dylan made no reaction but stared the man down, every muscle in his toned body a tensed spring waiting to be released. Though we had lived on Mars for ten years, Dylan took the opportunity in every town to train in gyms with simulated Terran gravity. They were expensive to use and rare to find, but he was not willing to let his skills lapse, acquired through years of military training. At that moment I was grateful for his determination.

The man lunged, and in a swift, blurred movement, Dylan pivoted to avoid the blade and delivered a disabling blow to the attacker's throat. Falling to his knees, gasping for air, he clutched at his injured windpipe. I watched as Dylan dug through the dying man's pockets. He pulled out the sheet the man had been studying in the tavern, examined it, then shoved it into his own pocket. Wordlessly, Dylan picked up the dropped weapon and with no hesitation buried it in his opponent's chest.

"What the fuck did you do that for?" I said, finally discovering my voice.

"Come on." He grabbed my hand and led me toward the airlock.

CHAPTER 4

Perspiration glistened on the balding head of Justin LaFoire. He struggled to maintain his composure in the presence of the Supreme Dictator. As intended, his emotional discomfort was compounded by the stress of the Terran-normal gravity maintained in the audience chamber. The long, thin, shaking limbs of his emaciated body belied a lifetime spent on Mars. Because the man's failure had displeased him, Mundi forced him to stand to deliver his report.

"Et effugium in…subiectum animan eius…"

"You're butchering the language. Speak in standard, you incompetent fool!" As a rule, Regis Mundi forbade the vulgar common tongue to be uttered in his presence. Learning new information about the incident at his facility was not the purpose of the interrogation. The details had been reviewed with his security chief. Mundi wanted to make an example of his former research director, and he still debated about what form that would take. Until a decision was reached, letting the whimpering idiot squirm before him served as his morning sport.

The nervous man offered an appreciative nod and continued.

"The subject escaped after an explosive device was detonated…"

"Yes, yes, I am aware of the sordid details of your failure. My question, which your miserable grasp of Latin failed you to comprehend, concerns the reason that particular asset was abducted."

Terror flashed across LaFoire's face. He struggled to regain his composure. "Subject 647 is the only one that exhibited encouragement the process might work."

Mundi fixed the man with a piercing stare and clumsily adjusted his portly form to lean forward in his chair.

"You managed to lose the only candidate that might allow me to control the discovery?"

LaFoire swallowed. "There was nothing definitive. The subject only exhibited the slightest indications that we are on the right path, Dominus. More experiments are required before we can declare..."

Mundi held up an imperious hand to halt the man's babbling. He stared judgementally for several seconds at the broken person before him. Brief recollections surfaced of this same man arrogantly declaring confidence of success. Shaking his head, he turned to the man who quietly stood at his side and spoke in Latin.

"Morgan, I want this fool crucified outside of the research facility—a reminder to his successor." He punctuated his statement with a grim smile.

The tall, muscled young man's reply demonstrated flawless mastery of the dead tongue. "As you wish, Dominus."

He signalled with a slight nod to the two guards who stood behind LaFoire. They seized him by each arm and dragged the weeping man out of the audience chamber. When the great door to the room had closed behind them, Mundi fixed his lieutenant with a thoughtful look, waiting for his analysis.

"This shows all the signs of rebel involvement, sire."

"Of course it does. But what does Talus Varr want with this subject? The experiments didn't result in the kind of control we need."

He rose from his throne and winced in pain. Morgan leaned forward to assist him, but Mundi waved him away. "Readjust the room to Martian gravity."

The younger man nodded and a preoccupied expression

crossed his face as he accessed the environmental controls with his cortical implant. Within moments Mundi relaxed as the pull on his ancient body lessened.

"Ah, much better. I've hated this accursed planet for most of my adult life, and yet, ironically, if I ever manage to conquer Terra before I expire, I'll never be able to live on its surface. The universe possesses a perverse sense of humour."

Morgan maintained silence.

Mundi chuckled and appraised his lieutenant with a critical eye. "You've learned the wisdom of keeping your thoughts to yourself. You remind me of your predecessor."

Sadness overcame him, and he mumbled to himself, "Oh, Felix, how I wish you hadn't betrayed me. I could use your council now."

"I apologize, sire, but I could not hear you."

Regis Mundi sighed. "Did you ever meet Felix Altius?"

"I only met him once, just before the—" He stopped himself.

Mundi frowned. "You were going to refer to the terraforming event, weren't you?"

The young man nodded. "Yes, Dominus."

"Yes, the great 'miracle' when the alien spaceship crashed into Mars and restarted the planetary tectonics. Now the dead woman responsible is celebrated around the globe as 'the Mother of Mars,' and my traitorous servant who aided her has fled into exile."

He glared at Morgan, studying his face for a sign of doubt. "You think me ungrateful and mad, don't you?"

"No, Dominus, I recognize what their interference cost the Martian people."

"If only others could be as astute as you. A terraformed planet was never destined to be. The only solution is for our people to assume their rightful place on a conquered and cleansed Terra. The so-called Mother of Mars used the nanites that were intended as my weapon of conquest to change everything. Now, because of her, people actually believe transforming this rock within a generation is possible."

"But sire, all is not lost. The discovery in the asteroid belt is rich with dormant alien nanotechnology."

"You are familiar with Felix Altius's reports?"

"Yes, Dominus. The capabilities of the nanomachines that compose that vessel are greater than the ones destroyed, and they offer far more potential than mere conquest. Melanie Destin demonstrated that they can be controlled when she directed the course of the terraforming ship. Her genetic material is still in your possession, and progress is being made —"

"I appreciate your enthusiasm, Morgan, but you heard that traitorous scum yourself. He only managed to achieve indications of 'potential influence' over the nanite sample we secured. It is a far cry from the power that woman exhibited."

"It is all the more reason to double our efforts to recover subject 647 from the rebels. My spy within their ranks informs me the stolen resource is not yet in their possession. There is still time."

"How deep is your agent placed inside the rebel hierarchy?"

"He meets irregularly with Talus Varr. Shall I order him to assassinate your enemy at the next opportunity?"

"No, you will do nothing until I tell you. Knowing Varr as I do, there will be contingencies in place to assure his death will not hamper his rebellion. We will not move until we can stamp out his movement forever."

"It will be as you command, Dominus. What are your orders about subject 647?"

"Spare no resource. It must be tracked down and recovered before it can disappear into Talus Varr's network."

Morgan nodded in acknowledgement with a pensive expression.

Mundi studied the younger man. "You're hesitating over something. What is it?"

"Apologies, sire, it is trivial; a rumour that came to my attention. It is nothing worthy of your concern."

Mundi smiled slyly as he resumed sitting on his throne. Collapsing into it, he sighed. "I will be the judge of what is important. Tell me."

The young lieutenant bowed his head. "It is a trifling thing, but activities around an old, related rumour are increasing."

"What rumour?" Mundi probed, annoyance in his voice.

"Certain interest groups across the planet are posting bounties for proof that the Mother of Mars still lives."

"What?"

"They are insignificant in number, sire, all seeming to vie with each other to prove their competing claims. I believe the organizers wish to bring any information they gather to you in the hope you will reward them. They are desperate fanatics, nothing more."

"How long have such rumours been in circulation?"

"About ten standard years. My research tells me they began with rumoured sightings in the communities around Olympus Mons and gradually spread to include the former terraforming settlements near the Valles Marineris. Most took the form of idle comments in chat groups on the planetary cortex. They remained an entertaining fancy until about two years ago. Multiple bounties have been issued in the past three months."

"What prompted this change?"

"Individuals wish to exploit the delusions of a small cult of worship that has formed around the woman."

"You will investigate this. Use your discretion to discover what stokes the optimism of these people and shut them down. The last thing we need is for the rabble to make a saint of her that Talus Varr can exploit."

CHAPTER 5

After we reached our transport, I relived the previous few minutes during our vehicle's airlock recycle sequence. When the amber light by the door indicated nominally breathable air, I ripped off my mask.

"What the fuck just happened back there?"

Dylan met my eyes through his faceplate. Without a word he turned his back and proceeded to the cockpit.

Long experience taught me he wouldn't answer until he was good and ready, so I followed him and sat in the passenger seat to sulk while I caught my breath. I regretted removing my ventilation pack prematurely, but I stoically suffered through the discomfort while the last of the air in the cabin recycled. He set the vehicle in motion and assured himself that the AI functioned properly. When satisfied everything was in order, he removed his mask and placed it on the console before turning to face me.

I waited for him to say something, but he dug into his pocket and handed me the crumpled sheet retrieved from our attacker. It was cheap, recycled plaz-stock, common throughout the surface settlements, and showed signs of long usage. On it was printed a ten-year-old holo-image of my face. Above my younger self the headline read, The Mother of Mars Lives, and beneath were the terms of a bounty for anyone who could prove I was alive.

"What the hell is this?"

"Isn't it obvious?" said Dylan. "The particular group that printed this believes you never died in that crashed ship. They are offering a reward that is a fraction of what Mundi would pay them for the same information. There are maybe a dozen similarly competing groups around the planet."

"That guy was no local. He wasn't even a Martian."

"No, he moved like an Earther. Ex-military by his fighting style." He removed the blood-caked knife from his belt and examined it before placing it on the console between us. "This is Terran marine issue. I think he was a mercenary looking for an easy score."

"Not that I'm ungrateful for your rescue, but why the hell did you kill him?"

"He was a bounty hunter, Mel. I couldn't risk him following or even passing on that he'd seen you."

I sat back in the seat, letting the full impact of it all sink in.

"I'll bet he couldn't believe his good fortune when he spotted me in that tavern."

"Guys like him do not rely on dumb luck. He'd been on your trail for some time. He probably saw or learned of you in that settlement during one of your visits and waited for your return."

A shiver ran down my spine as I recalled the feeling of being followed on my way from the clinic. "What are we going to do? There will be others like him in every town on our circuit."

"I've worried about something like this happening for a long time, and, frankly, I'm surprised it took this long."

"You never said anything."

He graced me with a tender look. "You're happier since we came down here; much more than you were on Olympia. Your work is fulfilling, and I appreciate how much it means to you. If I bothered you with my every concern, it would diminish that for you."

"But you suspected this sort of thing going on?"

"Rumours began stirring a couple of years ago, but when I checked into them they amounted to nothing more than wishful thinking. The people grow restless, and while they're afraid to openly support Varr's rebellion, it doesn't stop them from looking for a beacon of hope."

"Me?"

"You're responsible for a miracle nobody imagined possible. The terraforming of Mars is now a reality because of you. Naturally, people don't want to believe you perished."

The rumble of the engines filled the silence that fell for a moment.

"What should we do?"

He took my hand in his. "We could settle down somewhere. Some place we've never been where nobody will recognize us."

"And do what? Raise hydroponic vegetables and lots of children?"

"Would that be such a bad life?"

"Despite my posthumous title, I'm not motherhood material."

"Nonsense..."

"No, Dylan," I said, more forcefully than I intended. "I don't know how to be a proper mother. Mine was an alcoholic whore who turned me out when I was ten. I fended for myself in the streets of a Terran slum, foraging for my survival. I haven't the foggiest notion of what a normal domestic existence looks like. I'm not like you."

"Hey, maybe I grew up with parents and brothers, but I was taken away at an early age too."

"But you, at least, understand how a family functions."

He brushed my face with his fingers. "Families don't just happen, Mel. They're purposefully built, are never perfect, and they don't turn out like anyone plans. We're one now, just the two of us. Why not add to something good we've made?"

I broke from his touch and turned away. "I can't be a mother to another person. I'm a fucked-up genetic experiment. Who knows what freakish mutation I'd pass on?"

"Then we can adopt. There are enough orphans who need a good home..."

"No! I told you I'm not mother material. I never will be. Can we just drop the damned subject?"

We sat in silence for a long time. Dylan was annoyed with me, but there was nothing I could do about it. Any children raised by me would only end up as screwed up as me, or worse. Besides, as long as we lived on Mars we would constantly be looking over our shoulders, waiting to be found out or betrayed. That was no way to raise a kid. I was sure Dylan would come to his senses and see that eventually.

Rising from his seat, he kissed me softly on the top of my head.

"My father always told me that nobody is ever prepared to be a parent. The human race would have ended long ago if everyone waited until they were ready. Family happens to us when it is meant to."

He went to the galley and rummaged for something to eat.

"Your father sounded like a wise man," I called back to him.

"I suppose he was. He died while I was in military training. I really only knew him for a short time."

I hugged him from behind. "You'd be a marvellous father, Dylan. It's me I'm not sure about..."

He turned and embraced me. "Let's table the conversation for another time, okay?"

Relieved by the reprieve, I continued to hold him close and listen to his steady heartbeat. I was certain he believed I would change my mind. I was also determined that I wouldn't.

"Family or no, we still need to discuss what to do," he said.

"What if that guy was an aberration?"

"You mean to suggest he was the only person on the planet to take the rumour seriously?"

"Yeah. We don't have his psych profile. Maybe he was disturbed from PTSD or something."

"Mel, I don't think it wise to take this lightly."

"I'm not. But until it becomes apparent he was not an isolated case, I'm not prepared to give up my vocation. Too many people depend on me, Dylan. I can't simply abandon them without good reason."

"But these flyers are out and your picture is on them. If they see one of these they may put things together. The amount of the reward is temptingly large."

"I'm older and thinner now, and my hair is a different colour and style. To my patients I am Corrine Ross and always will be. The Mother of Mars is dead, and people want to place their hope in the myth, not the person. To find out she's me would be a grave disappointment. People don't want their myths dashed, be they Big Foot or Elvis."

"Who?"

"It's a Terran thing. You wouldn't get it."

Dylan's forehead wrinkled as he considered my words. "All right, here is what I'll agree to: we will proceed to our next scheduled destination. I'll case the town and see what rumours surface. If you're right and it was an isolated incident, there shouldn't be anything to hear about Melanie Destin. You keep a low profile. That means you go straight to the clinic and come right back here. No seeing new patients this time."

I began to object, but he raised a finger and cut me off. "These are my conditions, otherwise I'll program this vehicle to take us to one of the poles and lock you out of the controls. Are we agreed?"

Dylan didn't often play the overbearing protector with me, but when he did, I knew nothing I said would change his stubborn mind.

"Fine," I said, feigning a pout.

I wrapped my arms around his neck and gazed up at his handsome face.

"But I have conditions of my own. I'll only accept your terms if the hero who saved my life takes me back to the bedroom and has his way with me. It's a fantasy thing of mine."

Without a word, he scooped me up and carried me to our bed.

CHAPTER 6

The absence of pain confused her. Normally it happened when they stuck the hoses in her muscles, but not as much as when they turned on the machine. This time she didn't feel the needles being pushed into her limbs. Even when the blue liquid flowed through the tubes she felt nothing. The fluid should have burned. It always did.

Adrianna struggled to turn her head but could not. She tried to look at her arms and legs, but her eyes would not move. She could only stare, unblinking, at the blackness in front of her.

Someone waited on the other side of it. She didn't know who. She never did, but someone always sat behind the glass wall.

Adrianna didn't understand why it was dark this time. Often, the men who hurt her would make small changes in how they did things. She thought she remembered them using the word "variables." Perhaps they didn't want her to see the person this time. Maybe they believed things would be different if she couldn't watch them die.

Her feet tingled. The sensation crawled up her legs. She couldn't move her eyes to check, but she knew without a doubt that they were gone. The numbness climbed up her body, emptiness in its wake.

Her breath came in rapid gasps as it advanced to her chest. She wanted to pull herself out of the chair, but she no longer sat in it. Adrianna floated in the void, and she heard the scientists laugh at her.

She tried to scream, but the nothingness flowed from her mouth, then her nose, followed by her ears and eyes...

She found herself on the floor, drenched in sweat and wrapped up tightly in a blanket. The sheets on the small cot lay in disarray, and her pillow was nowhere to be seen.

Though she had told Carlos she wasn't sleepy, she couldn't recall falling asleep.

She glanced about the darkness.

He often vanished like that when he believed her to be sleeping. Sometimes she would pretend to sleep so that he'd be free to leave and do his business. This time she must have been tired.

She groped around in the dimly lit room to find her lost pillow. Hugging it, she sat on the edge of her bunk and listened to the noises outside. Daylight snuck through cracks around the door's edges. Her growling stomach confirmed that morning had arrived some time before.

Where is he?

Though he frequently went out alone at night to meet with others who might help them, he never stayed away this long. Perhaps something happened to him.

Will they find me? What should I do?

She cried out when something heavy thumped into the door. Crawling back until she pressed against the wall, she pulled the pillow tighter and peeked above it.

Something fumbled with the door latch, and she wished she could summon the monster. But it didn't work like that. Instead, she shivered as she waited for the men in white coats to come for her.

She screamed when the door fell open and a dark figure lurched into the room. It quickly closed the door and turned to her, a finger raised to where its mouth should be.

"Adrianna, it's me."

"Carlos!" Her fear flipped mercurially to joy, and she leapt from the cot to embrace him.

He winced at her hug, and she immediately disengaged.

"They hurt you."

"Gather your things. We have to go."

"Are they coming?"

He tousled her unkempt mop of hair and smiled. "No, I stopped them."

"You said this place was safe for us."

"It isn't anymore. But I found someone who can help us, and I need to take you to another place before I go find them."

"I can hide here."

"Too many people know we are here. I must take you to a safer place."

He moved past her and began to throw things into a backpack.

"I'm hungry."

"I'll cook something for us when we get there."

Adrianna smiled at that. She liked his cooking. It was so much better than the tasteless pasty stuff from the other place. The flavours of his food danced on her tongue and made her want to giggle with every mouthful.

Presently, Carlos guided her to the door. They paused as he cracked it open to peek outside. With a grunt of satisfaction, he grasped her hand and they exited into the street.

She squinted and held up her hand to block the bright light from the sunshine illuminated dome overhead.

Nobody had walked the streets when they arrived late the day before. Now they teemed with people going about their business. No one paid them any attention as they moved through the marketplace. The savoury smells from the food vendors reminded her of her empty stomach, and while she could not stop, she memorized each distinctive scent as they passed by.

Carlos behaved differently than before. They never travelled during the daytime, and certainly not with so many people about. He gripped her hand so tight that it hurt, and he pulled her along when she tried to pause and inspect the visual chaos of the market.

They exited the town square and passed down a series of

empty streets and alleys. As she'd learned to do, she memorized each turn of their route. Later he would ask her to trace out their path on a map.

They stopped, and he pushed her into a doorway. He craned his neck to peer further ahead at something.

"Stay here and be quiet."

Familiar with the routine, she squatted on her haunches and watched him slip across the street, careful to keep himself within the shadows. He never told her why she needed to hide at times like this, but she understood the people who looked for them wanted to hurt them.

Hugging her knees to her chest, she steadied her breath as Bettani once taught her. Carlos would soon return, and they would continue on their journey.

A small part of her, though, worried what would happen if he did not come back for her.

She didn't want to think about that. Instead, she continued to focus on her breathing.

Everything would be all right, just like Carlos said it would.

CHAPTER 7

Dani yawned loudly and stretched like a cat.

"Did you enjoy your nap?" asked the man in the seat beside her.

"Mmm, it was yummy." She blinked the sleep from her eyes and glanced about the small cabin of their ship. "How long was I out?"

"Five hours." Felix barely suppressed his smile as he focussed on the readout in front of him.

Dani loved it when he smiled. It took her almost six years to teach him how to look like he hadn't eaten a lemon when he did so. She allowed her gaze to linger. Even though Felix never seemed to be self-conscious about anything, she still liked to push him in her quest to see how human he could be.

She grew bored when he failed to respond. "Okay, perhaps I should earn my keep. How much longer until the tanks are full?"

"Another thirty-six minutes; you almost missed the entire operation this time."

"Rats," she said and became delighted when Felix broke into a toothy grin. "I'll make it up to you when we offload at Ganymede."

"You said the same thing last time."

"I did? You're making that up."

He turned from the console and raised one eyebrow sardonically. Dani giggled. His mock scorn wasted, he returned his attention to his work.

"I shouldn't laugh so hard. Now I gotta pee." She unbuckled to float free of the seat and pushed herself toward the rear of the cabin. On return a few minutes later, she said, "Peeing would be a whole lot easier if the gravity-plates worked."

"By my calculations, we can afford new plating after we arrive at Europa."

"Remind me how many different ways I've planned to spend this commission?"

"Five at last count."

"What can I say? I like my little luxuries, like bathing and eating. Speaking of food, when was the last time you had a break?"

"You would be embarrassed to hear."

"Seriously, Felix, I'll pilot the ship out to Tanis station after we finish the loading. You can get some shuteye. And eat something."

"I don't require as much of either as you. But thanks. I would like to catch up on my correspondence."

"You mean the snitch reports from your network? Can't you ease back on that a bit? In ten years we've not heard a peep that Mundi suspects where we are."

"I know the man, darling. His agents have looked for us sporadically over the past decade. The only reason we evade them is because of my snitch reports, as you call them."

Dani sighed and tried to sink into her seat, giving up when the lack of gravity made that impossible. "What an asshole. Shouldn't he be dead already? How old is he, ninety-something?"

"His resources ensure he'll be around for decades more. Be thankful he was unable to revive the program that created me. There is no telling how long he would endure within a synthetic body."

Dani regarded her lover, concern on her cherubic face. "Do you think that's why he kept you around?"

"That wasn't his initial plan. He found more use for me as his lieutenant, believing me to be more reliable and faithful than a human. Since my abandonment of him, I'm sure his motivation for my capture is to secure my body as his synthetic host."

She leaned over and kissed Felix on his hairless cheek. "You just keep up with those snitch reports, hon." Pushing back in her chair, her brow creased. "I hope Mel is all right. I wish they'd chosen to come with us instead of slumming it on Mars."

"She did not want to live in the outer system. Ministering to the health of the surface population was her greatest desire. Regis Mundi has no reason to disregard my report of her death, and Dylan is more than capable of maintaining her security. I am confident she is well and under no threat."

"I know you believe that, Felix, but you still have to learn about human intuition. I've worried about her for the last year."

He frowned. "Why haven't you mentioned this before now?"

She shrugged. "What can I say? You can't understand premonition. It would be like trying to describe the colour blue to a blind person."

"Nonetheless, the very fact that it disturbs you is a concern for me."

She smiled weakly and patted his hand. "I'm being an irrational human. How about we don't give it any further consideration until we have some facts to go by? Besides, I just remembered the emergency contact protocol you two worked out."

Felix replied, "I monitor those channels regularly. If Melanie ever believes herself to be in danger, she knows what to do."

CHAPTER 8

The light rainfall rolled off the front window of the transport as the AI drove it across the barren red landscape. Shallow, algae-covered pools from the accumulated seasonal rains dotted depressions in the terrain. They presented a navigational challenge for the computer in its attempts to avoid the larger ponds that would engulf the vehicle should we wander into one.

"It gets more challenging to cross this valley every year," I said, breaking the long silence that had grown between us.

"It won't be long before we need to find an alternate route or stop going to Nova Phoenix any more," replied Dylan. His eyes were closed, and he reclined with his stocking-covered feet on the console. I uselessly glared at him, annoyed that he knew me well enough to keep his attention on surfing the cortex with his CI when he made statements like that.

"We are not going to drop any of the communities we visit."

"Whatever you say, Doc. I'm just the hired help."

He remained pissed with me. The topic of children and family would not die, no matter how often I hammered a stake through its heart. Dylan stubbornly resurrected the discussion when he felt I was in a receptive mood; usually the morning after we'd made love. Most times I put an end to it and we moved on amicably. This morning it had resulted in a full-blown argument, and I ended up as the bad guy.

The moody silence condensed around us once more. He

wasn't prepared to forgive me yet, and I was not willing to apologize for something I believed to be true. I held no doubt I would be a shitty parent. Persuading him proved to be the problem. It stymied me, since after living with me for the past twelve standards he understood what a bitch I was.

"Whoa," he said, sitting up. He blinked against the glare through the window.

"What is it? Your favourite team lose again?"

He didn't react to my snark; all signs of his annoyance with me had dissipated. He seemed to be deciding how to break some bad news.

"Dylan, you're scaring me. What is it?"

"I need to show you." He bent over the comm interface.

In a normal relationship, he would have resolved my curiosity by pinging my cortical implant and directing me to the offending link. I had complicated matters by disabling my CI almost a decade before. It was the only guarantee I had of protecting my privacy. A minority of the populace never had one installed in infancy. Not having one made my alias as the Martian-born Corrine Ross that much more convincing. It also prevented a determined individual from probing an active CI for my real identity.

He moved away from the console to reveal a government communique.

"The writing is too small to read from here. What is it about?"

"You. This is an announcement from the security directorate. Any person with information leading to proof that Melanie Destin is still alive is to report it. There's a reward that makes the sum on that bounty hunter's poster sound like pocket change. Worse, there is a severe penalty for anyone who fails to turn you in."

I stared at him for several seconds, my mouth hanging open but no smart-ass comment available. Finally I managed to say, "I'm fucked."

"We both are. According to this I'm guilty for knowing you and not turning you in. Forget completely the fact that I abandoned my position as director of security and am a wanted man anyway."

"What will we do?"

He didn't answer but turned his attention to the navigation control and began running computations.

"What are you doing, Dylan?"

"I'm trying to see if we have enough supplies and fuel to reach the northern polar region."

"Why there?"

"Talus Varr controls that territory. Mundi won't be able to touch you, even if he finds somebody to rat you out."

"Fuck that! Going to Varr is the last thing I want to do. In time, he and Mundi will go toe-to-toe, and there's better than a fifty percent chance Varr will lose that fight and we'll be worse off."

"Mel, our list of available options is shrinking. If we don't join the rebellion, where do you suggest we go?"

I had no answer for Dylan. There was nowhere to go on the planet that we wouldn't be discovered. Dylan knew that as well as I.

"I don't want to turn up on Talus Varr's doorstep. He will only want to use me again, and that is something I don't miss."

Dylan took my hand in his, but I couldn't look at him. "He would exploit me as a rallying point for his rebellion. Having the resurrected Mother of Mars on his side would be a propaganda windfall. I would be under his thumb again." I looked up into his sad eyes. "I'd rather be the mother of a child than what that man would make of me, and you already know how I feel about that." I smiled weakly, and he squeezed my hand.

"We really don't have any other choices, Mel."

I nodded and turned to watch the ruddy landscape pass by. For as long as I could remember, I wanted to come to Mars and restart the shit-show I called my life. Talus Varr, or Walter Bickel, as I knew him then, had pulled me off the streets of New London when I was a young teen turning tricks for meals. He miraculously used his influence to gain my admission to the

Terran Medical Academy. Little did I appreciate at the time that his interest in me was not so he could feel good about his charitable altruism.

I was a lab experiment, part of a program Varr initiated to develop a mutant human capable of rescuing Mars from the brink of disaster. Nobody could have predicted that my mutation would give me influence over an alien nanotechnology that threatened to destroy all life in the solar system. I used that control to send that ship into Olympus Mons, but the fact that it restarted the planetary tectonics was a fluke. Now I was the eulogized mother of the new Eden.

Running to Varr and handing my future back to him would be tantamount to returning to my abusive pimp back on Terra. I would never give anyone that kind of control over me again.

"We can leave the planet," I said quietly, still gazing out the window.

"Where would we go?"

"I don't know. Titan, perhaps? The Galilean colonies, maybe? There are a lot of places where Regis Mundi can't reach us."

"Okay, I'm all for that. Our only problem is how. The government has such tight restrictions on space traffic that it's almost impossible to go off-world."

"I know somebody who can do it."

"Who?"

"Felix Altius; if anyone can get us off Mars, it's him."

"He vanished right after he falsified your death, Mel. You know where he is?"

"Not exactly, but I know how to reach him. We'll need a quantum radio, though."

"Oh, is that all? Those are so common. Why don't I just pick one up when we stop to reprovision?"

"Don't be a sarcastic asshole. Surely you could find one from your spy days?"

Dylan regarded me thoughtfully. "It was a long time ago. I have no idea if the installation even exists anymore, but we maintained a secret communications station in Rosetta."

"Then we need to go there."

"Mel, that is two thousand klicks from here, across some pretty rough terrain."

"Then that is advantageous to us. Anyone searching for me will be checking out the communities on our circuit and the roads connecting them. They will never expect us to go cross-country to Rosetta."

He stared intently at me, close to anger, but he had to admit I was right. It remained our only hope outside of running to Talus Varr. Dylan turned and addressed the navigation computer once again.

"If the radio idea doesn't work, we go on to Varr. It's on the route to his territory. Agreed?"

"Like you said, our list of options is pretty short. I agree."

"We can't make it unless we resupply. We'll have to stop at New Phoenix as planned."

"Great! You can restock the larder, and I can see my patients one last time."

"What the hell are you talking about? There is no way you can go to the clinic. That's just asking for disaster."

"There are some people I have to see. I can't just abandon them without good reason."

"There are lots of sick and injured in all the other towns on our circuit who will never see you again."

"But these people will be right under my nose. I can't just hide from them and pretend I never showed up."

"Why not? Mel, this isn't a game. You saw the kind of shit that happened at our last stop. Imagine what we'll face with the government bounty now out. We'll be lucky to get in and out before somebody identifies us."

"I can't let them suffer when I can help."

Dylan growled something under his breath and turned his attention to our inventory list. The cabin plunged into icy silence.

He was right, of course. The safest thing for us to do would be to sneak in, quickly resupply while encountering as few people as necessary, then high-tail it to Rosetta. But as far as I was concerned, the smartest thing was not always the right thing to do.

"Dylan, when did that bounty go up? How did you come across it?"

"It popped up while I surfed the cortex. I only saw it because I set a flag for government notices."

"Aside from you, a paranoid, fugitive, former spook, who else would reasonably be trolling the network for that sort of thing?"

"Hard to say. Civil servants and officials mostly, so not too many, I imagine. It tends to be the last kind of announcement people open, if they do at all."

"So it is likely that nobody has read that thing yet?"

"That works to our advantage. Where are you going with this?"

"For the past ten years I've been Corrine Ross to everyone. None of them will connect me with Melanie Destin until the announcement becomes more widely circulated. If I go straight to and from the clinic, I can do my thing before anyone realizes who I am."

"It's risky."

"Being born puts us all at risk. Do I have your support?"

He studied me longer than made me comfortable. Before I could resign myself to him killing my plan, he said, "Fine. Keep a low profile, stay out of crowded public places, and hold your visit to a maximum of the six hours I'll need to reprovision."

I threw my arms around his neck and kissed him. I was confident I would not be recognized and that I'd be able to help some seriously ill patients one final time before we dropped off the grid forever.

CHAPTER 9

Fewer people showed up at the clinic than I expected. I wanted to attribute it to the exemplary medical care provided on my previous visit, but the truth was the annual community festival took higher priority for a lot of those with minor issues. That was good for us in that the holiday would delay any chance of the government bounty announcement being seen until the next day.

As I packed my kit in preparation to leave, one of the admitting clerks approached me.

"Doctor Ross, I realize you were finished, but an injured man just came in and asked to see you."

Alarms went off in my head. "He asked for me by name?"

"Yes, he's sitting in the waiting area."

I parted the privacy drape and peeked at the only patient remaining. Though stooped and cradling his abdomen, he was tall, with a mass of long black hair and an equally unkempt, greying beard. Even under his loose-fitting coat he looked too well muscled to be a Martian. More likely a Terran, which gave me pause, considering my last encounter with an Earther only a few days before.

"Is there something wrong, Doctor?"

"What? No, not at all. What is his complaint?"

"He said he fell down a flight of stairs. He exhibits abdominal trauma and..."

"May I?"

He handed me the chart, and after satisfying myself that the admitting exam had documented extensive bruising and abrasions, I relaxed a bit. If he faked symptoms to gain access to me, he'd severely overdone it. "I'll see him right away."

He nodded and left. Deciding to play things safe, I donned a surgical mask to hide my features. The man might think me eccentric, but it would be harder for him to ID me as Melanie Destin. For added security, I quickly loaded a hypo-spray with a powerful anaesthetic and slipped it into my pocket just as the curtain parted and the man entered.

I introduced myself and directed him to remove his shirt and sit on the examination table. With a sidelong glance, he regarded me warily. Noticing his attention to my mask, I said, "I have a cold and don't wish to pass it on to my patients."

After he painfully sat and faced me, I got my first good look at his strangely familiar face. The beard hid most of his features, but looking past the clumsy cosmetic surgery, I knew those eyes. My heart skipped a beat and then jumped into my throat. Sitting in front of me was a ghost.

"Hello, Melanie."

My pulse raced. I stumbled back and knocked over a tray of instruments. Within seconds one of the nurses threw back the curtain to see what had happened. She stopped in her tracks and stared at me.

I pulled the mask from my face and forced a reassuring smile. "Everything is fine. I just got clumsy."

A perplexed look on her face, she checked out the two of us, then nodded and left. I returned my full attention to a man I never thought to see again.

Carlos Montoya had been my fiancé seventeen years before, during my time as a surgical resident on Terra. When I believed he'd died in a terror attack, my life fell into a horrible spiral. I much later learned about his secret involvement with Talus Varr and how he faked his own death and vanished. He now sat before me with a stranger's face, dangling his legs like a little boy.

Carlos shifted on the table and winced with the effort. He

tried to smile. "I suppose you have a few questions for me."

Still stunned by his unexpected resurrection, I sputtered wordlessly until I finally managed to say, "A few questions?"

Suddenly conscious we might be overheard, I reverted to a stage whisper. "You're fucking right I do. Probably more than either of us has time for you to answer."

I peeked out from the curtain for signs anyone was listening. Nobody was in sight, but deciding on caution, I led him around the corner to a bathroom.

"What the hell are you doing here and how did you find me?" I whispered.

"I've known your whereabouts for some time."

"Talus Varr."

"Yes, but I kept my distance, and I never had plans to reenter your life."

I raised my fist, so desperately wanting to inflict a fraction of the pain on him that his deception had caused me. He winced, and I stopped myself.

My burst of rage dissipated, I slumped against the counter.

"Why are you here?"

He pointed to his bruised torso and looked up at me. When he realized I didn't believe him, his expression saddened. "I need your help."

"What the fuck?"

"It isn't for me, Mel. I realize that's an impossible ask of you. But there is a little girl whose life is in great danger, and you're the only person I can turn to."

"You have a daughter?"

"No, she's not my child, but I am responsible for her safety."

"You have balls the size of coconuts to come here and ask for my help."

His eyes became downcast. "When I ... deceived you I did so for your protection—"

"Ha!"

"No, it's true. The only way I could protect you was to fake my death."

"I already knew all that. Your buddy Varr filled me in several years back."

"Did he tell you I've lived incognito since then, running errands for him and keeping myself hidden?"

My shoulders slumped. "No, he didn't mention that particular fact."

"That all changed a couple of weeks ago. Something happened on a mission I undertook, and my cover was blown. Mundi's people have been dogging my steps ever since."

"What? Do you realize what you did by coming here?"

He held up his hand, gesturing me to remain calm. "I terminated the ones who followed me here. I heard about the bounty. Believe me, if I had any other choice I wouldn't approach you, but as long as they're after me, the little girl is in danger."

"Why is she even with you? Who is she?"

He hesitated. "I rescued her from one of Mundi's research facilities. She's an orphan, Mel. They performed unspeakable experiments on her and had even worse ones planned. I'm trying to get her to safety."

"Why can't you call on your buddy, Varr, for help? Surely between the two of you there are multiple other people you can count on?"

"Talus's old network has been badly compromised since his exile. The few remaining don't want to risk exposure by helping me. Many of my own contacts are dead. I have nowhere else to turn. I fended off the last attack by Mundi's agents, but even if I can hide or fight off the next group, I'll eventually be caught. If that happens before I can deliver her to the people who can ensure her safety..."

"How would I be any better for her? I'm being hunted too. We're going into hiding as soon as we leave this settlement."

"I'm aware of your situation, Mel. By the time someone adds it up, they'll be looking for a couple. If you take the girl, she will enhance your cover story. Nobody will be watching for two adults with a child."

Tears flooded my eyes. "You asshole! We had plans for our life. You and I were going to have children; be a family. You took that away from us. From me! After what happened...after the life I've lived, I would be no good for this kid. Her life would be destroyed even by coming into contact with me. I'm toxic. Everyone who touches my life is worse off for it."

"Mel, that isn't true..."

"It is! And you're to blame. I had found the perfect fairytale existence, and you killed it with your lies and deceit. You and Talus Varr!"

Carlos sat in silence as I quietly wept, overcome by grief I had suppressed behind my bravado for seventeen years. The pain I experienced was physical, and it felt like a knife carved up my guts.

Tears appeared in his eyes as he watched my agony overtake the last shred of dignity I had.

"Melanie, there are no words that can express my sorrow for what I have put you through. I am so sorry and can completely understand why you would want to see me destroyed. But this little girl—she's eight years old and her name is Adrianna."

"Don't."

"Her life makes the horrors of your upbringing seem pale by comparison."

"Please stop."

"From her conception she's lived in a laboratory, subjected to endless tests and experiments. She's never known the warmth of human kindness, except for what her caregivers chose to provide. If Mundi gets his clutches on her again, she can only look forward to more of the same for her brief life. I know you despise me, but don't make Adrianna suffer because of that hate."

I had no more tears to shed. Drained of all energy, I could only listen as Carlos painted a horrific picture of the girl's life.

"Why would Mundi do that to her? It makes no sense."

"She is one of a group of children who possess a specific genetic marker. From the little we've learned, they are integral to the successful resurrection of the old synthetic human program."

"Why would they use kids for that?"

"I don't have the answer. All I can tell you is that Adrianna is the last survivor."

"Last? What happened to the others?"

Carlos shrugged. "Do you need to ask that?"

"What do you want from me?" I asked.

"I need you to transport her to a safe house in Espiritus. People, good people, are waiting to take her into hiding and care for her."

My first inclination was to tell him to fuck off. I couldn't afford this kind of complication in my life. If the girl really was a fugitive from one of Mundi's labs, I would be drawing a target on Dylan and me by taking her with us.

My wimpy, sentimental conscience was getting loud. Against my better judgement, I said, "This decision involves more than me. Dylan will be at risk. He needs a say in this."

"I understand."

"Tell me where you are staying and give me a couple of hours to discuss it with him."

"Thank you..."

"I'm not promising anything except that we'll talk it over."

Carlos put on his shirt and explained where I could find him.

He turned to exit and paused. "Dylan is a good man. I'm so glad you two found each other. He's made you happier than I ever could have."

With those words still ringing in my ears, he departed, leaving me with a lot of questions about my own judgement. It was too late to back out. At the very least, I needed to confer with Dylan. I owed the child that much.

CHAPTER 10

"You're serious, aren't you?"

Dylan acted surprisingly calm, given the emotionally charged info dump just laid on him.

"Of course I am."

He stared for several seconds then sat in his chair and continued to appraise me, as if he expected something more.

"Are you going to say something or just sit there and stare at me for the rest of the day?"

"I'm really at a loss for words, Mel. You dropped one bomb on me about your old lover showing up, followed by another one telling me you want to adopt his child."

"No! You didn't listen to anything I said!"

"Correction: I didn't hear anything you said after 'Carlos showed up today.'"

"I didn't use those words either. Trust me, I'm still processing his appearance too."

"Fine, now that I'm over the shock factor, why don't you run over the story with me one more time?"

I exhaled noisily then repeated the details of my encounter.

"What do you want to do?" he finally asked.

"Me? I want to hide my head in the sand. I want to turn on our vehicle and take off into the hills. I want to be anywhere but in this situation..."

"But you can't."

"Of course not! Dylan, there is a child out there who needs

help, certainly the kind of assistance that the likes of Carlos cannot provide."

"So you want to adopt her?"

"No, I don't! Weren't you...?"

He waved his hands to shut down my outburst. "Adopt isn't the right word to use."

"It fucking well is not."

"Mel, if this kid is going to live with us, even for a short time, you're going to have to clean up your language."

"This is not a joking matter, Dylan Hodgson."

"I'm not being funny. We should help the girl."

For the third time that day I was left speechless.

"The way I see it," he said, "having this girl...Adrianna?"

"Uh-huh."

"Having her stay with us for a couple of weeks while we transport her to the safe house will be an ideal chance to figure out if we want to start our own family."

"This is not going to be a trial of any sort."

"You keep telling me you'd be a shitty mother. I'm saying that this is the perfect opportunity to prove it to me. If you can manage to find a way to make that poor girl's life even more miserable by being her surrogate mother for two weeks, you'll have proven your case to me. Frankly, I don't believe you're that much of a bitch."

"You're incorrigible."

"Tell me I'm wrong, then."

I looked him directly in the eyes. "You're wrong. Transporting this girl is not about us. It's about getting her to a safe place. Within a matter of hours we won't be able to enter any settlement between here and the pole without running the risk of being turned in. We can't put her into that kind of situation."

"It sounds like you made up your mind before you even told me about her. Why did you bother? Why didn't you just tell Carlos to go screw himself and keep the matter to yourself?"

"I...I thought you deserved to know—"

"I think you actually considered accepting his proposal.

Deep down, you don't believe all the crap you spout about being a lousy parent."

I stared at the floor to hide the rising warmth in my cheeks. "She and I are damaged goods. Two wrongs can't make a right."

"You're mistaken, Melanie Destin. You both might help heal each other if you gave it half a chance."

The air grew heavy with silence as the sting of his words burrowed into me. What gave Dylan the right to think he knew me better than I did myself? He was the selfish one. How could he think using this girl would convince me that family bliss lay in the cards life had dealt me? What did I know about how to look after a child? I had been barely older than Adrianna when my drunk of a mother sold me to a pimp. Sure, that became an important 'what-not-to-do' life lesson, but it hardly qualified me to take care of a girl who likely possessed some severe psychological issues. If half of her described upbringing proved true, the kid would be more fucked up than me.

And Carlos? After years of struggling with the emotional baggage he left me with, he showed a lot of nerve coming back into my life. Why did he think I would even consider doing him any kind of favour to bail him out of his mess? Why the hell did I listen to his request?

I shook my head to clear it. It always came back to being about me. I hated when Dylan was right. The decision really needed to come down to the best thing for Adrianna.

Even if I was the mother of the year material, and she turned out to be well balanced, the situation was impossible. Spiriting her away from an abusive home would be challenging by itself. Hiding her from Regis Mundi's network of secret police became something else entirely. They wouldn't only be looking for her. We might as well paint a big sign on the roof of our vehicle for them to find us all.

I raised my head and lowered my voice so that Dylan had to lean forward to hear. "The safety of the girl is paramount. We can't take her without putting her at risk. To do anything else would be a selfish indulgence on our part. I'm going to tell

Carlos the answer is 'no.'"

"And what will happen to Adrianna when Mundi's goons catch up to her?"

"I have a list of people I trust. I'll make arrangements for someone to take her to the safe house. It's the best solution."

Dylan nodded, stood, and kissed me on the top of my head. "You're probably right."

The usual satisfaction I got when he let me win an argument didn't even poke up its head. Something didn't feel right about what was clearly the correct decision.

I prayed that I wasn't making a huge mistake.

CHAPTER 11

Worry about the girl preoccupied me as I made my way through the back streets of the settlement. Only when I bumped shoulders with someone and he glared at me did I realize how careless I had been.

The man's flash of annoyance vanished when I smiled and apologized, but I became keenly aware of my good fortune that this day was a holiday. The government news circular offering the bounty remained ignored, sitting in everyone's 'to-read-tomorrow' file. But what if that man had been the exception? I needed to be more mindful of my surroundings.

I surveyed the thinning crowd in the street. Most were headed home for the evening meal, concerned with their own affairs. If I could simply refrain from running into any more of them, I could continue on my mission unnoticed.

I tried to swallow the growing lump in my throat. Small families moved past, returning from the holiday festival in the central market. Parents and children alike wore happy expressions and laughed, delighted to simply have spent a few hours of their otherwise difficult lives together. It was the kind of life that Dylan wanted and the very thing I would never be able to share with him. Living a simple, anonymous life in a settlement like this, if we could pull it off, would never last. Sooner or later someone would uncover the clues and identify us. It surprised me how we had lived incognito for the past decade.

The issue of Adrianna aside, I had to give consideration to our future. The notice for information about Melanie Destin's existence was only the beginning. In time, Mundi's spies would gather enough anecdotal evidence and sightings of me to determine that I lived. Then the heat would be turned up and the net cast wider.

I deluded myself by imagining we could continue our charade in settlements we had never visited. We might manage to stay hidden for a year or two, but eventually one of us would make a slip or somebody would spot us and turn us in for the reward. Dylan would do his best to evade capture; he excelled at spotting things and never let his guard down. But we would be on the run for the rest of our lives, and our luck would not last forever.

We would both be executed. That was a foregone conclusion. By going into hiding with me he had abandoned his job as Director of Martian Security and made himself into my criminal co-conspirator. I remained a wanted fugitive. The false charges against me for the death of the high chancellor had never been dismissed. It didn't matter that someone set me up in a bid to bring Talus Varr down from his position in the Martian government. My flight with him and the subsequent assumption of power by his enemy, Regis Mundi had not done me any great favours.

As much as I hated to agree with Dylan, running to the protection of the rebels remained the only long-term solution for our safety on Mars. The only problem for me was I couldn't bring myself to do it.

I resented Varr's domination of my life more than anything else. He was responsible for my genetically engineered conception, and, ultimately, for my mother's abandonment of me. His continued interference had resulted in Carlos faking his death. Not content to leave me alone, he worked in the background for years to assure my exposure to the Ares weapon so my mutation would be triggered. Because of him I was now a fugitive and the mythical Mother of Mars. Every decision I believed to be of my own making had turned out be manipulated in some way by that son-of-a-bitch. The past decade had been the only time he had absolutely no influence over me. There was no way I would ever willingly return to his spider's web.

Getting off Mars began to look like the only solution, and it had to happen sooner than later. I had to contact Felix while I still had the chance. Although I promised Dylan we would wait until we arrived at our next destination, I didn't believe we could make it there before we were identified. Mundi not only had spies everywhere; he also had control of the government's vast resources.

In a way, Talus Varr made my decision inevitable. Under his direction, the orbital surveillance network was built, capable of locating anything or anyone on the planet's surface. Once Mundi's people figured out who Dylan and I really were, they would be able to identify our vehicle from orbit. If we got lucky and timed our trip with a dust storm, we might manage to make it to our destination undetected, but we would still have to wait for Felix's arrival.

When Felix Altius provided me with the subparticle key that would connect any quantum radio with his, I gave it to Dylan for safekeeping. What I kept to myself were the backup emergency contact protocols that Felix and I had established in case we could not find one. It was stupid of me to deceive Dylan like that, but he made no secret of his distrust of Felix, given their shared history. I trusted Felix because of his relationship with my best friend, Dani. If Dylan realized there was a way for him to locate me without hard-to-get tech, he would not be pleased. I, however, had learned a long time before not to close the door on any possible alliance that might save my ass.

From the street, I scanned for the place I had passed by on countless occasions without giving it any second consideration. I hoped my recollection of its location wasn't confused with a different settlement. I sighed with relief, however, when I spotted the communications building.

Every community on Mars had a public comm facility.

While the cortex allowed for regional networked communication, no planet-wide system existed for the populace to universally interact. The government learned lessons from Terra's troubled history with its own Internet and took precautions to limit unfettered communications across Mars. The result was the establishment of carefully controlled and monitored public facilities. Mostly people used them to catch up with relatives and didn't have anything to hide. People with less transparent agendas, however, were obliged to be more cautious.

Anything I intended to send to Felix would be closely scrutinized, hence his carefully considered protocols. He had no desire to be discovered by Mundi's spies either.

The place was not busy, with only a man and his children in one booth, sharing the day's events with some relatives. I paid my access fee to the attendant, who didn't give me a second glance and retreated to an isolated terminal at the back.

Real-time communication with Europa was impractical, so off-world messages were dispatched and received in a manner similar the ancient telegram or mail systems on old Earth. I would send a message and return later to pick up any response. Since these were ridiculously easy for the Martian authorities to monitor, a coded communication was required.

Felix was probably the only person other than Dylan whom I could trust to invent an uncrackable code. Before he and Dani departed Mars, he had forced me to memorize the coding key. Though I resented his patronizing attitude at the time, I was now grateful for the hours he spent drilling me.

With deliberate care I composed the message exactly as instructed and dispatched it from the comm terminal. To a casual reader it would appear as a birthday greeting from a local resident to a young nephew at Tanis colony on Europa. Even when the government's sophisticated code rippers dissected it, Felix's cypher would ensure that it remained innocuous. Only the recipient with the matching decipher key would learn of the true contents, that person being Felix Altius. It was an ancient method, long abandoned and forgotten.

Contemporary security technology, which searched for hidden data packets within the modern multilayered binary and trinary communication channels, would never detect it.

My call for help dispatched, I exited the building into the now empty street. I was a few minutes late for my meeting with Carlos. To ensure nobody followed, I took a circuitous route that took fifteen minutes longer than a direct one. It couldn't be helped. I didn't want to be the one responsible for leading anyone to him and the girl.

My travels brought me to a narrow, little used laneway, and I peered into the growing evening shadows. A lone doorway punctuated an otherwise featureless wall. Beside it dangled a useless and silent wind chime, just as Carlos had described. After one last check of my surroundings, I advanced toward the door.

Pausing before it, I strained to listen through the door for signs of occupation. Dead silence hung around me, forebodingly punctuated by the still ornamental chimes. With my pulse racing, I rapped on the rough surface of the door.

The loud creak of its rusted hinges startled me, and I jumped back. Instead of opening further to admit me, the door remained ajar, with no indication that anyone stood on the other side.

Thinking it must not have been properly latched and that my knock had pushed it open, I returned and cautiously opened it enough to squeeze through. The sight that greeted me made me catch my breath.

The interior of the room was in complete disarray, like a battle had taken place. Something terrible had happened.

CHAPTER 12

Dani chewed on what remained of her fingernails as she watched the giant rock slowly turn in the viewport. It didn't actually rotate, she realized—it only seemed to from the relative motion of her ship.

Wincing at a clumsy bite of her finger, she pulled her hand away and examined it. She shook her head at her mangled nails then returned her attention to the schematic displayed at the helm control.

"Easy, Sugar," she muttered to herself. "We don't want to startle him."

She fired the thrusters and halted her passage around the asteroid. Double-checking that her stationary coordinates were correct, she nodded with the self-satisfaction she knew Felix would discourage if he were present.

Well, he's not here now, is he? She blew a defiant raspberry.

Her petulant attitude faded as the difficulty of his part in this operation came to mind. Her fingers absently returned to her lips while her eyes turned to the communications station.

Blink, damn it! In spite of her encouragement, the light on the console remained dark.

Inhaling deeply, she held her breath for a short count before slowly expelling the air.

"Stay calm, Sugar. He's got this. He just needs a little more time."

As if in response, the indicator flashed green. Dani forced

her shoulders to relax then collected her wits in preparation for the next stage.

After only a brief hesitation to ensure she'd not forgotten a step, she activated the program that released the six drones from the storage hold. It was the third time they'd performed such an operation, but she still worried something would go wrong and her long-awaited chance would vanish in a puff of engine exhaust.

She wiped the sweat from her palms and settled down to run diagnostics. When green lights showed across the board, she bit her lower lip and sent the response signal to Felix. Within thirty minutes she would know if the efforts of the past six years had paid off. This was the last one—the most dangerous one; the final obstacle that stood between her and freedom.

For much of her life, the Jovian Collective had been something to fear. They had made miserable the lives of her family and the others who tried to eke out an existence in the shadow of Jupiter. There was not a single person throughout the Galilean colonies whose life was not affected in some way by them. They controlled all commerce between the colony moons, exacting crippling tariffs from any ship wishing to operate in the system. The inner worlds had all but ceased trade because of them, making a difficult life all the more challenging for everyone. It had been only natural for a naive, orphaned teen to aspire to join them to make her sad life better.

Dani shook her head as she reflected on the events that brought her to this place. After the deaths of her parents, she foolishly took what seemed to be the path of riches and joined the Collective. Within a short time, her developing talent for computer hacking came to the attention of Yarra Tambul. At the time he was nothing more than an ambitious thug who ran one of the organization's drug trafficking arms. The attraction between them was mutual, and she rapidly followed in his wake as he rose and cemented his position within the upper hierarchy.

They became a team with the single-minded goal of pushing

out the old leadership and running the entire collective themselves. It was a heady time, and the two of them believed they were invincible as every scheme and plot they devised resulted in ever more power. Little did Dani realize that her days were numbered the moment Yarra put a bullet in the head of Janzz, the leader of the organization for almost forty years.

As soon as he assumed control of the operation, she discovered how little her skills or affections were valued. Spurned for another woman, she became relegated to administrative tasks and given only the meanest taste of the wealth and influence she helped Yarra accumulate. It was then that she made the fateful decision to exact her revenge by stealing from him. She soon realized her mistake and fled for her life.

The flashing indicator that signalled Felix was in position pulled her back to the present. She deployed the drones to their assigned coordinates above Yarra's ship, hidden on the opposite side of the Trojan asteroid. Too small to be seen against the blackness of space, they sent no telemetry signal to betray their existence. Now running exclusively by program, Dani no longer controlled them and had no choice but to fulfill her part. Being blind and acting on faith did not frighten her as much as the knowledge that if something went wrong, she might never learn Felix's fate. Though they had successfully executed variants of this operation twice before, the consequences of failure this time terrified her.

Yarra knew they were coming for him. That alone made this undertaking more dangerous than any of the others.

When Dani and Felix fled Mars ten years before, they could go no place where safety was assured. They opted to return to the Galilean colonies as water haulers, using Felix's expertly forged identity documents. For four years they avoided any problems until a chance encounter with a tariff agent forced Dani to accept that she could not hide indefinitely. Rather than flee again, she allowed Felix to convince her of an alternate path that would forever free her of her fear of Yarra's revenge.

Over the next six years, Felix meticulously executed his plan to dismantle the Jovian Collective. One by one, using his covert skills, he eliminated the key leaders. Yarra suspected nothing of the plot until the recent death of his trusted lieutenant two months before. Fearing for his own life, he went into hiding, only to be uncovered by Felix's network of informants.

The readout in front of her counted down the seconds. The timing of her actions needed to be perfect, or Felix would be discovered in his attempt to board Yarra's ship. The idea was simple. She was to distract and frighten Yarra and his crew, allowing Felix, wearing an EVA suit, to enter the vessel and overpower them. For most people, this plan would be fatally stupid, but Dani was aware of Felix's capabilities. As a synthetic human, he was faster, stronger, and more intelligent than anyone she'd ever met. That he could singlehandedly prevail over a crew of ten she had no doubt, having seen him do so twice before. Still, she feared for his safety. She no longer could imagine a life without him by her side.

As the last remaining seconds counted out, she straightened in her seat and readjusted the microphone of her headset. She struggled to swallow, but her mouth was dry. At this moment she visualized the drones executing their program. One by one they would turn on the simulated targeting beacons directed at Yarra's vessel. Believing themselves discovered, the crew would be frantic in their search for something to target in response.

The countdown ended, and it became time for her to throw accelerant on the fire. She cleared her throat and flipped on the comm.

"Hello, Yarra. How's it going?"

Tension-filled seconds ticked by before a voice crackled in her ear. "Who the hell is this?"

"Aw, Sugar, you do know how to disappoint a girl. Are you sure you don't recognize my voice just a little?"

"Dani? Dani O'Hara?"

"You remember me. I'm flattered."

"What the fuck is going on? What is the meaning of this?"

"I'm disappointed again. I didn't think you were quite so

dense. I guess I'll have to explain. Six of my ships have missile locks on you. My intention should be pretty clear. I'm going to blow you to pieces if you so much as fart."

"Why are you doing this?"

"Yarra, that is such a stupid question. I'll give you a hint. It has something to do with the price you put on my head, asshole."

"This is some kind of bullshit trick. When I find out where you are..."

"Save your threats, dickwad. Who do you think snuffed out your lieutenants over the past few months? You're next. I just wanted to be the one to tell you."

A buzz of static interrupted Yarra's response. Dani jumped at a loud thump in her earpiece. Her heart skipped at the sound of gunfire and the shouts of panicked men. Her mutilated, bloody fingernails dug into the chair arms as she listened to the unfolding melee on the other vessel. She was desperate to call out and discover who still lived but afraid to do so in case Yarra answered.

A horrifying scratching erupted in her ear as someone aboard picked up the comm headset. Tears filled Dani's eyes, and she held her breath, listening for the voice of the survivor.

"Dani, this is Felix. The ship is secured."

Blood painted the ceiling and walls, and the air smelled of cordite.

Felix tossed the headset toward the dead man slumped over the console. Yarra had been the first to die, followed quickly by the remnant of his crew.

After reporting the success of the mission and relieving Dani's anxiety, he informed her he would make a sweep to ensure there remained no hidden survivors. A visual assessment of the overall condition of the vessel would also be necessary now that it belonged to them.

He regarded the impact marks on the hull made by the crew's low-calibre firearms. Not a single shot even came close to testing his lightweight personal body armour. Felix was disappointed by how poorly the Jovian Collective had trained its men. They were, no doubt, accustomed to ruling by reputation and intimidation and did not regard training in hand-to-hand combat or target practise necessary.

As he searched the corridors, he made a running commentary to Dani over his personal comm link.

"The ship was originally a water hauler, but it has been extensively modified. It is armed with missiles and a state-of-the-art ion drive."

"It makes sense, I suppose. Yarra's little empire required interplanetary travel capability for him to manage it."

"I'll need to run diagnostics on everything. If their maintenance protocols were as slipshod as their security training, I fear for what may be uncovered."

"Are you worried it's not space-worthy? I can't imagine Yarra taking that kind of risk with his own hide."

"I have no great concern. Based on my observations I don't anticipate any major refit will be needed. I think it will make a fine addition to our operation."

"Ooo, now that we have a fleet, I think I need a title. How about admiral?"

"The decision would seem to be out of my hands, Admiral," he replied.

"Have you seen any indication of the ship's name, smartass?"

Felix, who had been advancing through the darkened central corridor, played his searchlight along the opened hatchways. "There is nothing so far. Perhaps I'll learn more when I return to the bridge. Do you believe this might be one of your father's ships?"

"No, Papa only ran methane skimmers, but Uncle Cletus had three water haulers stolen from him by those bastards."

His magnetic boots clanked on the metal floor plates as he methodically searched the abandoned ship. As he neared the vessel's engine room, Dani contacted him once again.

"Uh, hon? A weird message packet just flashed up on one of your priority channels. At first I thought it was a report from one of your pals, but..."

"What is strange about it?"

"It has the correct prefix code, but there are no audios or vids, only text contents that don't make any sense. Do you want me to read it to you?"

"Yes, please. It will help occupy my mind while I search this unremarkable vessel."

"Okay, here it goes. Aunt Rimi and Uncle Bos wish you the happiest of birthdays and look forward to your next visit—I thought you didn't acknowledge your birthday?"

Felix clenched his teeth, and his brow furrowed as the meaning of the words became apparent to him.

He tramped back toward the airlock. "I'm returning to you."

"Why? What's going on?"

"I'll fill you in when I arrive."

Within thirty minutes of departing the newly acquired ship, Felix sat at his own vessel's communications terminal. His eyes were riveted to the monitor as he reviewed the message and checked the integrity of the file header data.

"What the hell is going on, Felix? Who is this from, and why are you so freaked out?"

After a final inspection of the screen, he turned to face Dani, concern written across his face. "It is a coded transmission from Melanie Destin. She and Dylan require our help to escape from Mars."

"Bullshit," said Dani. She nudged him aside and studied the communique. "How the fuck do you get all that from this stupid message?"

"It is embedded in the text using a code I taught her before I joined you. I promised to come to her aid if she ever required it."

"Does it say what kind of trouble she's in?"

He shook his head. "It only gives a location and the date they will arrive there."

"You're not telling me something."

"I am concerned about the manner in which this arrived. She was only to use this channel under dire circumstances because of the risk of it being intercepted. I fear they are in grave danger."

"From Regis Mundi?"

"Most likely, but I'll need to contact my remaining assets on Mars to be sure. In the meantime, we should make arrangements for my return there."

"You meant to say, 'for our return,' didn't you?"

"It will be far too perilous..."

"Now just a goddam minute—we just took down the biggest group of gangsters in this part of the system, and you think a quick run back to Mars is too dangerous for me?"

"I apologize. There is significant risk. The Martian authorities have imposed tight restrictions for entering their space. We will have to devise a cover to approach the planet without being fired upon."

A grin filled Dani's cherubic face. "They always need water, don't they?"

"Should I mention we will be executed if captured?"

"I trust implicitly in your sneakiness."

Felix smiled. "It may take more than stealth to pull this off."

Dani sat in his lap and wrapped her arms around his neck. "When do we leave?"

He shook his head. "We will depart as soon as your new ship can be readied for the trip."

"So right away, then?"

"Yes, immediately."

CHAPTER 13

I stood in the doorway, frozen by fear. Toppled chairs were scattered, some broken, across the floor. A table was overturned, and antique books and bric-a-brac lay tumbled from a damaged shelf. Bizarre shadows thrown by the light behind a crumpled lampshade posed menacingly on the walls. As if to contrast the visual chaos, the air carried the savoury scent of recent cooking.

Whatever happened had been unannounced and ill prepared for. Perhaps I had overestimated Carlos's competence as an agent of Talus Varr.

Listening for any sound that would indicate another presence, I heard nothing but my rapid breathing. I tiptoed my way into the room and picked a path through the detritus toward what I presumed would be the kitchen.

That room revealed its own mayhem, telling me that the battle behind all this had raged long and far; perhaps over the entire apartment. I was surprised the conflict had not prompted the neighbours to call the local constabulary.

At that thought, a new panic seized my heart. If they had been called, I could not afford to be discovered. I searched the small room for another exit, but a blue light in my peripheral vision distracted me.

A lazy gas flame still burned on the cooking unit, and the pot it had been heating was overturned with its contents dumped across the counter. I dipped my finger into the spilled stew and found it to be cold. The attack had likely occurred much earlier. Possibly the occupants who lived nearby had been attending the festival, and the authorities were not alerted. Perhaps I was wrong and they were now gathered at the front door.

A muffled thump from the back of the residence startled me. Every muscle in my legs screamed at me to flee, only overpowered from obeying instinct by my paralyzed brain. Afraid to blink lest the flutter of my eyelashes alert someone to my presence, I stood motionless like a frightened rabbit. My ears monitored the deathly silence in fearful anticipation of a repetition of the sound.

I don't know how long I impersonated a statue, but my need to breathe broke the spell. Curiosity won out over common sense, and I crept in the direction of the noise.

Wreckage from the epic conflict continued to present itself as I proceeded down the narrow corridor. On reaching the entrance to a single, large, dimly lit room that dominated the back half of the main level, I peeked around the corner. The scene before me represented the culmination of the struggle. Two men, too muscled to be native Martians, lay motionless. Beneath the nearest one spread a crimson puddle of congealing blood.

Not far from him, the second man was draped over something large and bulky. Awkwardly posed, his head was twisted to one side with a snapped neck.

My hand reflexively clamped over my mouth when he stirred. I stumbled backward into a wall and tried to flatten myself against it.

The man's back rose, his disarticulated head lolling to his shoulder. I wanted to scream, but nothing could fight its way up my windpipe. I could only stare at the supernatural horror resurrecting before my eyes.

With a loud grunt, he rolled to his back, his head facing unnaturally behind, to reveal the hidden third man who'd lain beneath him. The dead body resumed being an inanimate corpse while another, very much living man struggled to rise to his hands and knees.

My other hand raised a broken table leg it had somehow grabbed, and I readied it as a cudgel to defend myself from the apparent zombie rising before me. Before he could fully lift his torso from the floor, he cried out in pain. Clutching his lower abdomen, Carlos collapsed on his side.

Jolted from my paralysis, I dropped my crude weapon and rushed to his aid, startling him in the process.

"Mel, what are you doing here?" he rasped through gritted teeth.

"Apparently helping you."

I turned him to examine his injuries. My terror now displaced by my medical training, I dispassionately palpated his abdomen in the dim light. He winced at my touch, and my hand became sticky with the blood that soaked his shirt. Tearing a strip from it, I wadded it up and pressed it to bleeding wound.

"I should get you to the clinic."

"No," he gasped. His bloody hand squeezed my upper arm until I thought he might crush it. When the pain induced by his sudden movement passed, so did the pressure of his grip.

"You've lost a lot of blood, Carlos."

More calm this time, he repeated, "No."

Before I could argue, he shook his head. "You must take Adrianna to safety."

"The girl!" In all the hubbub I'd forgotten about her. "Where is she?"

"She's safe. They didn't find her."

As if on cue, in the part of the room the destruction had not reached, a small figure emerged from the shadows. The poor light from the corridor made her appear more like a misplaced doll at first. Thin and pale, her long tresses of unkempt auburn hair hung over her shoulders and partly obscured her face. She pressed her back defensively against the far wall, much as I had done. Her dark blue eyes, wide with fear, stared wildly at us.

She reminded me more of a feral animal than an eight-year-old girl. The sight of her mesmerized me. An unformed memory struggled for recognition as we evaluated each other. I had seen this child somewhere before.

A change in Carlos's breathing recalled my attention to him. The air gurgled from his windpipe as he fought for breath. His internal injuries were extensive, and I realized I could do nothing for him.

"You need medical help. Now!"

His attempts to dissuade me ended in a coughing fit, bright red blood spraying from his mouth. With much effort, he said, "No, I'm a dead man. You have to get her to safety."

Tears fogged my vision. "No, the two of us can take you to the clinic..."

"Mel, more of them are coming. We'll all be cut down before we can—" Another hacking fit wracked him. "They won't be looking for just you two. They won't suspect a mother and child. It's the only chance to save..."

When he could no longer manage to speak, his glassy eyes pleaded with me.

Tears now flowed freely down my cheeks. I nodded, hoping my acquiescence might ease his suffering. Relief on his face, his shoulders relaxed, and he slumped into my arms. I cradled him, watching powerlessly as his strength faded.

"There's a data safe...contact information...help you locate..."

He shut his eyes.

My heart in my throat, I shook him. "Carlos! Where is it? Where's the device?"

His eyes opened and locked on mine. A softness came to them for the briefest moment, reminding me of a time long past. Then, far too soon, they closed. He struggled to summon his last bit of strength. "Book...hidden...old trick...nobody reads...books...look..."

I hugged him tightly to my chest and counted his laboured breaths until he was gone. With no more tears left in me, I continued to hold him close, rocking him as if that would somehow ease his passage. This was the second time I had to say goodbye to him, and it hurt as much as the first; perhaps more. This time it was real.

Time seemed to stop as I cradled him in private grief. A rustling called me back, and I looked up to see the waif had come closer and now stood within arm's reach. Her eyes were transfixed on Carlos, studying everything about him. Slowly, she squatted down and reached tentatively toward his chest. Laying her hand on him, she whispered, "Thank you."

Her voice was so quiet, I strained to make out what she said. I felt like an intruder. What had their relationship been like? How long had they been on the run together? Was he a father to her? A brother? A protector?

When the tide of grief finally ebbed, I laid him down and covered his face with a jacket from one of the other men. Saddened and with nothing more to do, I turned to the girl.

The expression on her face was neither grateful nor helpless. Defiance stared back at me from those familiar eyes.

"Adrianna, my name is Melanie."

She continued to stare without responding.

"Carlos asked me to take care of you."

Still no reaction. Swallowing my growing frustration, I decided to get to the point. "Do you know where the—"

She turned abruptly and marched into the corridor. I remained kneeling and watched her disappear into the front room. Regaining my wits, I followed her, concerned she would wander out the door.

Rounding the corner, I found her standing next to the toppled shelf, holding an antique book. She thrust it toward me with both hands, and I reluctantly accepted it. We stared at each other again for a few seconds before I gave my attention to the object I held.

Books are a rarity on Terra and almost never found on Mars. This particular one seemed ancient, from the look of it, perhaps five or six hundred years old. I'd seen similar ones in Terran museums many years before, but they were in poorer condition and kept from curious fingers behind protective glass. The worn leather cover was embossed with intricate decorations, and the edges of the pages still showed traces of the original gilding. The title of the tome was engraved on the spine. I thought it was a copy of Milton's Paradise Lost, but the unfamiliar characters were ancient prestandard. A delicately worked metal clasp closed it and prevented the volume from being tossed open when it fell to the floor.

I reverently opened the cover. The interior pages had been cut away to form a hollow hiding space. Within lay a slip of paper with an address in Carlos's handwriting and a digital data safe. According to Carlos, everything we needed was now in my hands. The only problem was that I had no way to access the encoded information in the small metal case. He gave me no access code before he died, and I doubted the girl would know it. The only thing I had to go on was the note, and I made a huge assumption that it provided the location of the intended safe house.

Deciding it was a problem best tackled later, I shut the book and tucked it under my arm. I turned to Adrianna, who had been watching me like a hunted animal. She returned my gaze with a defiant one of her own. This kid was going to be a handful. The sooner I could get rid of her, the better for everyone.

CHAPTER 14

Adrianna was from sturdy stock. Once we left the apartment, she became a study in calm determination to remain on the move. Distracted by Carlos's death, I was not attentive to our surroundings and frequently made wrong turns.

The girl however, never paused. More than once she pulled me by the hand down an unfamiliar alley. It appeared she and Carlos had spent some significant time exploring the less frequented avenues of the city. Our weaving path took us through back lanes and little used streets, and she occasionally led the way when I found myself lost.

New Phoenix was one of the largest settlements on Mars and a busy supply hub for the region. Its enormous distribution facility was able to accommodate our surface vehicle, eliminating the necessity for us to camp outside of the dome. After more than an hour of walking the maze of streets, we stood fifty metres from the entrance to the massive structure. All that remained for us was to find a way inside the confusing labyrinth of the building, hopefully without drawing attention to ourselves.

That would be a trick. The only people entering or exiting were the workers or the transport operators. Certainly no eight-year-old girls were commonly observed. If our survival depended on anonymity, this was a terrible place to be. We might as well just stand in the middle of the town square and broadcast our identities. I wished I could talk the problem through with Dylan. If anyone I knew could come up with a plan, it was him. It was one of the few times I ever regretted deactivating my cortical implant.

I queried Adrianna. "Do you have a CI?"

She wrinkled her nose and frowned at me like I spoke gibberish.

"Okay, I'll take that as a no."

She eyed me warily before returning her attention to the activity outside the building. I worried she was concerned I might abandon her to save my own skin. I was about to reassure her that would not be the case when she pointed to something farther up the street.

Two men argued while a third one, grimacing in pain, sat on the ground holding his foot. While delivering items to the distribution centre, they had been pushing an enormous motorized hand-truck when the fellow was injured. The offending low, five-metre-long, wheeled platform was piled with boxes and oddly shaped packages destined for the warehouse inside.

With an idea only half formed, I told Adrianna, "Wait here for the chance to hide on that thing."

Smiling for the first time since meeting me, she nodded. Shaking off my unease, I moved out from the shadows and ran to the scene of the accident.

"Hello, I'm a doctor. What can I do to help?"

The two companions ended their argument, and after only a brief hesitation, competed to explain their differing theories of what had happened. Not waiting for them to get their stories straight, I knelt beside the injured man and introduced myself, being sure I kept one eye on Adrianna's hiding place. After receiving permission to do so, I examined the injury while his now silent work mates looked on with concern.

"Are you really a doc?"

"Yes," I said, realizing such a rare occurrence had captured everyone's attention. "I come through here every few months. You're fortunate I was passing by."

While all three men were focussed on me, a small figure

slipped from the shadows and made its way toward the back of the hand-truck.

"It doesn't seem to be broken. If we tape it up and put ice on it, you should be fine in a few days. Is there a first aid station around?"

"Yes, inside the distribution centre," said one man.

I helped the injured man up and supported him on the way to the building. His two workmates resumed guiding the motorized hand-truck and proceeded ahead of us. I snuck a peek at the back of the vehicle as it moved past, but I didn't see Adrianna among the boxes and packages.

It took me about twenty minutes to properly wrap the damaged limb and ensure my patient understood my instructions. By the time I was finished, the others had disappeared within the enormous warehouse. I volunteered to tell his companions about his condition and send them back for him.

Armed with vague directions, I located them as they removed the last of the items from the truck. After accepting their thanks, I watched them depart and I wondered where Adrianna had hidden. I poked about the various berths and open doors looking for her, to no avail. As my anxiety rose, I heard a faint hissing come from a bay I had just examined.

Peering into the darkness, I was ready to dismiss the sound as my imagination when a gentle tug on my sleeve startled me. Pleased with herself as only a child can be, she grinned up at me. I couldn't help but smile at her in return. Maybe this kid would grow on me after all.

CHAPTER 15

The winds raged outside, hurling grit against the windscreen. Visibility was down to fifty metres and threatened to reduce further as we entered the storm's heart. While our machine was capable of navigating unassisted using the AI's enhanced thermal imaging, Dylan still brooded over the controls.

Our premature departure from New Phoenix eleven hours earlier necessitated evasive navigation on our part; basically heading due east until we encountered the storm, then veering off toward our intended destination, Espiritus. While the sole purpose of the manoeuvre was to cover our tracks and avoid casual visual detection from orbit, we both realized it was a temporary advantage at best.

Adrianna was the deciding factor for our early departure and would likely be the reason Mundi's people found us sooner than later. Unless we got lucky and located a place to hide before we were spotted, this shaped up to be a short trip.

I caught Dylan's eye as he looked up from the readouts, brow furrowed. His expression softened.

"We're making good time. There's still a chance, especially if you're correct in assuming you weren't seen."

"Still..." I let the sentence drop off as I regarded Adrianna. She was curled up in my usual travelling seat, looking blissfully peaceful as only a sleeping child could.

"Mel, you made the only possible call. Leaving her behind —"

"Was an unacceptable option. Yeah, I know. I can console myself with that thought as I'm awaiting execution."

"They won't find us; not soon, anyway. We can still make Wells Canyon before they realize what happened to her."

"But once they figure out she's not anywhere back in New Phoenix, even the cover of this storm can't prevent our detection from orbit. We're screwed, Dylan."

He nodded and returned his attention to the console. He knew I was right; he just didn't want to admit it to me.

"How's your first day as a father turning out so far?"

My comment coaxed a smile out of him. "You're being awfully flippant about something you were adamantly opposed to only fourteen hours ago."

"Gallows humour, I suppose." I turned again to watch the sleeping girl's chest rise and fall. "I went to Carlos settled on turning him down. Even when I found him fatally wounded, a part of me still believed there was a way to save him and locate someone to care for her. But when I saw her for the first time, Dylan..."

"Your maternal instincts kicked in?"

"Fuck, no! I felt like I looked in a mirror. That scruffy waif reminded me of myself all those years ago on Terra. I knew I could never leave her to be found by Carlos's killers. It would be like abandoning myself—it sounds stupid."

"No, it doesn't." He reached out and touched the back of my hand.

"So now what...Dad?"

He chuckled. "Now, we keep moving until we get to Wells. If we can conceal ourselves beneath those overhangs, we have a chance."

"And after that? We can't hide under a rock forever."

"One crisis at a time, please. I'm making this up as we go along. I'm glad you decided to send a message to Felix and Dani ahead of schedule, even if it was a surprise to me."

"I don't know if he received it..."

"Not much gets past Felix Altius's attention. If we don't meet him when he arrives, he'll begin a search for us. I may not like him, Mel, but I respect his abilities...and his honour. If he pledged to come to your aid when called, nothing will prevent him from doing so."

"Yeah, I suppose. Besides, Dani would probably kill him if he refused."

Dylan laughed for the first time in hours. "Yes, she likely would. Your friends are scary."

Our brief respite was interrupted by an alarm from the console. Dylan turned back to see what it was, and I turned to the still sleeping Adrianna. The child was exhausted from being on the run. This might have been the first chance for her to sleep in ages.

A grunt from Dylan attracted my attention.

"What is it?"

"Nothing good. Our long-range scanners show someone headed our way."

"Maybe it's Felix?"

"I doubt it. We are still six days away from our scheduled meet-up."

"Mundi?"

"Most likely."

"Can we make it to Wells?"

"They're moving too fast to be using ground transportation. They'll be on us in twenty minutes."

"How the hell did they find us?"

Dylan ignored me. Instead, he fixed a critical gaze on Adrianna. He retreated to the back and returned with his eyes glued to a small device in his hand. His frown deepened as he slowly moved it around the cabin, finally coming to rest over the girl.

"She has a tracking beacon on her."

"The fuck you say!"

Dylan gently rousted the child and ran the scanner up and down her body. She sat impassively, as if such examinations were the norm. He settled it over the back of her neck.

"It's subdermal."

"Shit!" I bounded out of my seat and grabbed my medical

kit. Rummaging through it, I retrieved a scalpel and moved toward Adrianna. At the sight of me her eyes grew wide. She screamed and pushed herself into the chair.

"I don't have time for this bullshit. Dylan, hold her down so I can get at it."

He hugged her until her screams were muffled against his chest. I felt the area Dylan had identified and discovered a small lump beneath the skin. Deftly, I worked the instrument, trying to be as quick as possible to shorten the ordeal for Adrianna.

"Got it," I said, triumphantly holding up the rice-sized device.

Dylan grabbed it from me and examined it before he threw it on the floor and crushed it under his heel.

Without a word, he hurried to the navigation console. The vehicle swayed and bounced as it turned to our new course and sped up considerably. Such a move was ill-advised under the present storm conditions as we ran the risk of rolling over an undetected obstacle, but there was little choice.

After waiting for a few minutes without any comment from Dylan, I inquired, "Did it work?"

He shook his head. "If it did, we've only delayed them..." He was distracted, absorbed in finding a solution to our problem. I tried to wait patiently.

Adrianna cowered from me when I looked at her. I wondered what they had done to her.

"They aren't changing course. We've bought ourselves maybe ten minutes."

"What are we going to do?"

Dylan's answer was to walk to the storage locker and pull out two environmental suits. "See if you can adjust the smaller one to fit the girl."

For short excursions outside, a breathing mask usually sufficed, but the fact that he handed them to me told me he planned for us to be out in the storm for an indeterminate duration.

Adrianna pulled back as I advanced with hers. Not wanting

to induce a full-blown tantrum, I knelt to her level. "Look, kid, we're in a time crunch here. I need you to put this on so I can fit it to you. We're going outside."

She eyed me stonily, but eventually she nodded and allowed me near. As I finished adapting it to her small frame, Dylan emerged from the back, wearing military power armour.

"When the hell did you get that?"

"I brought a few things ten years ago I thought we might need."

"And that thing was hiding back there all this time? I really am a lousy housekeeper."

He glanced at me without a flicker of amusement then checked the console once more. Shaking his head, he muttered to himself. "A wide-range thermal scan...about a minute and then, another two... Get suited up now, Mel. We haven't much time."

As I rushed to don my environmental suit, he made adjustments to his armour.

"What is the plan?"

"I'm going to approach close to an outcrop I spotted. You two will hide there. Whatever happens, keep your heads down and stay out of sight behind the rocks."

Without waiting for any response from me, he advanced to another locker and removed a lethal-looking firearm. It was more like a small cannon than a gun.

"Where will you be during all this?"

"I'm going to take up a defensible position as far from you as possible," he said.

Realization of his plan dawned on me. "You're using our vehicle as bait?"

"We have one shot at this. If there is more than one ship pursuing us, we're fucked."

The transport lurched to a stop as Dylan had programmed it to. Knowing the time for chit-chat was past, I helped Adrianna into her breathing mask before donning my own. The door in the back opened, and the three of us jumped out into the blowing sandstorm.

Though the winds appeared savage from inside the vehicle, outside they amounted to little more than a strong breeze, leaving our biggest issue as visibility. Dirt and grit swirled about Dylan. With his helmet now on, he looked like some kind of formidable combat robot.

The comm receiver in my ear buzzed with his voice. "Head over there."

I looked where he indicated. A shadow poked through the dust, roughly the size and shape of a toppled multistorey building.

"The outcrop should be about fifty metres away. Whatever happens, stay hidden."

I realized there was a good chance I might never see him again, and fear clutched at my heart. I wanted to say so many things to him; all the little shit that goes unexpressed from day to day until we forget to ever say it.

I addressed the back of his fading figure. "I love you. Please be careful."

"I will," his disembodied voice replied in my ear. He pressed a button on the control panel on his forearm, closing the rover's door. Then, like some kind of ghost, he faded from view.

I grabbed Adrianna's hand, and the two of us ran to the formation. We scrambled up the sloping face, and a short search revealed a small cleft in the rock face for us to hide within. Just as we settled, the loud whine of an aircraft rode on top of the wind over our heads.

Our perch afforded us what should have been an ideal position to see for kilometres. As things were, the storm obscured the scene, and all I could discern was a vague shadow in the shape of our vehicle, fifty metres or so away.

From the direction of the growing noise, a dark form coalesced above our transport. With spread wings like a giant raptor, it hung motionless, assessing the vulnerability of its prey before plunging down for the kill.

An explosion startled me. A bright orange flash from the aircraft told me Dylan's first shot had been true. Unfortunately, it had not been fatal. Engines screamed to a crescendo as it rotated, and thunderous flashes of returned fire burst from its side.

Another blast erupted on the hull as Dylan managed a second volley. This time, the damage was more significant, and the ship rasped desperately, the whine rising and falling as the pilot attempted to wrest control of his failing vessel. The spectral wings listed alarmingly to one side, and the doomed craft descended rapidly toward where it had fired its guns. Seconds after it vanished into the blowing grit, a hollow boom shook the ground, accompanied by the screech of rending metal and composites.

Clutching each other, Adrianna and I crouched motionless, listening for any sign of the returning marauder. The only sound was the whistling of wind and the ticking of sand grains as they bounced off the rocky outcrop.

When I could stand the silence no longer, I risked activating my comm. "Dylan? Are you there?"

Static in my ear was my only reward for breaking protocol. The aircraft went down in his general direction, and I didn't care what he told me about remaining hidden. I scrambled down the rocks and had reached the bottom, ready to dash off in search of Dylan, when I remembered Adrianna.

I waited while her short limbs hurried her down the hillside. Her hand locked in mine, I pulled her toward the downed airship. An explosion knocked us both off our feet. As we rose again, the obscuring dust ahead of us glowed orange from the burning wreckage. The air darkened further as smoke from the fires mingled with the suspended sand before being whisked away on the wind.

My heart beat a rapid tattoo as I called in vain for Dylan. Stepping around smouldering chunks of fuselage, I strained to peer through the pall of dust, desperate to find him.

A tug at my sleeve by Adrianna directed my attention to something a few metres away. Advancing on the slowly moving object, we discovered it was not Dylan but an injured member of the ship's crew, or what was left of him, practically torn in half by the crash. His legs were missing entirely. The dying man dragged himself pathetically across the sand. Gasping in the thin air, his trailing entrails leaked what blood remained in him on the parched Martian soil.

Distracted from his hopeless quest, he stared at us, a desperate plea on his face. Adrianna, to my surprise, did not cower from the horrible sight. Instead she met the man's stare with a coldness that sent chills down my spine, as if she willed for him to die in front of her.

There was nothing I could do for him except put him out of his misery. It was the merciful thing to do, but my inclination toward him was more in line with Adrianna's. My vow to do no harm became a convenient justification to leave him to his fate. It was a deliberate misinterpretation of the Hippocratic Oath, but I didn't care. For all I knew, this man had killed Dylan.

Wasting no further thought on him, I led Adrianna into the swirling smoke and sand to look for Dylan.

We groped our way across the crash site for an hour, finding nothing but twisted metal and scorched ground. We encountered no more survivors, or bodies for that matter, and despair rose up like a tide threatening to drown me.

A crackle of static in my ear and the fragments of words stopped me in my tracks.

"Dylan? Is that you?"

I interpreted the word "yes" struggling to emerge from the noise bursts in my earpiece. With a surge of newfound energy, I searched further until, a few minutes later, I found him.

He was in bad shape. His damaged armour had taken the brunt of the impact from a piece of the doomed ship draped over him. His helmet's faceplate was cracked, and dried blood trailed from his nose and mouth, but his eyes were open and he recognized me. That he had internal injuries was a certainty, but he lived, and I couldn't contain my joy.

Afraid to hug him, I placed my respiration mask against his helmet. Though his radio was damaged, he could hear me through the contact.

"I thought I lost you," I said, tears streaming down my cheeks.

"I was starting to worry about you." He winced in pain with the effort.

I needed to find a way to free him and return us to our vehicle. The debris pinning him was huge, too large for me and a child to lift. The only reason he wasn't crushed was because of his armour. If I couldn't come up with a way to extricate him, and soon, he would die.

CHAPTER 16

Perspiration trickled into my eyes, despite the dropping temperatures. With darkness an hour away, little headway was made in extricating Dylan. The environmental controls of his damaged combat armour would not permit him to survive, exposed as he was, to a Martian night. Even if I freed him and dragged him back to our rover, presuming I could still locate it, he might yet succumb to his injuries. I had no way to assess the extent of them.

I welcomed the respite from my futile struggles when he waved for me to come to him. I pressed my faceplate against his. "I can't budge the fucking thing."

He nodded lazily, his eyes drooping as he fought the pull of slumber.

"Dylan! Stay with me. Don't go to sleep."

His eyes snapped open. "Then you should get me out of here, because..." Fluttering eyes rolled to the top of his head.

"Hey!" I shouted, rapping his helmet with my knuckles.

"I'm okay. Just tired."

We both knew better. He was losing blood, and we were running out of time.

"How's the girl?"

I forgot about her while struggling with the immovable wreckage. Panicking, I raised my head and searched about. She sat with her back to us, digging in the sand with a small metal plate from the debris field. I envied her childish ability to compartmentalize her emotions. It was a survival mechanism I knew well at her age but found increasingly more difficult as the years passed.

Then a thought struck me. "I am such an idiot! Kid, you're some kind of genius."

I called her over, and we searched for another, similar sized fragment. Pulling her around the right side of Dylan, I pointed to the red earth and told her to dig. Within five minutes we moved enough soil that I could drag him out from under the pinning object.

I assessed the condition of his armour. It was scraped up and dented but had retained its structural integrity, giving me hope that Dylan's injuries might be treatable.

His eyes were closed and remained so, no matter how much I shouted and jostled him. Desperate, I pressed my faceplate against his and held my breath as I listened for any signs of life. I fought the urge to pull off his helmet and administer CPR. Exposing him to the dropping temperature and the oxygen-starved atmosphere would be fatal. A faint fogging of his visor told me he still breathed, so I allowed myself to relax a bit and collect my thoughts.

Searching the strewn debris nearby, I collected enough material to form an improvised travois. With Adrianna's help, I rolled Dylan on it and secured him with some cables I recovered from the remains of a console.

While the two big problems of freeing Dylan and devising a way to move him to our rover had been solved, one critical difficulty remained. I didn't know where our vehicle was. Finding it in the dust storm was challenging enough, but the growing darkness made the task impossible.

Then came my second opportunity of the day to feel foolish. Lifting Dylan's arm, I located the control he had used to shut down the transport. Its configuration was unfamiliar to me, so I experimented with buttons in the hope I might trip on the engine or exterior search lamp: anything that would provide an indication of the vehicle's location.

I pressed every combination I could think of, each time

followed by a scan around us for any suggestion of success. Nothing worked. For all I knew I had raised and lowered the door ramp and nothing more.

My shivering rattled my teeth, and I pulled my arms around Adrianna to share as much body heat as the insulated suits would permit. We didn't think to bring a torch or a survival pack with us in our haste to escape to the outcrop. Total darkness had descended, and the temperature continued to plummet.

The only things visible were the illuminated faceplates of Dylan and Adrianna. She shivered, huddled into my side. Dylan's armour would protect him from freezing far longer than our flimsy environmental suits, but by morning he would still be dead, along with us.

I admired his peaceful face, made ghostly by the LEDs. The only apparent damage was the long crack in the hardened clear composite of the faceplate. The lights told me the armour still had power, and most of its systems functioned, including the infrared scanner built into the visor. It was ironic that the only person capable of locating our vehicle was in no condition to do so.

My mind wandered as I examined the elegant combat suit. Modularly constructed, it was designed to be donned quickly, as Dylan had demonstrated earlier. It was similar to those injured Terran soldiers wore when they were brought into the ER during the Lunar Rebellion. I remembered the care we had to take because of the redundant oxygen and power supplies within the headgear itself.

The cold made my thinking sluggish. I shook my head to clear it and make room for a crazy idea to form. After I checked the clasps on my own breathing mask, I returned my attention to the one that held Dylan's helmet in place. It was possible my scheme might work, but I had to be fast and pray that my assumptions about the design were not in error. If I were wrong, I would be the first to die, gasping for air. At least I wouldn't freeze to death.

I took several long slow breaths to oxygenate my lungs, then, holding my breath, I took off my respiration apparatus. The icy cold stung my face, but I forced myself to keep my eyes opened and quickly removed the only thing keeping Dylan alive. With shivering hands, I put my discarded ventilation mask on him and sealed it. With my face and fingers numb, I threw his helmet on my head and pulled up the collar of my environmental suit to make a crude seal.

Its lights flickered and dimmed but remained on. Unable to hold my air any longer, I exhaled and reflexively inhaled fresh, icy, breathable oxygen. Taking only a moment to be grateful I still lived, I activated the standard HUD display with a head movement and turned on the infrared scanner.

I didn't search long before the thermal outline of our rover appeared. Making a mental note of location and distance, I drew a line in the sand beside me pointing toward the machine. I took one last look as a confirmation it was real, then as fast as my cold hands allowed, I reversed the operation and returned our helmets to their rightful owners.

CHAPTER 17

The child stood motionless and stared at him. Dylan, who drifted in and out of consciousness, did not notice her strange attention, but I was creeped out enough by it for the both of us.

The only time I'd heard her speak was the sad farewell to Carlos. Since then, her only form of communication with me was a series of saucy looks and a lot of attitude. She seemed fixated on Dylan as much as she was mistrustful of me.

She proved helpful in pulling him back to the vehicle, more so than my expectations from an eight-year-old girl. After we transferred him to the bed and removed his armour, she assumed her vigil while I performed my examination of his injuries.

Aside from a concussion, a broken leg, four snapped ribs, a punctured lung, bruised spleen, and some frostbite, he emerged from the ordeal relatively unscathed, considering an aircraft had dropped on top of him. I was able to treat him with the emergency equipment I kept on hand, and he now rested under sedation.

Adrianna stood at his side during the four hours of surgery, only breaking her discipline to resentfully drink some water when I ordered her. She ignored me entirely when I told her to get some sleep. I suspected she would remain on guard until she was confident Dylan would recover.

The truth was, I had no idea how to deal with the little shit.

I was reluctant to sit down with her and attempt any kind of conversation for fear she might actually speak to me and tell me of the horrors Carlos suggested she'd lived through—or maybe something worse. The kid was messed up, I had no doubt. The sooner I got her to the safe house, the better. Then she would become someone else's project.

The attack on us had delayed that handoff. I had no way of knowing if our vehicle was specifically identified before Dylan shot the ship down. It was five more days until the planned rendezvous with Felix. We couldn't afford to loiter, waiting for him after dropping off Adrianna.

Though considerable distance was between ourselves and the outcrop, the fear of being detected again loomed large in my imagination. Inspection of the navigation computer told me our best option was still our first plan, to hide out at Wells Canyon for three days before making the run to Espiritus. A quick handoff of the girl and then we could leave the planet before anyone realized.

The weather forecast showed the storm would be going strong for another week, which would help. Besides, Dylan could benefit from the rest while we waited. Satisfied with my decision, I settled into the pilot's chair while the darkness rolled by.

I was startled awake by a bump of the vehicle. With my heart beating wildly, I looked about to orient myself. The familiar surroundings of what had been our home for ten years assured me I had been dreaming, and I relaxed back into my seat.

The blackness outside had lightened to deep tawny, telling me that the sun had risen. Sitting beside me, motionless, was Adrianna. Her arms were folded across her small chest, and anger smouldered behind her dark blue eyes.

"How long have you been there?" I did not expect any response.

"He should be in a hospital."

I stared, speechless, at her for a few heartbeats.

"I beg your pardon?"

"He needs a doctor."

I frowned. "I AM one."

She inspected me critically then turned to the watch out the front window. "You're not very good."

"What the f—?" I squeezed the arm of the chair until my fingers ached. "What are you talking about?"

"He's still hurt."

"Of course he is. He's recovering and will need some time —"

"You didn't fix him."

"Where do you...?" I stopped myself and replayed the entire surgery from memory. When finished, I glared at the child. Her accusing expression had not changed.

Growling under my breath, I rose and went back to check on Dylan.

He slept fitfully despite the painkillers pumped into him. I felt his forehead and was taken aback by how cold and clammy it was.

No longer sure of myself, I fetched a bioimager and scanned him from head to toe. Nothing conclusive showed. The girl's accusation had rattled me, despite how ridiculous it sounded. How would an eight-year-old know anything? It was absurd to consider. And yet, her unwavering certainty coupled with Dylan's condition had me questioning my competence.

Not quite willing to turn in my medical degree, I resolved to put the matter to rest. Since the communities I visited didn't have access to many modern treatment options, over time I had assembled an array of black market components as a necessity. Though I hated to put money into the hands of thieves, I could not legitimately dismiss doing so on the basis of moral or ethical superiority. There was a time not so far in the past when I supplemented my income by a similar means.

Some contraband surgical nanites had recently found their way into my medical supplies. Though I'd already used some in my treatment of his injuries, I injected Dylan with the last of my supply and turned to the medical monitoring station. As I suspected, the tiny machines homed in on a reopened internal wound. Cursing under my breath, I programmed them to recauterize the site and prayed it didn't happen again, since I had no more to treat him with.

After sitting with Dylan for a while to assure myself his condition had stabilized, I returned to the cockpit and resumed my seat beside Adrianna, determined not to give her any satisfaction by telling her anything. She regarded me without emotion, the accusing look now a thing of the past.

She rose and went to the back of the vehicle. When curiosity became overwhelming, I followed and found her sitting next to Dylan, watching over him once more.

I regretted my decision to delay our arrival in Espiritus. I needed to swallow whatever feelings I had over the next few days, but the sooner I rid myself of this kid, the better I would feel.

CHAPTER 18

Although I embedded our rendezvous time and location within the coded message to Felix, I showed up early and waited with my stomach in knots. I fretted I'd screwed up somehow and sent him to places unknown or that my cry for help was not received. Never once did it cross my mind that he might refuse to respond.

I was surprised to spot Dani first, casually browsing among the kiosks in the market. Though Felix was nowhere in sight, I was confident he was not far away, watching for trouble. When her eyes found me, her face lit up and she let out a squeal of delight, which was drowned out by the noise and bustle of the marketplace. Realizing her error, she sobered and strode purposefully toward me through the crowd.

On reaching me, we ducked between two stalls and she embraced me with an unrestrained bearhug. Felix's sudden, spectre-like appearance behind me interrupted our reunion.

"I was worried you didn't receive my message," I said after greeting him with a more reserved embrace.

"No chance, Sugar. Felix doesn't miss anything. I can't get away with a thing." She winked at him.

Not willing to risk being in the open longer than necessary, the three of us departed and made our way toward our vehicle. I filled them in on the details of everything that happened to us and prepared them to meet Adrianna.

"She's a bit odd, as you might imagine," I said.

"Nonsense, Sugar, I'm sure she's a delightful little girl. I look forward to getting to know her."

"That will not be possible, my love. Based on Mel's story, we must be expedient in our delivery of the child and our own departure," said Felix.

"Well, that's just too bad. She sounds like somebody who could use some friends. Have you given any thought to bringing her with us instead?"

Felix broke the awkward silence that grew as I searched for a response to Dani.

"That would be ill-advised."

He looked at me knowingly, and I subtly nodded my thanks to him.

The arrival at our vehicle initiated another round of greetings with Dylan. When he winced in pain at Dani's enthusiastic hug, the nurse in her took charge. She decided he needed to rest and that Felix was, indeed, correct that our departure should be sooner than later.

"You and Felix take her to her new home," she told me as she smiled at the girl. "I'll watch over Dylan while you're gone and help pack things up."

Dani knelt to look the child in the face. She stroked a loose strand of unruly, auburn hair from the girl's eyes and spoke to her in a soft voice. "You can't be in safer hands than with these two, sweetie. They will make sure you get to a fine home."

She then leaned forward and hugged Adrianna. To my great surprise, she returned the embrace.

With nothing left to talk about, we departed to fulfill Dani's promise to her.

Felix strode beside me as if he owned the town. In a sense, he almost had at one time. As Regis Mundi's erstwhile lieutenant, he practically ruled over all the magnate's diverse corporate and political interests. If he had chosen to remain in service after the dictator's assumption of power on Mars, no doubt he would be the practical governor of Espiritus and every other settlement on the planet.

Love had changed all that. Nobody imagined, least of all

Dani and Felix, what kind of relationship would develop from their unconventional introduction. At first I thought Dani suffered from some version of Stockholm Syndrome, but in the brief time they were together, I came to understand a more perfect match could never be planned.

Dani had a proclivity for exotic lovers of either gender. It only seemed natural after the fact that she would fall in love with a synthetic human. For his part, something about her affected Felix. I thought it was for the better.

The girl walked on my other side, maintaining her customary silence. Since our disagreement over Dylan's treatment, she had started to speak more. I was graced with monosyllabic responses to my attempts to chat, but for anything requiring a level of conversation, she remained mute around me.

With Dylan, however, she was a different person. She giggled at his jokes and they shared stories, taking the time to grow comfortable with each other. It was as if both of them had found something in the other that had been missing in their life. I couldn't wait to rid myself of the little bitch.

Espiritus was large enough that we could blend in with the crowds of pedestrians choking the narrow streets. The evening press of people migrating from work to home delayed our progress, but provided us with a degree of anonymity as we passed for a family of three. His sharp, synthetic eyes detected surveillance cameras long before I ever could, giving us ample time to select an alternate route.

We arrived at the address and paused at a distance to survey the situation.

"I didn't spot any monitoring systems along this street," Felix said.

"It's probably why Carlos's people selected it for a safe house."

Felix nodded. "We should still proceed with caution. Mundi's people will be on the alert for you two. I suggest you remain concealed here until I can reconnoitre."

Without waiting for my response, he left us and made his

way up the abandoned lane. He strolled past the door, never changing stride and never looking up. He appeared to be lost in thought, and I wondered how the hell he would notice anything. Continuing to the end of the block, he vanished around the corner.

Time passed, and I was worried something had happened to him until Felix stealthy approached us from behind.

"There is no sign the door is watched. We can proceed."

We emerged from our hiding spot and advanced toward the residence. After only a brief hesitation, I rapped on the door. My pulse raced, and I forced myself to control my breathing. I repeated my knock, but there was no response.

His brow creased, Felix checked both ways down the avenue before holding an ear to the entry. Seeming satisfied by what he heard, he tried the latch, which yielded. He pushed the door open.

Darkness and the smell of dust were all that greeted us. After one more check of our surroundings, Felix ushered us through the portal and closed it in our wake.

We stood just inside the threshold, alert for any sign of an occupant. Felix's eyes adapted more quickly than mine, and he proceeded ahead into the gloom. After a minute of listening to the faintest of footfalls, a light came on, blinding me briefly.

The now brightly lit room revealed itself to be devoid of furnishings, and a film of the omnipresent Martian grit covered the floor, undisturbed except by our footprints.

"The place is abandoned," said Felix. He regarded me with an unasked question.

"This is the address I was given."

"It has been empty for some time, judging by the thickness of the dust. Was there no other information?"

"Only this," I said, removing the data safe from my satchel.

Felix examined it. "This is a sealed archive: military grade encryption. Were you told what it contains?"

I shook my head. "No, and the key code to access it probably died with Carlos."

He handed it back to me. "Our options are limited. Either

we open it and possibly learn of a place to deliver the child, or we must take her with us off-planet."

"Fuck!" I immediately regretted my outburst. Felix had only given voice to what I already figured out.

"I'm sorry, Felix. You're right, of course. Do you think Dani can decode it?"

He looked to Adrianna, who returned his gaze, the almost perpetual scowl creasing her brow. Returning his attention to me, he said, "It is possible she can. Her abilities are prodigious. You must, however, prepare yourself for the possibility we may never discover its contents."

I tried to imagine Adrianna as a happy little girl, living a normal life with a family who loved her. "Yeah, maybe, but I still want to try."

We exited the house and retraced our route. After five minutes of walking, without explanation, Felix led us down an unfamiliar street, followed by turns into two more unknown lanes.

"Felix, this isn't the way we came."

"No."

He increased our pace and ushered us into a dark blind alley. "Wait here for me."

Before I replied, he vanished. I squeezed Adrianna's small hand. "We'll be fine. I'm sure he'll only be a moment."

She wrinkled her nose at me then rolled her eyes. It took every ounce of self-control I could muster not to smack some respect into her. No sooner had the idea entered my mind than I became sickened by it. That was the pattern of my childhood. She might be a disrespectful little shit, but she didn't deserve to be beaten for it. Maybe it really would be best if someone else cared for her.

Felix's return rescued me from my self-examination. Clutched in front of him by the scruff of the neck was a strangely submissive man. He had a reddening spot on the side of his face, and some blood dribbled from his recently broken nose. Felix threw him to the ground at my feet.

"We were followed," he said emotionlessly.

The cowering man had long, thin limbs and the gaunt, malnourished look typical of someone whose ancestors had arrived on Mars generations ago. Though Felix was a head and a half shorter, the fellow had not been a match for him.

He seized the Martian by his lapels, lifted him to his feet, and slammed his back into the alley wall, pinning him there.

"I believe you know what my question will be," he said.

"Look, you don't need to rough me up anymore. I'll tell you anything you want to know."

"Let's begin simply. Why were you following us?"

"I...I was paid to watch the apartment you guys went into. I was supposed to find out as much as I could about anyone who went there."

"Who do you work for?"

"Lots of people. This job is freelance. I picked it up on the Cortex and don't know who's behind it."

"What were your instructions?"

"Once I learned where you went, I was to contact the guy and collect my payment. That's all I know."

"So you have no idea who your employer is?" I asked.

"No."

"This is crazy," I said. "Why didn't they just set up a surveillance camera?"

"I don't know any more than what I just told you."

Felix answered, "There are methods to detect or even thwart automated systems, as you may be aware." A subtle smile curled up the edges of his mouth. "Physical observation is preferred in certain circles."

"So you know who hired him?"

In response to my question, Felix seized the man's head with both hands and twisted it violently until a sickening snap signalled the breaking neck. He released the dying man and allowed him to fall to the ground.

I fell to my knees beside him, but I was helpless to aid the man.

"Why did you do that?"

"He is an agent in Regis Mundi's network. His report would

be damaging."

"But he couldn't identify us. He didn't know where we were going. There was nothing useful he could give to his employer."

"He would pass on that a child arrived at that residence in the company of a man and woman. That and anything interrogation would extract would be sufficient to deduce who we are. Without such information in their hands, we still hold an advantage."

If anyone knew Mundi's methods, it was Felix.

Adrianna stood over the dead man, studying him like he was a specimen. Any other child would scream hysterically. This one had seen violence and death before—a lot of it. She was anything but normal.

Felix helped me to my feet.

"We must return to the others and develop a plan of action. Once this informant's body is discovered, it won't take long for Mundi's agents to cast a wider net. This settlement is no longer safe."

"But where can we go?"

"Perhaps the data archive will give us some idea of our next step. Unless you are amenable to taking the child with us off-planet? We can leave tonight."

I took another look at the troubled little girl.

"Let's get back and see what Dani can do."

CHAPTER 19

Neither Dani nor Dylan made any attempt to hide the surprise on their faces.

Dani gestured toward the girl. "What the hell happened?"

"The rendezvous was a setup."

"Carlos sold you out?"

"That makes no sense," said Dylan. A few days of rest had done wonders for him. Still in a lot of pain, he was at least moving about now.

"Likely your contact was compromised and abandoned the location," said Felix. "There was no sign of violence. I suspect Mundi's agents, having missed their quarry, posted an observer should anyone come calling."

"Mundi?" said Dani. "Were you spotted?"

I glanced at Felix. "The situation's been handled." I was reluctant to provide Dani with the ugly details of what her lover was capable of. "Nobody knows we were there."

"So now what happens? Are we taking Adrianna with us?"

Explaining the situation to her, I removed the data safe from my satchel and placed it in her hands.

"It's been a while," she said, turning the box over as she examined every facet of the enigmatic package. "It may take some time."

Without waiting for a response, she sat in the pilot's chair and activated our vehicle's main computer. With nothing more interesting to watch than her typing code, I elected to find something to eat.

Realizing I was probably not the only famished one, I asked Adrianna, "Are you hungry?"

Never taking her eyes from Dani, she shook her head. It suddenly struck me that nobody had thought to ask the girl what she wanted. I squatted down to her level.

"What would you like to do? Do you want to leave the planet with me?" I had no idea what prompted me to ask the question. Bringing her along with us was the very last thing I desired. I would be a bad enough mother to a normal child. Life with this one could not turn out well for either of us.

She fixed me with those big, deep blue eyes for several uncomfortable seconds.

"Yes."

"You do?" I sputtered.

A hint of a devilish smile turned the corner of her mouth. "Yes, I'm hungry."

You little shit.

Feeling foolish, I led her to the kitchen area and prepared a sandwich for each of us.

Over the next two hours there was nothing to do but wait for Dani to work her magic. Dylan returned to our bed to rest while Felix jacked into the Cortex to monitor for anything suspicious. Sitting on the floor, hugging her knees to her chest, Adrianna was absorbed in her own world.

I felt pity for her. I recalled the horrific picture Carlos had painted of her life. Spending an entire lifetime as a lab rat would mess anyone up. The girl seemed functional, though I suspected multiple psychoses lurked under her recalcitrant personality.

"Uh, guys?" said Dani. "There's a problem."

Felix and I hovered over her shoulder, but she waited until Dylan emerged from the back to join us.

"This archive is military and has a homing beacon, which I tripped."

She allowed the flurry of exclamations to continue for a moment before she raised her hands to calm us.

"I deactivated it, but it still managed to set off a signal burst for about thirty seconds."

"We need to get moving right away," said Dylan as he coaxed Dani from the pilot chair. While he started our vehicle and got us under way toward the settlement's airlock, she continued to report on her findings.

Dani moved to a second computer station and brought up a display of the contents of the data safe.

"I'm pretty sure this device doesn't belong to Regis Mundi. Everything on here is from one of his research facilities, and every file shows signs of tampering. Whoever hacked the encryption left some tell-tale damage. It was a clumsy job, but if this belongs to Mundi's people, I find it odd they would include data stolen from him in it."

"Carlos was involved with Talus Varr," I said. "He stole the information for him. Probably the signal you tripped went out to the rebels."

"It would make sense that he wanted to deliver this to them," said Dani. "Maybe the girl was part of the package?"

Adrianna seemed disinterested, absorbed with her own thoughts. It wouldn't surprise me, though, if that was a ruse to convince us she wasn't paying attention.

Lowering my voice, I said, "What's in the files?"

Dani glanced toward the child then whispered, "She's a clone. Her DNA record is included here."

"Is there any indication of who the source is?" asked Felix.

Dani shook her head. "Nothing like that. She is referred to as subject 647. Everything indicates she is the only one to survive."

"There were others from the same donor?"

Dani shrugged. "Your guess is as good as mine, Mel. But 647 is a scary number if there were."

I returned my attention to the girl: grown in a lab, along with hundreds of others exactly like her. Why? What was so important about the donor's DNA that Mundi's scientists felt they had to mass-produce clones? Maybe they had a limited donor sample and could not acquire more; someone either dead or beyond their reach.

Felix stared intently at the screen, paging through multiple documents too fast for me to read them.

"What is it, Felix?"

"It appears cloning is not the only activity occurring in Regis Mundi's laboratory. Many of these files are familiar to me. They are from the original synthetic humanoid program that resulted in my birth."

"You told me that project was abandoned," said Dani.

"Mundi discontinued the effort when I defected from his service. He perceived no advantage in spending so much for servants who could betray him as easily as humans. Yet these documents suggest its revival."

"What's the connection between clones and synthetics? What is he working on?" I asked.

"It is not clear from the contents of this safe," he replied.

"Whatever it is," said Dylan from the pilot's chair, "Varr's people thought it important enough to steal that data and abduct the girl."

"What are we going to do?" asked Dani.

"The first thing we're going to do is put a lot of distance between us and this place. We'll be through the airlock in five minutes."

"We can't leave with Felix and Dani," I said. "Their ship is here, and they'll be stuck on Mars."

Dylan brought the vehicle to a halt. "Well, a decision needs to be made."

"Dani, you and Felix need to go," I said. "Get away from here before the authorities find you."

"But what about you, Sugar?"

"We can't go; at least not yet. This data was important enough for Carlos to sacrifice himself. By leaving, we may be permitting something terrible to happen."

"I must agree with Melanie," said Felix. "The fact that Regis Mundi chose to resurrect the synthetic humanoid program is disturbing. By itself, it might merely be an attempt to prolong his life by artificial means. But knowledge the project also involves human cloning suggests something else is at play that must be stopped, if only for moral reasons."

"So we're all agreed then?" said Dani. "We will try to find Talus Varr and deliver the girl and the data to him."

Felix responded to her, "There is no reason to put your life at risk."

"Screw that. I was sent away by you once for my safety. It isn't gonna happen again, hon."

"All right, then," I said, "it's decided. We'll go to the rebels."

CHAPTER 20

Morgan monitored his pace as he traversed Olympia's long, curving corridors. Only the concern of being seen and the subsequent damage to his authority kept him from rushing. Even if he didn't care about what the others thought, it would never do to appear winded before his master.

Referring to the old fossil as "Master" or "Dominus" had seemed demeaning when first required of him. Though grown accustomed to using the terms, the expectation irked him. A lifelong republican, the idea of a Supreme Dictator would have once been repugnant. Had fortune left him on the planet's surface, he may well have joined the uprising, and he would be dead for the effort, a gaping crater now occupying where his home settlement had been.

It was the first of three communities ordered obliterated by asteroid bombardments. They served as examples of what happened to those who opposed the new order. Much of the remaining populace renounced any sympathy for Talus Varr's fledgling rebellion and reluctantly accepted Regis Mundi as their new ruler.

Morgan's rapid rise through the ranks to become Felix Altius's successor was nothing he planned. Yet here he was, the second most powerful man on Mars. Though on occasion nostalgic for the old republic, he did not want a return to the old ways. He had gained far too much.

One of the greatest threats to his security was Mundi

himself. The old man was mercurial, and his moods needed to be gauged carefully. Many, less cautious retainers had met unexpected ends, and Morgan learned from their failures.

The bigger problem for him and everyone else was that Mundi was dying and had appointed no heir. This, of course, created ample opportunity for many within the inner circle to jockey into favourable positions. He remained constantly diligent lest those seeking to displace him found a means to do so. And so he walked to his destination, betraying none of the anxiety he felt.

The guards admitted him, unchallenged, into the private infirmary. Even though it was located deep within Mundi's apartments on the orbital habitat, the dictator still did not feel comfortable without his Praetorian Guard to protect him.

Morgan stood quietly by the door and waited as the doctors fussed over the old man lying in bed. He frowned as they applied the bandages to his hand. When Mundi spotted him, the medics were impatiently waved away.

"Come closer and give me your report."

The frown returned to Mundi as he examined his bandaged appendage. "I'm in a race against time, and these idiots tell me it's the best they can do. What do you think?"

Morgan regarded the proffered hand from a discreet distance. "Did they replace it, Dominus?"

"No, the cowards wouldn't consider that. All they dared attempt was grafting new muscle. It will be a couple of days before I regain the use of the hand, but it will do nothing to relieve my arthritis. They are not yet ready to grow the bones, and an entire body is out of the question at the moment. Of course, everything would be different if they could recover the clone. What is your progress on that front?"

Morgan's throat tightened. "It was tracked to New Phoenix, and two agents attempted a recovery."

"Attempted? So the subject escaped them?"

"The suspected architect of the plot was killed, but not before he could retire our operatives."

Mundi raised his voice. "So what happened to their

quarry?"

"It was aided to escape by..." How could he tell his master what he barely believed to be possible?

"Well, spit it out, boy! Who helped?"

Morgan tried to swallow past his parched throat. "Available information suggests it was Melanie Destin."

"The Mother of Mars? Are you certain?"

"I'm not yet convinced it is her, sire..."

"You realize the implications of this, don't you?"

"Yes, Dominus, but I caution you this intelligence is based on questionable data and..."

"Well, if it isn't her, someone took the clone. At what stage is your follow-up investigation?"

Morgan wished for more time. A few hours more might give him something substantial to offer the old man. Thinking it best to avoid any mention of the lost pursuit aircraft, he girded himself to tell Mundi what he needed to know most.

"All our sources indicate they plan to transport the girl north, into rebel-controlled territory." There, it was out in the open, and his failure was now exposed.

"A lone woman and a small girl slipped past the network of informants you persuaded me to finance, is that correct?"

"Sire, if it was Melanie Destin, she avoided detection for ten years. You must consider the allies she..."

"Do you know the price of your incompetence?"

"Yes, sir, I..."

"I don't think you understand. I am dying. My physicians can only postpone the outcome a human lifetime of excess guarantees."

Morgan grew uneasy as Mundi studied him. He had to make sure he did not signal an inappropriate reaction to what the old man assumed to be a revelation.

"Recovery of the clone will allow me to extend my life." He dashed a surgical tray across the room. "Of course, that will never occur because of the collective bungling of everyone!"

Morgan lowered his eyes to avoid Mundi's. No response would be helpful. He had to let the man vent and hope to survive.

"I need Melanie Destin, if she lives. Only her cells are adapted and have the potential to bond with the synthetic flesh. Only she will guarantee, not only my survival in a body that will last for a thousand years, but the ability to control the alien nanites."

"Master, I am following several leads. I only require a little more time, and I will recover subject 647. If the woman is with her, everything you desire will be yours."

"Time is my problem, Morgan. There is little left for me. Even if you retrieve them, it only postpones my demise. My idiot scientists think replacing me part by part will accomplish what only a new body can."

"Then allow me to shorten the time. Give me the authorization to pursue my quarry into rebel territory."

"What do you require?"

"Armoured combat ships to fend off any enemy forces we encounter. I believe they are aiding the flight of the clone. They will be heavily armed, and military assets are necessary."

"Very well, you may do what you ask. Just insure you bring me what I need, or do not return."

Morgan nodded and took a step backward while he turned the last, most dangerous intelligence over in his mind. If he declared his information then failed to deliver, he would be finished. Only the capture of Melanie Destin would compensate Mundi for the disappointment.

On the other hand, if he could provide Mundi with everything the old man ever imagined, the rewards would be incalculable, but only if predeclared. If he remained silent and delivered without revealing what he knew, his success would be interpreted as serendipity, and Mundi never rewarded luck.

"Is there something else, Morgan?"

"Sire, there is one more thing which I believe you should be aware. Felix Altius is on Mars."

"This is confirmed?"

"Yes, Dominus. He was sighted only once in Espiritus but is now off the grid. We identified the ship he arrived in, and it is under surveillance."

Mundi slid off the examining table and paced the space between them, lost in thought. Morgan imagined many possible reactions to this news; thoughtful reflection was not one of them.

"You must discover the reason for his return. It will be difficult. I'm sure most of his old contacts are still in place, aiding him to avoid capture."

"My network identified him once. It can locate him again."

"I want him captured, unharmed, do you understand? He is precious to me and must not be damaged."

A pall of doubt covered Morgan. Had Mundi forgiven his erstwhile lieutenant?

"M'Lord, he betrayed you. I would have thought you wished his head?"

"Oh, yes, he was indeed false. Were he not unique, I would allow you to kill him. I have a much different fate planned for my old friend."

"Sire?"

"Instead of removing his head, I will empty it and transfer my own mind into his perfect, synthetic body. Then I'll possess all the time I shall ever need."

Taking his leave, Morgan departed the infirmary and proceeded to his office to begin planning the operation. The small, fearful voice inside him held a small hope that neither Destin nor Altius would turn up. If they did exist, both would be almost impossible to capture and might never be taken alive. If that happened, he might as well plan on putting a bullet in his own head.

Felix Altius was a most formidable opponent by himself, but if, as Morgan suspected, he'd returned to aid Melanie Destin, then the stakes had been raised to heady heights.

The woman was no doubt accompanied by her lover. An alliance between he and Mundi's former lieutenant would be unassailable. Dylan Hodgson had been his superior before his disappearance. Morgan never believed the conclusions of the investigation that predicted his defection to Terra. The man betrayed his duty and aided the fugitive woman in her escape from justice. If she still lived, it meant he was with her. Mundi might want to keep her and Altius alive for some insane purpose, but there was no reason Martian law shouldn't be carried out on her companion.

The more he considered the matter, the more he relished the idea of taking on his former mentor. Though he had once admired and emulated the man, he'd proven himself an unworthy son of Mars. Ten years had made Morgan stronger, better trained and cannier than the young officer his erstwhile commander knew.

That being said, he couldn't afford to take his old superior for granted. Someone had destroyed the pursuit aircraft sent to apprehend the clone. If the traitor had been responsible, that would represent but a fraction of the danger he presented.

It was right to request military support. Any rebels they might encounter in their hunt would present an insignificant threat when compared to the allied skills of Dylan Hodgson and Felix Altius.

CHAPTER 21

A week can really establish how small even the biggest land transport vehicle is, especially when five people are crammed inside.

Dani stumbled out of the lavatory, a frown creasing her freckled brow. "Any chance our fearless leader will permit us a thimbleful of water to bathe with today?"

I returned her scowl. "Why do you need to ask that every morning?"

"Well, mostly because I don't enjoy smelling like the inside of an old shoe, like you, Sugar."

We glared at each other through slitted lids for a few seconds before Dani broke first. She fell back against the wall in an uncontrollable giggling fit.

"Seriously, Dylan," she gasped after regaining her composure, "could we please use a bit more water today?"

"I'm afraid we've a limited supply and a long journey ahead of us," he said from the pilot's seat.

"I can't believe you two lived like this for ten years."

"We deal with the same issue aboard our spaceship, my dear," said Felix. "We have larger storage capacity than this vehicle. It wasn't designed for five."

"Well, I'd like to at least wash my armpits. After the four of you have been through, only dust comes out of the tap."

"That doesn't sound right," said Dylan. "There should be enough water for each of us to sponge ourselves off every day."

"Well, somebody is a water hog," she said.

"I've behaved myself," I said.

Felix added, with no hint of humour, "I have no sweat glands and do not require bathing."

"Eeew!" My nose crinkled.

"It's true," said Dani, smiling at her lover. "He always smells fresh and yummy."

Dylan returned to the topic at hand. "Well, I don't use my quota. If Felix isn't using his, what happened to all of the water?"

Everyone looked to the small form sitting on the floor, knees pulled up to her chin.

"Adrianna?" I called.

She drew her legs tighter and hid her nose behind them.

"We've had this conversation once already," I said to her.

Defiant blue eyes peeked from under an unruly mop of auburn hair.

I sprang from my chair. "You little bugger!"

Dani intercepted me. "Whoa, Sugar, don't go bat-shit crazy on the poor kid."

"That 'kid' is wilfully defying me..."

"She's a child, Mel. They try to get away with shit...er, stuff."

"Why are you taking her side? She's screwed you out of your water ration."

"I've survived worse. So have you, if I recall correctly."

I suddenly felt very small with everyone staring at me.

When only a little older than Adrianna, I was already an accomplished thief and con artist. I needed to remember she hadn't benefited from a life as screwed up as mine. I should have been the adult, yet somehow I reverted to my own childhood's street gang survival behaviour.

"You're right, Dani. I'm sorry I overreacted."

"I'm not the one you need to apologize to," she said, glancing toward the girl.

"She's the one who..."

Dani's cocked eyebrow stopped me cold. The warmth rushed to my cheeks as my jaw flapped mutely in search of any words that would not further incriminate me.

Gathering what remained of my dignity, I removed myself to my bed in the back of the vehicle.

What was it about Adrianna that made me so stupid? She hardly said a word and stayed out of everyone's way; the perfect "seen and not heard" child every parent had hoped for since forever.

It was the unexpressed message behind those familiar eyes. It was like she read what was on my mind and hated me for something I'd never acted on or expressed in front of her.

I felt petty for disliking a little girl, but she was the reason we were in this mess. Because of her, Dylan had almost been killed. I could barely consider her without anger boiling up inside me.

Yet if I took the time to reflect rationally, none of it was her doing. There was something about her, through no fault of hers, except for living, that compelled me to dislike her.

No, that wasn't right. I hated her and felt guilty for it.

Dylan's call from up front yanked me out of my funk. On return to the cockpit, I avoided eye contact with the child.

"We have a problem and need to make a decision." He looked to Felix to relate what had been explained in my absence.

"The storm is breaking up and will die out in six hours. Once it abates, we will be visible to anyone."

"Weren't we always vulnerable to thermal imaging?" I asked.

"That's the other disconcerting news," said Dylan. "There is absolutely no indication we are being tracked."

"That's a good thing, isn't it?"

Felix shook his head. "Not necessarily; we are detecting no activity on any of the communications bands. Our long-range sensors indicate no sign of anyone in this vicinity."

"We are in the middle of nowhere, aren't we? Maybe we've already entered rebel-controlled territory and Mundi's people won't follow us."

"If that were the case, we would detect standard comm

traffic, but there is nothing," said Felix.

"I don't understand what that implies."

"It means," said Dylan, "someone has dropped a suppression net over us."

My uncomprehending look prompted him to explain further. "It's a passive monitoring technique. It's operated over a confined area in the hope your unsuspecting target will reveal himself by leaking some kind of signal."

"We aren't sending any signals, are we?"

"Our long-range sensors generate one but are programmed to operate at low noise levels. Their signal masquerades as background static," explained Felix. "We are undetectable unless we slip up and accidentally broadcast our position. The fact that we have not detected any thermal scans from orbit suggests they suspect our ability to detect them. They are making great efforts to keep us in the dark and unprepared."

"They want us to relax and let down our guard?"

"Yes, by the time they strike, we would receive little warning."

"That seems like an awful lot of work to catch a simple country doctor on the run," I said.

"Yes," said Felix, "they probably anticipate resistance. If they've determined it is Melanie Destin they seek, they will be aware of Dylan's presence. The ship you destroyed more than likely confirmed such suspicions and compelled them to act with caution."

"So what do we do?" asked Dani.

"Our options are limited. We can locate a defensible position sheltered from orbital observation. If we remain silent, we can hope they'll abandon the search in this area."

"So cower in a cave or under another outcrop like we did before?"

"There are several possible locations along our route. They would be obvious follow-up candidates should our enemy decide to assume a more direct method."

"Playing hide-and-seek doesn't sound like a game we can win. We'll run out of food and water," I said. "Are there any other options?"

"We continue as we are," said Dylan.

"Just pretend nothing is happening?" asked Dani. "I mean, I'm a naturally hopeful person, but that idea sounds just a little...well, stupid."

Dylan frowned at her. "We don't know where rebel-controlled territory begins. There isn't exactly a line on the map, but we should be close. If we maintain our course for the next day or two, we'll wind up in an area defended by the rebellion. Mundi's people would be shot down before they could land."

"Unless they intend to employ the military. An armoured unit would normally be vulnerable to a rebel defence, but a quick extraction strike might stand a chance of success," said Felix.

"Whose side are you on?" I asked him.

"It is a tactic I would consider were I still leading Mundi's forces."

"Well, I vote for pushing on," I said.

Everyone agreed it was the most palatable option, so we all settled in for the monotony of the journey ahead.

As the day wore on, we all fell into activities to alleviate the boredom. Felix and Dylan constantly monitored our instruments, course, and surveillance data. Dani occupied herself with her reading, and I passed the hours lost in thought, watching the dusty landscape pass by.

Adrianna assumed her customary position in the copilot's chair, observing Dylan, asking him questions and giggling at his jokes. He was the only one with whom she would converse beyond monosyllabic responses and the odd grunt. Dani too could engage her in conversation, but not with the same kind of rapport.

He truly enjoyed the little girl's company, and she responded to his kindness by opening up and revealing her true personality. He was the only one of us she was not guarded with, and with the passing days the two grew closer. They shared a bond; Dylan saw her as the child he wanted, and he was the closest thing to a caring adult she'd ever encountered.

As they interacted, I realized how much my stubborn refusal to start a family with Dylan hurt him. He came from a large one and no doubt missed the tender bonds of affection he'd been raised with.

Yes, we were close soulmates of a kind, but we both were painfully aware I was damaged goods. I couldn't give him what he desired. He would say he had everything he needed, but seeing him with Adrianna told me the truth.

The girl, deliberately or not, was working her way into Dylan's life. The longer she stayed with us, the stronger their bond would become. It would be difficult for him surrender her when the time arrived, though he would endure it for the good of everyone involved.

I was worried the hole in his heart from their inevitable parting would be one I might never be able to fill. I would have to keep an eye on their relationship. I did not yet know what I could do to prevent the pain he would experience, but I would need to think of something.

CHAPTER 22

Unable to sleep, Dani joined Felix in the cockpit and shared the silence with him. The dust storm had died out during the night, and she now surveyed the myriad stars that faintly illuminated the landscape.

Jupiter was not difficult to locate, its swollen yellow orb outshining the brightest star. She imagined she could make out the passing shadows of the Jovian moons across its striped surface but knew her eyesight was not that keen.

"Can you see home?" She spoke softly, not wanting to waken the others.

He directed his attention toward the horizon and after a few seconds pointed at the same object Dani had identified.

"I wish I could see it through your eyes from here," she said. "I never thought I'd be homesick for Europa."

Felix offered a reassuring smile. "It's still there. This will be over soon."

A rustle of fabric behind them drew their attention to Adrianna, rubbing the sleep from her eyes. Her usually unruly mop of hair was exceptionally dishevelled.

"Did we wake you? I'm sorry, sweetie," said Dani as she extended welcoming arms to the little girl.

As had become early-morning custom, she crawled into Dani's lap. The child's head rested against her breast and was enveloped in a motherly cuddle.

Dani couldn't help but appreciate the privilege of being one of two people the girl had taken to, the other being Dylan. Though nothing had been said to her to prompt her selection of them, she seemed drawn to the only ones who had grown up within a family.

The horizon brightened, heralding the first sunrise Dani would see since her return to Mars. Faint snores drifted from the back of the craft where Dylan and Mel slept. Adrianna's now alert eyes sparkled as she followed the rhythmic breathing.

Giggling, she whispered, "He sounds funny."

Dani smiled conspiratorially. "Are you sure it's him?"

Adrianna stifled her laugh with her hand, and Dani hugged her, a wide grin lighting her own cherub face.

Adrianna's demeanour sobered, and she said, "She isn't nice."

Dani's heart fell as she struggled for a response. Mel had not been kind. She'd not been cruel, nor even showed meanness, but she didn't show any warmth either. She made little effort to hide her annoyance over the burden Adrianna's care created. In many ways her friend had behaved in a childish manner.

For all her achievements over life's adversity, Melanie Destin was still a damaged little girl herself. Adrianna brought that out in her, making her less than her best self around the child.

"She's not nice to him." Her big blue eyes stared challengingly at Dani.

"Oh, Sugar, that isn't true. Why do you say that?"

The girl buried her head back into Dani's breast. "I wish she would go away and leave us alone."

The penny dropped. She was infatuated with Dylan. As a father figure, a big brother, or her own concept of a protecting knight, it didn't matter. As far as her eight-year-old sensibilities told her, they belonged together.

At a loss for words, Dani could only look to Felix, who merely shrugged and maintained his focus on whatever he had been doing.

Someone stirred behind them, and Dani was grateful to see Dylan emerge from the back. Adrianna slipped down and padded over to greet him with an affectionate hug.

"Good morning, squirt," he said to her. "Have you eaten?"

Dani watched as the little girl pulled him by the hand to the galley. There was no doubt in her mind her assessment of the situation was correct. Dylan, like most men, would likely be oblivious to what was going on in Adrianna's heart. He had no idea what pain was yet to come when the child lost the one person who mattered to her.

Dani wiped a tear away. Part of her wanted to dissuade Adrianna; prepare her for the reality of her life. She would shortly end up being handed off to the rebellion and to some unknown fate. Given the choice, she would want to remain in Dylan's care, and preferably without Mel tagging along. But nobody was going to let her choose, and she would become more damaged. At the very least, Dani had to find a way to warn Dylan what was happening.

Chewing an energy bar, he returned to the cockpit and plopped into a passenger chair. Adrianna unhesitatingly climbed into his lap and began to consume hers.

"I see the storm broke overnight. I take it everything is still quiet?"

"For the most part," said Felix. "However, since the storm's passing, I detected some odd fluctuations in the background signal on our sensors."

"Do you think it's because of a change in the weather conditions?"

"Perhaps, but I need to investigate further."

Felix rose from the pilot chair and moved to a workstation beside the galley. The navigation computer maintained their course, and Dylan seemed to be in no hurry to assume his shift monitoring the operation of the vehicle.

Dani fidgeted in her seat, noting the interaction between Dylan and the girl. Though no words were exchanged, they appeared to enjoy being in each other's company. If the morning's pattern held, when Mel emerged from the back, Adrianna would become sullen and return to her familiar spot on the floor; the cub deferring to the lioness.

"Dylan, can you please give me your opinion on this?" asked

Felix.

Helping the little girl slip from his lap, he went to Felix's side and looked over his shoulder at the computer screen.

"I've never seen a pattern like that," he said.

"It is familiar to me," said Felix. "It is a code of my design."

"Mundi?" Dani asked.

"Yes, they appear to have grown impatient and are communicating, most likely coordinating an attack on us."

"We must be close enough to rebel territory to prompt them to act."

"I've detected no other anomalies suggesting they are in the area. Perhaps that has emboldened our pursuers to strike quickly while the opportunity exists."

"Any idea of how long we might have?" Dylan asked Felix.

"There is no movement on our long-range sensors. If the assault comes from orbit, then I estimate twenty to fifty minutes."

"We need to find a defensible position." Dylan resumed his place at the navigation computer.

"They will be better prepared than during your last encounter."

"You're sure there is no sign of rebel activity in this area?" asked Dani of Felix.

He shook his head. "But they may be employing technology I am not familiar with to mask their presence."

"Maybe we could put out a distress call of some kind," she said.

"Doing so could hasten our own demise. Such a signal will help to pinpoint our location."

"The data safe," said Dylan. "It sent out a beacon before Dani disabled it."

"I remind you there is no guarantee it was intended for the rebels."

"But they are the most likely recipients. Can you turn it back on, Dani?"

"Yes, but is that a good idea?"

"At this point, my love, it might be the only action that can help us," said Felix.

She retrieved the item and began to work on it. Out of the corner of her eye she spied Adrianna hovering at Dylan's shoulder, absently wringing her small hands. Not seeming to want to disturb him as he worked, she still looked on worriedly.

Dylan looked up and offered her a reassuring smile.

She rubbed the small scar on the back of her neck. "Are they looking for me again?"

"We're doing our best to make sure they don't find you."

"I don't want to go back."

"I know. We won't let that happen." He winked at her then returned to his work.

Dani sighed and surveyed the exposed electronics on the desk before her. "I'm ready. Are we sure about this?"

Dylan nodded.

Her deft fingers reconnected the disabled relay. She sat back, still staring at the data safe. "It's doing its thing. I hope we're not calling the wrong people."

CHAPTER 23

I awoke to unfamiliar noises from the cockpit. Still rubbing the sleep from my eyes, I emerged from the sleeping area to a tense scene. Dylan was still dressed only in the undershirt and shorts he slept in. He and Felix conversed quietly, hunkered over the navigation computer. A frightened-looking Adrianna cuddled in the lap of an equally concerned Dani.

"What's going on?"

Dylan glanced up, frowning, and turned back to the screen as he answered. "We've been spotted. We're working on a plan."

"Why didn't anyone wake me sooner?"

Abashed, Dani replied, "Sorry, Sugar. It all sort of happened at once."

With the men clearly preoccupied, I sidled next to her and spoke in a lower tone. "I can't believe you guys forgot about me. Tell me everything."

She filled me in on the recent development, and with all the scary facts now out in the open, a silence fell. Adrianna pressed herself into the protection of Dani's arms.

I smiled and reached up to tousle her hair, as Dylan did. She pulled back from me and clung tightly to Dani. My friend shrugged and tried to give me a reassuring smile, implying the girl reacted to the situation and not me. We both knew, of course, that was complete bullshit.

Adrianna clearly held no affection for me. For days had I

watched her to warm Dylan and Dani. She transformed from a sullen, mistrustful creature into a normal child in their presence. She even got along with Felix, though in a more guarded fashion. But between the two of us was only conflict. Neither of us managed to do anything right in the other's eyes, and a silent truce had developed between us. She generally stayed out of my way, and I left her care to the others.

I was not particularly proud of myself. It was not as if I hated children; far from it. They had turned out to be some of my favourite patients over the years. I treated many of them as they grew from infants to kids about Adrianna's age. I shared laughs with many and was comfortable being with all of them.

Adrianna brought out the worst in me, as if I was afraid of her on some subconscious level. The way she looked at me was like she owned a claim on my soul and wanted it back. For my part, something about her unsettled me. It wasn't that she was a clone; our mutual distrust developed long before that disturbing fact presented itself. Our feud ran deeper and was almost primal. I couldn't put my finger on what it was about. If I believed in reincarnation, I might have thought we were mortal enemies in a previous life.

Dylan approached us. "We have a scheme that just might get us out of this."

"Why do I think I'm not going to like it?" I asked.

"Do you recall how we dealt with the last attack?"

"Shit! We're not going to do that again?"

"Felix and I discussed it at length. The plan is sound..."

"Yeah, right up to the part where the ship crashes on top of you. No way! Come up with something else. These guys aren't going to fall for the same trick twice."

Felix joined us. "Dylan's tactic holds the highest probability for your survival."

Dani regarded him with moistening eyes. "What about yours?"

He stared at her for several seconds. "The three of you will require environmental suits. There isn't much time."

She burst into tears. "Isn't there another way?"

Felix knelt in front of her and caressed her face. "I have no intention of dying, my love. But to be at my best I have to be assured of your safety."

"Dylan," I said, "isn't there anything else we can do? Something that doesn't involve you two taking them all on?"

"Mel, you saw Adrianna's file. She's far too valuable to them to allow her to escape. There is a better than even chance they plan to kill us all."

I turned to the girl, still huddled in Dani's lap. I wanted to resent her but could only feel compassion for how terrified she must be. I remembered living in almost constant fear for my survival at her age, being hunted by the sex gangs seeking fresh girls for their stables. I had a feeling Adrianna fled from something far more sinister and would rather die than return.

"The only way Mundi's people will attempt an incursion into rebel territory is if they intend a surgical strike," said Felix. "They can't risk spending any more time on the ground than necessary. We only have to make the job more difficult for them than they anticipate. If we can hang on long enough, they'll be forced to withdraw or be taken down by rebel forces."

"Why can't we all just abandon the transport and hide?" I asked.

"They'll destroy the vehicle and scour the area for everyone. We need to keep them preoccupied and make enough noise for the rebels to find us."

"Assuming they are coming," she said.

Felix frowned. "You three will take the survival pack and remain hidden. If Varr's people heard our signal, they'll eventually find you."

"And if they don't?" I asked.

"They won't ignore a battle in their own territory," said Dylan. "They'll come."

"Fine," I said, "but I want a weapon."

"Mel, we've tried it. You can't shoot to save your life."

"I'm not that bad."

"I can use a gun," said Dani, tears running down her cheeks. "Give me one. At least we won't feel vulnerable after you idiots die."

The men looked at each other and seemed to silently communicate in that macho way of hero types. Dylan left and returned with a lightweight projectile rifle.

"Do you remember the basics I taught you?" he asked, holding it out for me.

Dani seized it from him and inspected the working parts, slapping it around like she was a space marine.

She looked up at Dylan. "We're good."

I stared at her in awe. "Honey, I thought I had a past. We need to talk."

CHAPTER 24

Ten minutes later the three of us crouched behind a low outcrop, watching our vehicle trundle off into the narrow canyon without us. Getting out had been tricky since part of the boys' plan involved not letting it appear to anyone observing that anything was out of the ordinary. That meant we couldn't stop the transport to let us get off.

Much better prepared than the last time, I watched through the binoculars I pulled from the survival pack. For such a small package, it was impressively endowed. It held a first aid kit, an emergency transmitter, a secondary O2 resupply for our suit rebreathers, a portable heater, a storm-rated tent, food rations we could stretch to last for ten standard days, and enough drinking water to supplement what our environmental suits could not recycle.

I did not see Dylan or Felix depart the moving rover, as the plan called for, but I was confident they managed to do so and were now concealed among the rockfall on either side of the canyon. They chose this location because it limited the number of directions from which an attack could come.

It didn't take very long before the distinctive whine of engines from an approaching aircraft echoed around us. A dark shadow passed over as an enormous flying wing, bristling with guns, entered our view and tentatively hovered over our tracked vehicle as it continued obliviously along its programmed path.

Explosive gunfire erupted from the muzzles of two sets of weapons on the ship. Sprays of red soil sprang up and raced like the footsteps of an invisible charging beast toward our ground car. Its front and rear tracks burst apart as the projectiles targeted them, leaving the cabin unscathed.

Its prey now immobilized, the airship descended like a carrion bird. Simultaneously, as it touched down, its back opened to disgorge a dozen armoured soldiers. When the last of them departed, the craft lifted into the air again and disappeared over the valley walls.

Even with my military exposure limited to the occasional story from Dylan, I knew this was a more disciplined group than the ones we caught unawares before. Assuming a staggered formation, weapons raised, the seasoned troops cautiously advanced on the disabled transport.

Just as I began to worry that Dylan and Felix might not have escaped the vehicle, gunfire echoed and five of the advancing group fell to the ground, their armour blown apart like cardboard, no match for Dylan's choice of firepower.

Realizing the trap they'd fallen into, their leader swiftly mustered his surviving command toward the only source of cover, our damaged vehicle. Two more of the men were picked off before the remaining five slipped behind the only protection available to them.

Gunfire continued to echo through the canyon. The desperate assault team fired blindly into the surrounding hillside. Despite the sophisticated tracking capability contained within their helmets, they appeared unable to pinpoint the location of their attackers.

Before my hopes for a quick victory could rise, the sound of the returning airship's engines nearly deafened me. A black spectre roared down, lethal weapons unfurling retribution as it strafed the hillsides in passing.

It soared over the transport and rose high until within seconds it became a tiny black dot against the sky, the deafening engine's screams mercifully reduced to the rumble of distant thunder.

As if recovering from the shock of the attack, gunfire began anew, the besieged soldiers now targeting one particular location along a canyon wall. My heart lodged in my throat as I scanned the hills for any indication of who they were shooting at. Dani's hand fell on my arm as she extended her other one for the binoculars. It took her only moments to locate one of our men.

"Dylan's pinned down," she shouted before switching her gaze to the other side of the valley. "I can't see any sign of Felix. I hope..."

As if in answer to her worry, the now familiar sound of a heavy-calibre weapon resounded, and two more of the attackers were dashed aside like paper dolls. Two of the surviving men redirected their firepower at the opposite hillside in an attempt to pin down Felix.

With the loudening roar of the returning aircraft rattling my ears, I gasped in realization of what had happened.

Fully expecting a trap, our enemy had purposely deployed those twelve soldiers with the certain knowledge that most of them would die in an ambush. Their goal was not to capture the occupants of the vehicle but to flush out the location of its defenders. With the positions of both Dylan and Felix now established by the surviving troops, the raptor would be able to pick them off.

The craft now slowly approached the battlefield. It opened fire on the positions the pinned men had targeted. Heavy rounds blew rocks apart and sent an avalanche of detritus down both cliff sides.

The airship continued its unrelenting barrage as it set down and discharged another squad. Instead of taking off again, it maintained covering fire for the troops as they split into two teams, each headed toward the assaulted positions.

I jumped as a loud explosion threw up dirt and rock near us. Seconds later another blast erupted closer to the battle, prompting the new group of soldiers to halt their advance.

A third projectile found its mark and the landed aircraft was blown to pieces, sending shrapnel in every direction.

The stunned assault team, scattering in disarray, scrambled for any available cover.

A mechanical roar deafened me as three armoured tracked vehicles roared past our position and approached the battlefield. Through the thick black smoke from the burning wreckage I made out another two advancing from the opposite end of the valley.

A brief firefight erupted between the tanks and the pinned ground troops. Realizing the futility of their situation, first one group, followed by another, raised their arms in surrender.

Seeming to appear out of the thin air, armed men emerged from concealment among the canyon rock fall; their ochre-coloured armour had camouflaged them perfectly. They converged on Mundi's defeated men and relieved them of weapons. To my great shock, any wounded they found were summarily executed.

The survivors were gathered together and forced to kneel with their hands on their heads. I feared we would witness a mass execution but relaxed a bit when the prisoners were instructed to be seated and a guard was posted over them.

I'd always dismissed the stories about rebel brutality as government propaganda. What happened made me reevaluate my romantic admiration of Talus Varr's rebellion. As noble as the cause might be, their tactics were nothing of the sort. There was nothing admirable about how those wounded were dispatched.

My initial relief at our apparent rescue soon devolved to concern when there was no sign of Dylan or Felix emerging from their cover. The entire valley was filled with thick black smoke from the burning wreckage, and I had difficulty seeing their location. I began to crawl over the ridge that hid us to get a clearer view, but Dani grabbed my arm.

"Felix wants us to sit tight, Sugar."

We had no comm with us, since Dylan didn't want to risk giving away our position. "How the hell would you know that? Are you communicating on your CI?"

She pointed to her head. "Duh, the links are short-range

and need a relay network. I'm just following the instructions he gave us."

Overcoming my embarrassment, I said, "Do you think they're okay?"

Dani placed a comforting hand on my knee. "They're both fine." Her reassuring smile was barely discernible behind her faceplate. "We're not to reveal ourselves until we're sure it's safe."

Given what we'd just witnessed, I thought that was a good idea.

The smoke cleared enough that we could again observe the canyon walls where our boys concealed themselves. Movement caught my eye, and I grabbed the binoculars from Dani.

Four ochre-coloured figures moved among the rocks. They were armed with lightweight firearms and had them raised as they approached what had been Dylan's position. I hoped he'd managed to move during the fracas.

The troops halted and aimed their weapons at a particular spot. Slowly, another armoured figure rose from concealment, hands held high in surrender. They'd found Dylan, and my relief at seeing him turned to dismay when they herded him toward the other prisoners. He took his place among them, and I could only imagine the anxiety he felt in the company of those who only minutes before tried to murder him.

"I don't like this. We've got to do something."

Dani grabbed my arm and held tight. "Just hang on, Sugar. Nothing we can do will help."

"Of course there is. If those rebels learn we're the ones Mundi's men attacked, we can straighten this entire mess out. Besides, they're who we've been searching for all this time."

"And what will happen to Felix?"

"What do you mean?"

"You saw what they did to those wounded men. Once everyone is questioned, they'll more than likely be executed too."

"That makes it even more critical that we tell them Dylan is with us."

"But think about Felix, Mel. He's easily recognizable and known to have been Mundi's right-hand man. Once they capture him, his life will be very short." Tears fogged her visor.

"He hasn't been with Mundi for a decade."

"Do you think they'll care?"

"Why didn't you two say something about this before? We could have found another way to handle this." I looked at Adrianna, who was focused on the unfolding events in the valley.

"Because the plan was to go to Talus Varr. He knows about the circumstances around Felix's defection. These guys don't, which makes this a totally different situation."

I turned back to the scene of the battle. Dylan still sat with the prisoners, and eight more men had been added to the group scouring the side of the canyon where Felix still hid.

"We've got to do something, Dani. They're going to find him, and we're the only ones who can vouch for him."

"Or we'll be labelled as Mundi's agents and shot along with everyone else. Felix said to stay put. I trust him, Mel. You should too."

Uncertainty showed in her eyes before she returned her attention to the unfolding events. Felix was a brilliant tactician and a more than capable warrior if it came down to a battle, but he was outmatched by this squad of rebel troops. He wouldn't be stupid enough to resist them, but what would happen when they captured and identified him as Mundi's former lieutenant? Most of the rebels had lost someone to the dictator's brutal regime. It didn't matter that Felix had betrayed the Supreme Dictator; these people were just as likely to take out their revenge on him as turn him over to Varr.

"Oh no," said Dani, watching through the binoculars. "They found him."

Not wanting to commandeer them from her, I strained my eyes to make out the distant details. A group of seven or eight rebels surrounded a figure rising from the rocks, hands raised above his head. Unlike the others, Felix did not wear body armour, and the only thing that prevented his immediate recognition was the helmet he wore. They wouldn't tear it from his face, but it wouldn't be long before his identity would become apparent to them.

I looked to Dani, who returned my gaze, fear and uncertainty written behind her own breathing mask. In my mind, there was only one thing to do.

I crawled over the ridge and began walking toward the scene. After only the briefest of hesitation, both Dani and Adrianna followed me. With the rebel's attention on their prisoners, we wouldn't be spotted until we got nearer to the action. That gave me some time to figure out how I was going to present us and not join the growing circle of captives.

CHAPTER 25

It took the rebels longer to spy us than I imagined it would. We neared the rearmost tank, and an inattentive sentry finally noticed two women and a child walking past him. He wasted no time redeeming himself and summoned half a dozen of his comrades. They surrounded us, their weapons pointed menacingly.

Within sight of Dylan and the other captives, they ordered us to our knees with our hands behind our heads. I craned my neck to locate any sign of Felix and was rewarded with a blow between my shoulder blades.

"Hey," shouted Dani.

The soldier who hit me did not appreciate her concern for my welfare and turned toward her, his rifle raised to strike. Before he took another threatening step, a screaming hellcat with wild auburn hair assaulted him.

What Adrianna lacked in body weight and fighting skills, she more than made up for in ferocity. Having jumped on the unfortunate soldier's back, she clung around his throat with one arm while the other grabbed at his helmet. She dug her small fingers beneath its rim and struggled with both hands to pull it up and off his head. Secured to her victim's back by her skinny legs wrapped about his waist, she pulled his head back with all her strength. Though she had no chance of removing his headgear, she knocked him off balance, and the two of them toppled to the ground.

He rolled over in the red dirt, trying to dislodge his diminutive attacker but only succeeded in further entertaining his raucous comrades.

Tiring of the entertainment, a soldier with an officer's epaulet on his shoulder patch seized Adrianna by the scruff of her neck and pulled her off the man. He held her out at arm's length, avoiding her wildly flailing limbs. I was certain that if she wore no breathing apparatus, her teeth would also be involved in her attack.

"Somebody take control of this!" he ordered.

Two men secured Adrianna's arms and legs before her captor released his hold.

"Don't hurt her," I shouted, prepared to receive another blow for my words. Instead, I noted their efforts to avoid harming her.

The officer extended his hand to help me to my feet.

"Please accept my apology. That man will be disciplined for his treatment of you." He looked at the now restrained Adrianna. "And for his mistreatment of your daughter."

Believing it wise to not correct him, I replied, "I think he got the worst of that."

He laughed. "He'll probably never hear the end of it." Sobering, he said, "If you can control her, I will release her."

I knelt before her. "Everything is okay now; nobody is going to hurt you. They'll let you go if you promise to behave."

Dani stood behind me and reaffirmed my words. After considering the offer, she nodded tersely. The soldiers cautiously released their grip on her, and she ran into Dani's arms.

If he was surprised, the officer said nothing, offering instead to conduct our conversation in the relative comfort of one of his vehicles.

We were escorted to the largest of the units and offered uncomfortable seats in the confined interior. The air smelled like Martian soil and body odour; kind of like my environmental suit after a few days of continued use.

His back to us, the commander removed his helmet,

revealing a dishevelled mass of straight, jet-black hair. When he turned, the face that matched the hair was unmistakably Asian. The sight of him took me aback, and I tried to hide my surprise. I'd never met a Martian of any pure ethnic origin.

He extended his hand. "Please permit me to introduce myself; I am Yu Chen, commander of the fourth armoured battalion of the Free Republic of Mars."

"I am Doctor Corrine Ross, and this is my good friend Dani O'Hara."

He raised one eyebrow. "If we are to take each other seriously, I suggest we dispense with pretence. I am well aware of your true identity."

My face warmed as the blood rushed to my cheeks. I looked at Dani for a moment then decided there was no benefit arguing with him and everything to lose. I needed to gain his trust if we stood any chance of securing the freedom of Dylan and Felix.

"Then I'll begin again. I am Melanie Destin."

He accepted my proffered hand. "It is a great honour to meet the Mother of Mars and her daughter."

My blush deepened. "Adrianna's not mine."

He carefully studied her then directed his attention to Dani.

She shook her head. "Don't look at me."

Turning back to me, he said. "What is her relationship to you?"

"She's...an orphan."

I couldn't read him. After his calling me out on my name, I didn't want to further antagonize him with lies. I decided to anticipate his next question. "We are taking her to Talus Varr."

"Really?"

That was easy to interpret. He didn't believe me.

"We sent the coded signal that led you here."

"What signal?"

Shit!

"We discovered you during our response to the enemy incursion."

Shit, shit and triple shit!

"I am, however, interested to learn more."

I considered asking to speak to his commanding officer but doubted that would be well received, or if there actually was anyone else. More important, the amount of time remaining before his men identified Felix and Dylan was shrinking. I debated the risk of coming clean.

After a glance at Dani, I related the entire story to him. He betrayed no reaction as I described the death of Carlos, the rescue of Adrianna, and how we came to possess the alarmed data safe. I took great pains to explain who Felix was and his whereabouts during the last decade, as well as Dylan's recent history. I knew I took a big risk in outing them, but I figured it better their identities be revealed voluntarily by me than discovered through interrogation. Above all, I emphasized my past association with his boss.

After I finished, Chen was unreadable while he studied me. Seconds became a minute, and just when I thought my next words would be to beg for our lives, he called to one of his officers.

"Separate the two prisoners taken from the hills and place them under guard in unit B."

He addressed me. "I will verify your story with them. If there are no anomalies, we will take you to our base from, where you will be transferred to central command. I also need to examine the device."

I nodded to Dani, and she pulled it from her pack. He examined it closely and said, "This will be returned to you shortly if you are telling the truth."

Then his demeanour changed, and a gracious smile appeared. "In the meantime, I offer you what meagre hospitality we can. You must be famished." He signalled to the remaining officer and instructed him to provide us with food, water, and a place to rest.

Noting my hesitation, he said, "Your companions will be well treated and fed as well. After I question them you will be permitted to join them."

After he departed, while we waited for the promised rations,

Dani whispered, "Do you think he believed you?"

"I hope so. He isn't the type who is easily bullshitted."

Adrianna cuddled in Dani's arms during our interview with Chen. I smiled at her. "You were impressive out there, kiddo. Remind me not to piss you off."

She giggled. Encouraged, I added, "Maybe when we get out of this, we'll ask Dylan or Felix to teach you some self-defence moves so you can really kick ass next time."

A grin spread across her face, and on mine as well. It was the first positive interaction between us in days.

CHAPTER 26

Yu Chen returned two hours later. He approached us with a friendly, relaxed manner.

"I am satisfied you were truthful with me, Doctor Destin. You will be treated as my guests during the trip to our base, with the exception of the synthetic."

"Why not him?"

"Dylan Hodgson presents no problem for me. He was under the direct command of Talus Varr at the time of his defection, and there is little reason to suspect his sympathies lie with our enemy."

"And Felix?"

"There is the complication of his former relationship with the dictator."

"But that association was before Mundi returned to Mars. Felix hasn't had anything to do with him for ten years."

"Yes, and that is the sole reason he is still alive. May I be blunt?"

"I wish you would, please."

"Altius's role as Mundi's lieutenant gave him great notoriety. Murder, espionage, blackmail, political, and corporate destabilization were the tools he employed on behalf of his master. We suspect he is responsible for the assassination of the high chancellor and subsequent chain of events that brought Mundi into power. His present loyalties notwithstanding, he still must answer for much."

The colour drained from Dani's face, and tears pooled in her eyes. "What's going to happen to him?"

"That isn't my decision. We'll turn him over to Talus Varr, along with yourselves."

He left unvoiced the implied threat that all our fates had yet to be determined.

"You may visit him freely, but he will remain under guard."

He looked apologetically to Dani. "I'm sorry, but that is the best I can offer."

"In that case," I said, "I give you my word we will not cause problems for you."

"Thank you for understanding, Doctor. Would you like to join them now?"

"Yes, please."

We donned our gear and departed the confinement of the attack unit. Though I still breathed recycled air from a tank, I sighed with relief when we exited the stale-smelling vehicle. The former battlefield had been transformed into a military camp, with portable shelters set up and soldiers going about the routine of repair and maintenance of their equipment while they had the opportunity.

As we passed our own damaged transport, I noted men repairing the drive track and random projectile holes in the passenger compartment.

Noting my interest, Chen said, "I thought you would be more comfortable inside your own unit during the trip."

"I appreciate it, thank you."

Near one of the other armoured vehicles, I noticed five prisoners being marched under guard toward the edge of the encampment.

Breaking away from our group, I followed the parade around the tent to satisfy my curiosity. Neither Chen nor our escort attempted to stop me. Dani and Adrianna hurried to catch up.

"What's going on, Mel?"

"I'm not sure. I'm just curious about something."

Rounding the corner, I was presented with a scene that

made me regret my impulsiveness.

Two rebels guarded ten of the government soldiers, all lined up on their knees. The squad leader approached the first of Mundi's men and spoke to him. After a moment's hesitation, the captive soldier removed his helmet, exposing himself to the toxic CO_2 atmosphere. As he held his breath, the rebel withdrew his sidearm and shot the prisoner in the head.

Dani screamed and shielded Adrianna from the sight. Speechless, I witnessed the ritual repeated for each of the remaining captives. None cried or begged; all accepted their fate with an eerie stoicism.

A movement beside me caught my attention, and I turned to face Yu Chen.

"What the fuck is the meaning of this?"

"They are enemy combatants, and our resources are too taxed to keep prisoners."

"So you just murder them?"

"These men requested this."

"What the hell are you talking about?"

"Each is given the choice to be left here to find his own way back, or this."

"They would never make it back to civilization. Both choices are a death sentence."

"Perhaps, but there is also a chance that they might be picked up by one of their own patrols along the border. It isn't that far away."

"I don't understand why they would choose this."

"Because if they managed to return to their unit, they would likely face a worse fate."

With the prisoners now dead, the rebels methodically stripped the armour from the corpses.

"Military equipment is difficult to come by," said Chen.

The taste of vomit lingered in my mouth. "Waste not, want not, I suppose?"

"Something like that, Doctor."

He returned to the camp. With nothing left to witness, I followed, grateful we did not face a similar choice at the moment.

CHAPTER 27

The journey to Varr's secretive location began when our vehicle was deemed repaired. It suffered more damage than apparent to my eye, and despite the best efforts of Yu Chen's mechanics, the machine was barely functional. Their makeshift repairs got us moving, but barely, and our progress was slow. We stopped frequently to shore up the mended parts and ensure something more critical didn't break down.

I wondered why we weren't escorted by one of his attack units while Chen went about his regular patrol. It seemed strange to me that our conveyance to Talus Varr was of such importance that he would neglect the defence of their border.

The commander wasn't concerned about it. "We monitor a vast area and have been out here for almost three months. Our relief is en route."

Our little parade across the Martian wilderness took on a tedious routine. Our vehicle's main power plant was compromised, forcing us to abandon one of our two radioactive cores. As a result, in addition to the other damage, we only operated for short intervals. Six hours in transit were followed by four of rest, repair, and irregular recharge of our supplementary solar array.

After the first couple of days, I persuaded Chen to let Felix ride with us instead of under the watchful eye of his men. When it became apparent that the condition of our machine would not permit escape, he agreed.

While our hosts repaired our vehicle, I examined our men. Dylan's armour had once again served its purpose, protecting him from significant harm, but some of his previous injuries were aggravated. Felix managed to fare better, despite his lack of protection.

"I had sufficient cover," said Felix, who acquired only a few cuts and abrasions from flying rock debris. His artificial biology healed at an impressive pace, and he required little attention from me. I had no idea if infection could occur in his synthetic body, but I tended to his dressings regardless.

"I don't understand how they can treat you like their enemy after what you did to defend us from Mundi's goons," said Dani.

"They are understandably mistrustful, given my reputation."

"That happened before you even came to Mars. It shouldn't be any of their concern."

"There is the matter of the high chancellor's assassination," I said.

"You weren't involved with that, were you?" asked Dani.

"There is no evidence to support such a charge," he said.

My gaze remained fixed on him. "No," I said, "whoever did it made sure everything pointed to me."

Avoiding my dig, he said to Dani, "Since Talus Varr is aware of Mel's innocence, another scapegoat is necessary. My conviction will link Regis Mundi to the crime, eroding his support and strengthening the cause of the rebellion."

"So you're a pawn?" said Dani. "That's not fair."

"No, but it is politically expedient."

"Well, Varr knows the truth. He'll set everything straight soon enough."

Felix smiled reassuringly at her, but it faded when he saw me watching him.

I knew damned well Mundi was behind the assassination. As his major-domo, Felix was more than likely the plot's architect. But I overcame my resentment toward him after he and Dani became close. His relationship with her had changed him for the better, but even though I now loved him like a brother, I never lied to myself about what he was capable of.

And I was not deluded about Talus Varr's capabilities. It was not a stretch to imagine him exploiting the capture of Felix. Hell, he would probably exploit the Mother of Mars with equal enthusiasm. The two of us landing in his lap would be like a wet dream come true for the old bastard.

"Yu Chen approached me a couple of days ago," announced Dylan, who I thought asleep, reclined as he was in the pilot's chair. He sat up and leaned forward, awaiting our reaction to his non sequitur.

"So?"

"What he wanted might provide a solution to Felix's problem."

I scowled at him. "He asked you to join the cause again, didn't he?"

"The rebels realize the advantages to having us sign up."

"You mean it's advantageous for them to recruit me, don't you? We've been over this a hundred times, Dylan. I don't want to be Varr's poster girl for his rebellion."

"Goddammit, Mel, why don't you try thinking of somebody else for a change? If you offer yourself willingly to Varr, you can pretty much demand anything you want, including amnesty for Felix."

"So if I become his little whore, I can negotiate my fee?"

Wide-eyed, Dani asked, "Is this true, Mel? Can you get them to release Felix?"

"I don't know, Dani. The conversation never got that far."

"So he asked you? When did you plan to tell me?"

"Yu Chen brought the subject up a couple of times. It isn't like I refused a formal offer or anything."

"How could he make one?" replied Dylan. "You insulted him before he had a chance."

"What the fuck are you upset about? He was hitting on me, so I told him to get stuffed."

"Mel! You didn't tell him that?"

"Dani, I..."

"What makes you believe he came on to you?" said Dylan.

"You're old enough to be—"

"His older sister? Is that what your were going to say, asshole?"

"Oh, fuck off," he said. He retrieved his breathing mask and stormed from the vehicle.

An ugly silence lingered in the cabin like a garlic-charged fart.

Her presence ignored during the argument, Adrianna arose from her customary place. If looks could kill, I would have died a thousand painful deaths in that moment. She retrieved her own gear and followed Dylan outside.

Though daggers were not behind Dani's sad eyes, disappointment was. "Dammit Mel, we're in this mess because you called and asked for our help."

She joined the parade of the offended.

Felix and I sat in silence. I couldn't bring myself to look at him, so I studied a new stain on the floor.

"How about you?" I asked.

"Your history makes your position understandable."

"What the hell do you mean by that?"

"Merely that given your childhood experiences, reluctance to allow yourself to be prostituted once more is natural."

"Why don't they understand that?"

"You are asking the wrong person, Melanie."

"You're the only one still speaking to me."

He considered his words. "Your refusal to consider Chen's offer makes them anxious. They perceive a limited number of outcomes."

"And you don't?"

"I enjoy more options than you wish to recognize."

I raised my eyebrow in a silent question.

"If so inclined, my escape would not be difficult."

"But we're in the middle of nowhere. You wouldn't survive."

A hint of a smile turned the edges of his mouth.

"Okay, maybe you, of all people, would. What about Dani?"

"I didn't say all options are favourable."

"So what is your point, Felix?"

"Only that you might have more choices than you realize."

"They aren't obvious to me."

"What is the one variable we've not yet discussed?"

Feeling like the slow student in class, my brow knotted. Then, like a bothersome bit of food between my teeth finally popping free, it came to me.

"Adrianna! Varr wanted her badly enough to sacrifice Carlos."

"We must deduce the reason."

"Maybe she's an integral piece in Mundi's plans, and capturing her screws him. What is so important about her? It can't be that she's a clone."

"Are you certain?" he asked. "Whose is she?"

"I...I don't have the foggiest."

"You didn't examine the DNA record in the data safe?"

"We've been kind of busy, and now the equipment is wrecked."

"I thought it would be the first thing you did."

"What good would that accomplish? I wouldn't know the donor anyway."

He did that thing with his eyebrow again, and I once more felt like his failing pupil.

I extended my hands dramatically. "What?"

He shook his head. "Do you not imagine you've seen the girl somewhere before?"

"Yeah, but..."

"Tame the wild hair and the shape of her face becomes familiar. Her features, the cadence of her speech, even her gait all belong to a younger version of yourself."

"Bullshit. Why hasn't anyone else mentioned this before?"

"She is still young, and her characteristics not developed. The others may have dismissed the resemblance as coincidental."

"No, no, no, this doesn't make any sense."

"It might if you consider it. What other person would be of such interest to Regis Mundi and Talus Varr than someone genetically modified to control the Ares weapon? Both are aware of the ship hidden in the asteroid belt. Its composition of the same metananites which now terraform Mars would be known to them. Your ability to manipulate the technology is of incalculable value."

"But I had to be exposed to the nanites to activate my mutation. They are all gone; either changed into terraforming engines or lost with their mothership."

"We must assume Regis Mundi's people obtained an unaltered sample, presumably from that alien vessel. I dutifully reported its location to him before my epiphany and departure."

"That still doesn't explain where they got my DNA." The answer dawned on me as I spoke. Many sources existed in the course of modern everyday life. Obtaining a record of mine would be child's play.

"Even if they got my pattern from the records, it would just provide a matrix."

"The technology that created me would supply a means for its synthesis."

"I'm afraid I don't follow you."

"Unlike you, I am ignorant about the process of my creation. However, I do know that I was synthesized from a human template."

"They modelled you from another person? Who was it?"

"I don't know, and I am not an exact replicant. The DNA was modified to take advantage of the materials composing my cellular structure. The secret died with the scientists who made me, but the basic principal is understood. This could explain why Mundi revived the project."

"So, if you are right, eight years ago somebody dug up my genetic pattern and manipulated synthetic tissue to build a clone of me?"

"It may have been more recent than that. Artificial age acceleration would be likely. It reduces the time required to discover random aberrations in the developing subject."

"That explains why they cloned over six hundred others. How old do you think she is?"

"It's difficult to say. Based on my understanding of the process, I would guess this version of her is no older than three standard years."

I appraised him through narrowed eyes. "How old are you?"

He smiled.

My appreciation of Adrianna had changed considerably. Ironically, though her origin was as inhuman as anything I could conceive, I felt closer to her when I admitted to what had been obvious to my subconscious: she was me.

Unlike Felix, whose appearance made it apparent he was different, she appeared to be a perfectly normal eight-year-old girl who looked eerily like me. I wondered what enhanced abilities lay hidden within her by virtue of her hybrid biology. More importantly, once her inherited mutation from me was activated, how would Mundi exploit her to manipulate the alien nanotechnology? She was not exactly the most cooperative of children.

"Regis Mundi's reasons to get the girl back are pretty clear. What bothers me is what Talus Varr intends to do with her," I said.

"That puzzles me as well. Terminating the child is a more efficient solution."

"It disturbs me how casually you said that. But you're right."

I looked into his unnatural, milky blue eyes and realized there was no other choice. I couldn't allow her to come under Varr's control any more than I could permit him to exploit Felix's capture for political gain. My selfish fear had blinded me, and though I owed everyone a sincere apology, it would have to wait.

I needed to negotiate with Yu Chen about my terms for joining his rebellion.

CHAPTER 28

Finding Yu Chen to discuss my change of heart proved more challenging than I imagined. Naively, I planned to approach him on one of our regular stops. It turned out he had more responsibilities than overseeing our convoy.

"I have been looking for you to continue our earlier discussion, but you're a very busy man, Commander Chen."

"I'm sorry, Doctor, but I thought you made yourself abundantly clear on the matter."

"I'm afraid I was tired and more concerned with tending my husband's injuries when we last spoke. I was unjustifiably abrupt and rude toward you, and I must apologize. Hopefully you can find it in your heart to forgive me, Commander?"

Some of the few useful skills from my early years on Terra involve managing men's emotions. Learning the proper words and tone to disarm an otherwise potentially violent john had saved my life more than once. Manipulation was the only weapon available to a young teenaged girl, besides a hidden shiv for when all else failed.

"It would be ungallant of me to refuse. Your unnecessary apology is accepted."

The break in the conversation dragged itself into an awkward silence.

"I'm sorry, Commander. You're busy. I can talk to you later." I turned to leave, feeling incredibly foolish. It wasn't like me to freeze like that.

He laid down the document in his hand. "Actually, I have some time now, Doctor."

After dismissing the only other soldier present, he invited me to sit with him at his small, makeshift desk inside the cramped military vehicle. It was strewn with plaz-paper maps and data pads and a couple of old fashioned books by Terran authors I was passingly familiar with.

"In our last conversation, you mentioned something about a possible role for me. Please tell me more about your idea."

"Well, your practical skills as a physician would be more than welcome, but I believe you can serve a greater purpose, if you are willing to consider it."

"I really don't know what I can provide beyond medical assistance. I wouldn't be much good at anything else. I can't even shoot, despite several attempts to learn."

"I would be more than pleased to teach you how to handle a firearm. But that is not the sort of role I was referring to. I am thinking of you more as an inspirational leader. Surely you realize your reputation as the Mother of Mars. Your active endorsement of our righteous cause against Regis Mundi's dictatorship would be invaluable."

I blushed at the mention of that title. I hated the honorific Felix had given me when he declared me dead in that alien ship crash. I thought it presumptuous to apply it to me posthumously. To accept its application to me as a living person seemed the epitome of arrogance.

"Please forgive me for being blunt, but why does a patrol commander make such offers on behalf of the rebellion? I thought Talus Varr was your leader."

He smiled. "Ah, I can see your point. I am not merely a soldier, Doctor. As the regional administrator for this territory, my authority is second only to his. Despite appearances, my responsibilities extend beyond supervising your transport within our little convoy. Six other similarly equipped mobile squadrons answer to me. Together, we maintain a close watch on the vast, fluid border."

"What do you mean by, 'fluid border?'"

"Without the resources to amass large armies, both sides resort to hit-and-run tactics. We each try to destabilize the other's control over this region. They incur into our territory; we push them back and return the favour. It's a stalemate with neither side enjoying a clear advantage."

"That sounds more like chess than war."

"Our engagements with the dictator's forces are more akin to a game of hide-and-seek along an imaginary line in the sand." He waved his hand over one of the maps on his desktop. "Frankly, we're outgunned and can't afford an all-out assault. That limits our tactics. Unlike the Terran-Lunar conflict, we see no value in carrying out terror attacks against an otherwise sympathetic population."

"Your supposed sympathizers show you little open support."

"The threat of an asteroid being dropped on you from orbit can be intimidating. After Mundi ordered the destruction of those cities, our leadership chose to withdraw to the unpopulated region near the northern pole. We operate from hidden, underground bases to prevent the dictator from locating and bombarding us as well. With no targets on the surface for the asteroids parked in orbit, the conflict became relegated to sporadic action along the border we maintain."

"You mean that you fight them when you happen to run into each other, like the other day when you came across us."

"I know it sounds lame from a military perspective."

"I can't speak to the tactics of waging a war of rebellion, but I don't understand how you can ever achieve a victory over Mundi doing what you are."

"We cannot defeat our enemy in an open conflict. We choose to destabilize him and force him to expend valuable resources swatting at us like a swarm of annoying insects."

"You're hoping he makes a blunder that you can exploit."

"It will take years; decades perhaps, but eventually our moment will come."

"Or you'll be overwhelmed by some new weapon his scientists develop." I thought of Adrianna and the unknown goal Mundi's people had for their experimentation on her.

"We are not without our own resources, Doctor."

His openness surprised me. It told me there was little chance of us departing his company alive if we didn't join the rebel cause. His comment also shed significant light on the reason Varr was so interested in getting his hands on Adrianna.

The manner in which this rebellion was conducted would be comical if not for the devastating nature of the tool Mundi used to suppress any growth in support of the cause. The Martian dictator employed the same tactic adopted by the Lunies during their independence war.

I lived on Earth when the last asteroid assault happened. Almost a billion people wiped out in a single blow terrified the Terran government into settling the conflict at any cost. Even though their military might was vastly superior, Terra lost because they chose the moral high ground and did not attack civilian populations in kind. Varr's reluctance to involve Mars's population had backed him into a similar corner. He needed something to employ against an enemy who had no scruples.

"Our discussion has wandered, Commander Chen. What sort of role do you envision for me?"

"You are revered across the planet for bringing about a sustainable acceleration of the New Eden. When the people learn of your return, they will rise up to throw off the yoke of oppression..."

"Whoa, cowboy. Let's not get carried away trying to turn me into some kind of religious icon."

"You would become a miracle for the people to rally under. If I may now be blunt, Doctor, we really do not require your cooperation. A few edited vids of you, alive and well, and the people will never need to see or hear you again. Those who encountered you over the past decade will serve as witnesses to your resurrection. You will be a symbol, whether you cooperate or not."

There are worse ways to be remembered than as Saint Melanie, Mother of Mars. That still didn't make the notion one I liked, but he was absolutely right about not needing me to participate.

"If all you say is true, why aren't I dead in the sand back there with Mundi's soldiers?"

His smile returned. "You are correct, Doctor. There is another, unspoken reason you still live. I, however, am not privy to what it might be, so my orders are to transport you and your companions to Talus Varr."

I stood. "Why did we even have this conversation, Commander? What did you hope to achieve?"

"You approached me, remember? My family has terraformed Mars for generations. We arrived with the first Chinese colony expeditions from old Terra, and our lifeblood is in the soil. When you crashed the alien ship into Olympus Mons and restarted the planetary tectonics, it was like an answer to the prayers of my forefathers. Your name is spoken reverently among my relatives. Your spirit has resided with those of my honoured ancestors since I was a young man.

"When, a few days ago, I discovered who you are, it was a great adjustment for me to accept you as an ordinary woman. It was like the Melanie Destin I believed in had died and been replaced by you: a flawed, selfish, foul-mouthed woman. Your very humanity offended me. I thought that if I persuaded you to embrace your mythology, you would rise above yourself and become the person I believed I knew."

He lowered his eyes and bowed his head. "My offence against you is unforgivable."

Holy shit! I couldn't imagine what the experience of having his childhood god supplanted by me was like. I was also insulted by his low opinion of my character but decided it was time to be a bigger person than he believed he knew.

"Commander...may I call you by your name?"

He looked up and nodded solemnly. "I am Chen."

"Chen, I think maybe we've gotten off to a poor beginning. Perhaps we need some time to get to know each other? You never know, you could learn to like the real me. You might even persuade me to become your poster child."

"I would like that very much, Doctor Destin."

"Mel." I extended my hand. "Why don't we start by having

you teach me how to shoot a weapon? It might come in handy if I join the rebellion."

A hesitant smile appeared, and we shook hands.

He was obviously not the person who would make the decision about Felix's fate. We would have to wait until we were brought to Talus Varr. Dani wouldn't be terribly thrilled about that, but if I became Chen's friend, perhaps he would be on my side when I raised the issue with his boss. I had to try and hope Felix had a better backup plan than escaping into the wilderness.

CHAPTER 29

The monotonous cycle of stops and starts began to get on everyone's nerves. While Dylan and I had made up for our nastiness to each other with our usual post-argument rutting, Dani still hardly spoke to me. When the convoy stopped, she was usually the first to exit the vehicle, Adrianna in tow. They made a point of avoiding me during the rest interval, disappearing into the camp until it was time to resume the journey.

I thought she behaved childishly, and I made the mistake of telling her so. That little lapse in judgement resulted in her spending the next twenty hours in one of the other vehicles until Felix finally coaxed her back to ours. After that, the most I could get out of her was an eye roll or a derisive sneer.

The conflict between us only strengthened the growing bond between her and Adrianna. With it apparent that neither Dylan or I wished the other harm, she spent less frequent visits with him and more time with Dani. She was still happy to spend time with him, but only when I was not around to sour her mood.

Felix was of no help whatsoever in dealing with his lover. He refused to take sides, which Dani then blamed on me. I was sure that if one of Mundi's asteroids came crashing down on our heads, her last words would be an admonition that it was all my fault.

With the girls gone on walkabout and the men engaged in

repairing systems ignored by the rebel mechanics, I was left to my own devices. While wandering about the camp, lost in thought, I jumped at a touch on my shoulder.

"Commander, you startled me."

"I'm sorry, Mel. You seemed distressed, and I only wondered if there was something I could do for you."

"Not unless you..." I stopped myself from giving voice to my revenge fantasy. "Yes, you can give me that shooting lesson you promised."

Delighted, he led me to one of the tracked vehicles from which he retrieved a lightweight, snubnosed assault rifle. We then walked beyond the perimeter of the encampment, where he proceeded to construct a small cairn from the omnipresent rocks strewn across the ground. When he was finished, his pathetic half-metre-tall monument looked as if it would tumble over in a stiff breeze. Arms akimbo, he surveyed his work. His breathing mask obscured any sign of the pride I suspected was plastered to his face.

"Is that supposed to be, my target?"

"Yes, it's perfect." He grabbed my hand and pulled me away until we stood a hundred metres from it.

I laughed at what I thought was his idea of a joke at my expense. "I can't see it from here."

"Look through he scope," he said as he handed me the rifle.

I'd watched Dylan practise hundreds of times over the years, but try as I might, I was a hopeless shot. Though he tried to teach me how to shoot on several occasions, my incompetence soon exasperated him and the lessons ended. Now, not sure how to properly hold the thing, I did my best to imitate him.

Awkwardly, I raised it to my eye until it knocked against my faceplate. Fumbling with it, I found the pile of rocks in the sighting apparatus and jerked the trigger. The target remained undisturbed.

Without as much as a chuckle, Chen approached me from behind and gently grasped my shoulders. "Here, let me help."

He adjusted my posture and my grip then coaxed the sight back up toward my visor. "If you wore a helmet like mine, the

HUD would be linked, so you could aim it from any position." His strong hands pressed on my upper arms as he stood behind me. "You'll have to learn to use the weapon's optical mechanism."

I allowed him to help me adjust the gun. "I'll bet it's a lot easier without a breathing mask on."

He chuckled. "If you look around inside the eyepiece, you'll notice various data readouts. We'll just focus on a couple of them for this first time out."

After filling me in on how to aim the damned thing, he instructed me to squeeze the trigger. My finger jerked and a click emitted from the weapon. Nothing happened.

"Is this thing working?"

"The recoil dampers absorbed the shock. You just missed."

I looked through the scope once more. The untouched pile of rocks silently mocked my marksmanship.

"I thought you couldn't miss with these things?"

Chen laughed. "Where did you hear that?"

I was glad my breathing mask hid my blushing face. "I guess I assumed with all the gizmos and everything that an AI was operating in the thing."

"There is a rudimentary AI in the rifle, but it isn't infallible. A lot of variables can influence a projectile. That is what some of the other readouts are for."

We spent the next hour practising, with Chen encouraging every minor success I achieved. As the time passed, his helpful hands often found themselves on my shoulders, waist, or hips, lingering just a little too long after my stance or posture had been corrected. Despite his dedication to my education, I was a terrible shot, though he was much too polite to say so.

Returning the gun to him, I said, "I hope I'm never threatened by rocks."

Laughing too hard at my stupid joke, his hand found the small of my back to prompt our return to the encampment.

After we returned the firearm, I noticed Dylan walking brusquely toward our vehicle, a piece of machinery in his hand. A sick feeling came over me as I wondered how much of our target practise he witnessed. I hastily thanked the commander and followed my retreating husband.

Inside our transport, I found Dylan with his head buried under a panel, cursing a blue streak.

"What's wrong?" I asked.

The expletives halted and a pregnant silence filled the air.

"This fucking part they gave me won't fit."

He emerged from under the console. His face was flushed. "These guys are incompetent. It will be a bloody miracle if these assholes don't get themselves wiped out sooner than later."

"Isn't that a bit harsh? The mechanic just made a simple mistake with the part."

He growled under his breath and examined the uncooperative piece of equipment. "How was your shooting lesson with Chen?"

I laughed. "You know I'm hopeless with a gun."

He redirected his attention to me, seeming to scrutinize every feature on my face before he returned to the object he held. "He seemed to have no problem finding his target."

"Ohh, you saw that?"

"I think everyone in the camp did."

"Don't be ridiculous."

"Well, some of us did."

I knelt next to him and rubbed his thigh. "I didn't want to shut him down if he was only going to flirt. We need his support if we're going to help Felix."

"Was the potential damage to your reputation worth it?"

"He was giving me some harmless attention."

"He pawed you like he hasn't had a woman in months."

"He wasn't pawing me. Look, if anyone knows how to handle a horny man, it would be me."

"So you figured it wouldn't do any harm to resume your old profession to get Felix off the hook?"

"I hardly prostituted myself, Dylan. What the hell is going on?"

He dropped the useless piece of machinery to the floor and

crossed his arms. "Ever since you made it clear you don't want a family, things haven't been the same between us."

I shifted to sit beside him and embraced him. With my face buried in his shoulder, I said, "We've kind of been stressed, what with getting chased and shot at and all."

He chuckled and hugged me. "You know what I meant. I hoped having Adrianna with us would bring out your maternal instincts. Instead, you two fight like you hate each other. I guess I'm disappointed that you were right about being lousy motherhood material."

I buried my face deeper into the fabric of his shirt.

He pulled me close. "Well, aren't you going to say, 'I told you so'?"

"Um, there might be a reason—a good reason why the kid and I don't get along."

I filled him in on the conversation Felix and I shared about Adrianna.

"That's messed up, Mel. It's like you both hate yourselves."

"I would normally accuse you of being dramatic, but you're right—sort of. I think it's more of a primal response to something unnatural about her. She's not fully human, Dylan. She's not completely my clone. She's a human-synth hybrid mutant."

"I just see a cute kid who's had a rough life."

"Yeah, one of six hundred identical sisters grown in a lab."

"Felix is synthetic. You don't hate him."

"I know; it's hard to explain. When I look at her, I feel violated; like Mundi stole a part of my soul and put it into that...creature."

A thump from the back of the vehicle startled me. Adrianna stood at the exit lock, breathing mask in her hands. Her face was wet with tears, and pain filled her eyes.

Shit! The kid overheard us.

Before either of us could react, she closed the airlock door and was gone.

"Why didn't you tell me she was here?" I said as I struggled to my feet.

"I didn't know. She must have returned while I was getting my part."

I reached the door first when Dylan stopped me. "I'll go after Adrianna."

"No, it's my fault. I should—"

"Do you really think she wants to be found by you, Mel?"

"I've got to tell her I didn't mean it..." My wet cheeks surprised me as much as my words.

"We can do damage control after we find her. Go tell Felix and have him join me. If anyone can track her better than me, it's him."

"If Chen's men spot him leaving the camp, they'll shoot him, and maybe you too."

"Then you'll need to persuade your new admirer to help with the search as well." He kissed me on the cheek to take the sting from his words. "That shouldn't be too difficult since she is the prize they want to deliver to Varr."

We parted ways, and I went to locate Chen first. Wind whipped up dust devils, and the sky over the horizon darkened with the approach of another storm. My gut was tied in knots as I ran across the compound. Our time was running out before the planet would claim her small body. I could never live with that outcome on my conscience.

CHAPTER 30

The small figure hid behind the tracked vehicle and waited for any sign of pursuit. She shivered in the dropping temperature and hugged her knees to her chest to keep warm. Behind her, the skies blackened with billowing clouds of dust, and the wind blew her unruly hair about her face.

Adrianna fought to calm herself, just as her caregiver had taught her when she was still at that place. Bettani showed her how to slow her breathing and relax her muscles so the probes did not hurt so much. She had been the only one there who was kind.

Dani was like her. The way she talked and laughed was even better, because it happened more often. Dani never did the things that Bettani was forced to do. Adrianna wished she could go find her but dared not leave the hiding spot.

Adrianna crouched lower when she saw Dylan and Mel exit the vehicle. Mel would probably punish her for running away. The small girl's heart raced when for one, brief moment it appeared Dylan might come toward her. Then disappointment descended when he ran in the opposite direction.

She enjoyed her time with Dylan. He was better to her than Carlos, who rushed them from place to place and always seemed angry. She didn't think he was ever cross with her, though, because he cared for her, fed her, and kept her safe. She was sad he died.

Adrianna was glad when Mel fixed Dylan's injuries and

hoped it meant she was not like the other caregivers she'd known. She was wrong about that. She didn't understand why Dylan was Mel's friend. They always argued, mostly about what they were going to do about her.

After Dani explained families to her, the idea sounded like the best thing in the world. It would better if she and Dylan could become one with Dani instead.

Mel approached her hiding place. She told her legs to run, but they could only shake and would not obey. Closing her eyes, she wanted to do the other thing to protect herself; the bad one that hurt people. But she needed the tubes in her to make that happen, so she could only sit still and wish to not be found.

Mel passed by, and Adrianna allowed herself to relax a little. Absently, she rubbed the fading bump on her head, remembering how she'd received it. Mel's behaviour confused her; she was sometimes protective and mean at other times. Often she would imagine her harsh words before they were spoken.

Mel was right, though; she was a creature, and not even Dylan or Dani would really want her because of that truth.

Soldiers emerged and gathered together, distracting her from self-pity. Their boss spoke and told them they must find her. Memories of that other place flooded her memory. If these men caught her, she would receive cruel treatment and beatings.

She had to get away.

Looking over her shoulder, she watched the growing wall of dust. Dylan had gone toward it. If she found him, he would protect her. Maybe they could hide together until everyone gave up and left them behind. Then they could be a family, just as they both wanted.

She permitted herself a smile at the thought and ran in that direction. Something in the cloud sparkled and attracted her attention. She stared at the spot, her stomach tightening with a familiar fear.

It happened once more. A flash of light glinted off

something at the front of the storm. Several more metallic reflections popped on and off within the shifting dust as an object coalesced into a recognizable form. It looked like the airship that had attacked before, she was sure of it, except now there were many, and they drew closer at an alarming speed.

Not thinking of where she would go, only that she must hide, Adrianna fled in the opposite direction. She didn't care if anyone saw her. Before long the approaching ships would begin shooting, and she would be forgotten. Her short legs carried her rapidly across the barren, rock-strewn plain as the sky darkened with the descending storm. She risked a glance behind but could see nothing except the enveloping dust and billowing grit.

Her wild, loose hair whipped about her masked face, and tiny grains of sand stung her exposed skin. Searching frantically about, she realized she was lost. She thought of returning to the camp, but her footprints had vanished, filled in by the blowing detritus.

Unable to see more than a few metres, she stumbled forward in an effort to put distance between herself and the others.

It would be better to die in the wilderness.

CHAPTER 31

"We need your help!"

Dani and Felix were enjoying a visit over a cup of coffee inside the large rebel troop transport. It served as a canteen for the soldiers during our frequent stops.

She scowled and returned her attention to her cooling drink. "The last time we helped you we ended up here."

I narrowed my eyes. "We don't have time for this debate. Adrianna has run off."

"What happened?"

"Does it really matter why? She's out there and the storm's approaching."

Felix stood and reached for his respirator. "Where did you last see her go?"

"She ran out and was nowhere to be seen by the time we followed her. Dylan has gone to check the other vehicles, but I'm worried she may have fled the camp."

"Bad weather is blowing in from the northwest. She doesn't have much time," he said as he moved to the airlock.

"Wait. You're still considered a prisoner," said Dani. "If they see you leave, they'll shoot you."

He turned to me. "Have you informed Commander Chen?"

"I was going to tell him next."

"Good, they will search the entire camp first. I'll slip away in the confusion and scan for any sign of where she went."

Dani grabbed her own respirator. "I'm coming with you."

Felix touched her arm gently. "I can move more quickly alone, my love. Time is not on the girl's side if she gets caught in the storm."

"Come with me to find Chen," I said, "then we can search for her together."

For the first time in days, Dani looked at me without the resentment behind her eyes. She nodded and we all went outside.

The sky had darkened while I was inside. Without a word, Felix hurried to the southern side of the camp. If anyone could pick up her trail, it was he. His heightened senses allowed him to observe things most others, including Dylan, would overlook.

Yu Chen was hunched over a computer console in conference with one of his men. His scowl faded when he saw me. "I'm afraid I'm rather busy at the moment, Mel. Is this something we can discuss later?"

As I informed him of the situation, his frown returned. "The approaching storm is interfering with our instruments. I was about to break camp and put us on high alert in case of an attack."

"There is a little girl lost somewhere out there," I said, my voice cracking.

His features softened during the few agonizing seconds he spent examining Dani and me. "We should be able to find her quickly if everyone helps."

Before I could thank him, he issued orders for a complete search of the camp by every available person. As he did so, Dani turned to leave.

"Dani, please come with me? I'm afraid she won't want to return with me if I stumble across her path."

Anger flashed in her eyes. "What is it with you? Why do I constantly find myself bailing you out of problems of your own making?"

"I would do the same for you."

"I want to believe that, Mel. I really do. But in the years I've known you, it has never happened that way. I am beginning to wonder if you are my friend, or if I am only yours."

"Look, Dani, I can't afford the time to defend myself now. I'm going out there to find Adrianna, and if I do, I'll try my best to make good by her and bring her home. After that is over and she's safe, I'll be happy to have an argument, a catfight, or a shooting duel with you, whatever it takes to settle this thing between us."

A hint of a smile turned up the corner of her mouth. "You can't shoot."

"I know."

"Let's just find her. This quarrel can wait." She put on her breathing apparatus and left.

My disappointment must have been written all over my face.

"I'll accompany you to search for the girl," said Chen.

He donned his mask and grabbed a backpack from a rack by the door, which I presumed contained an emergency medical kit. I felt stupid for not thinking of that contingency myself.

When we exited the vehicle, the storm was practically on top of us.

"Let's scour the outer perimeter," he said. "My men pretty much have the interior covered and will join us if necessary."

I looked out at the vast landscape and felt despair. Though seemingly empty at first glance, there were thousands of boulders and depressions in sight that could conceal a small girl who did not wish to be found.

Chen's hand grasped mine. "We just have to think like a child might."

With that in mind, my eyes settled on a sizeable boulder a few hundred metres away, and I started toward it with a determined gait. My heart in my throat, I reached my objective to find nothing behind it but a pile of fine red sand.

Before my emotions could convince me otherwise, I jogged to another likely hiding place, Chen in my wake. On finding it too unoccupied, I surveyed the landscape once more. The descending sandstorm had reduced visibility to less than a kilometre. On the other side of the camp, the billowing dust was much thicker and would soon make its way in our direction. My pulse raced.

"She could be anywhere," I said.

Chen pushed me to the ground. "Get down!"

In response to my unvoiced question, he pointed to our encampment. Above it, from out of the blowing sand, emerged first one, then a second attack airship, similar to the ones previously encountered. They were soon joined by two more.

Flashes of muzzle fire erupted from some of Chen's men. Their hand-held weapons had no effect on the hovering ships, which responded with far more devastating consequences. Barely discernible through the thickening dust, I watched soldiers fall like scattered chess pieces as the menacing airships fired relentlessly at them. A vehicle exploded in a flash that lit everything with a brilliant orange glow.

Chen's hand rested heavily on my shoulder as we crouched behind the boulder. If he was concerned I might foolishly bolt toward the conflict in an effort to save someone, he needn't have been. My knees were locked in abject fright, and I doubt I could have run away if the attackers chose to come after us in that moment.

During the decade since my encounter with the alien nanites, I occasionally wondered if they would ever obey my commands again, now that they were deployed within the planet's interior. I wanted them to rush out of the soil and engulf the attacking vessels, consuming them to their base molecules. But nothing of the kind happened. Mundi's ships continued the devastating assault, and after a few minutes that felt far longer, it was over.

With all gunfire ceased, the only sounds were the blowing wind and the whine of engines as one of the airships settled to the ground within fifty metres of us. The back opened and dozens of armed men emerged, each one more prepared for battle than any of the rebels had been. They advanced on the camp and vanished into the dust.

Every sporadic pop of gunfire startled me. I strained to see anything beyond the pall of the engulfing storm, but the only thing in view was the menacing form of the aircraft that stood between us and everyone else.

What I could see of Chen's face through his mask was stony as he looked toward the scene.

"How did we not see them coming?" I whispered unnecessarily through our private comm link.

"The electrical activity of the storm confused our instruments. They hid within it," he said. "We use the same tactic against them, but rarely through an aerial assault. It's too dangerous since the ships would be flying blind. They must have had compelling reasons to take on that risk to attack us."

My thoughts turned to Adrianna and her value to Mundi. How many of his minions had perished in pursuit of his prize? What were a few more if it increased his odds of success?

A figure stepped out of the ship and descended the ramp. Even wearing a breathing mask, I recognized his physique and mannerisms. Though we had only met once ten years before, he was unmistakable to me. During Dylan's time as Head of Martian Security, Chas Morgan was his right-hand man. Though young and inexperienced at their last meeting, Dylan had introduced him as the most promising cadet to emerge from the Military Academy in decades.

Those words were high praise coming from Dylan. He wasn't conceited or arrogant in any way, but he was the best soldier, spy, and dedicated son of Mars the planet had ever known. To encounter anyone who could hold a candle to him was a rarity, so when Dylan praised the young man, I knew he meant it.

Morgan had definitely made something of himself if he was commanding this attack unit. I doubted Mundi would have entrusted such a critical mission to a simple underling.

I found myself hoping that if Dylan were somehow captured by these men, their prior relationship with would be helpful in how he would be treated. The downside of Dylan's capture would be a confirmation that I was running with the rebels and most likely result in a thorough sweep of the area. Maybe if they found me, they would give up their hunt for Adrianna.

At that moment I hoped the girl was far away and beyond

their clutches. She'd suffered too much at the hands of these monsters. As for me, things looked pretty bleak.

CHAPTER 32

Morgan stood at the foot of the ramp and surveyed the scene. For the first time in weeks he felt as if he had a handle on the situation. After the previous two disastrous attempts to capture the renegade, Melanie Destin, fortune had finally smiled on him.

Not only had his source confirmed that she travelled with this particular convoy, but he also assured Morgan that the missing clone and Felix Altius were present. Apprehending all three would more than make up for the losses incurred for the mission.

When the location and route of the rebel caravan was confirmed, he needed only to await the appropriate moment to strike. The notoriously fickle Martian weather had threatened to be uncooperative, but the unexpected development of a storm system permitted him to attack before the enemy entered too deeply into their own territory.

Though he intended to take all the credit for the mission's success, Morgan was acutely aware of how close the entire operation had come to failure. Only the presence of Mundi's agent within this rebel unit had given him any advantage. He had no idea who the spy was, which made his next choices difficult. When the rebels were rounded up, he had no way to identify the valued asset. He certainly did not wish to blacken this victory by inadvertently executing the man, but he couldn't come out and ask for him to step forward either without compromising him.

Calling his lieutenant over, he said, "Gather them here. Kill only those who refuse to surrender. I'll hang any man who does otherwise."

Within thirty minutes, the first of the captives began to assemble in the appointed area. None wore battle armour—a testimonial to the stealth and swiftness of the attack. He wondered which of them the agent might be, or if he had even survived. His pulse accelerated at the contemplation of that possibility, but he soon convinced himself that it was war, and accidents happened. It would of course be regrettable but easily explained to the satisfaction of his Dominus, especially if he presented the three he hunted.

When the apparent last of the prisoners had been herded into the assembly area, the lieutenant approached to give his report.

"Every survivor is now present, sir."

With growing panic, Morgan studied the defeated group of men. "There should be a woman and a child travelling with them. Where are they?"

The soldier's eyes grew wide behind his helmet visor. "We found no women or children. There are none among the casualties either."

"Search again, thoroughly this time. They must be hiding. And I need a list of who is captive and who is dead."

The officer saluted and ran off to carry out the order.

Morgan summoned one of the men acting as guard. He meticulously described Felix Altius to the soldier and ordered him to physically inspect everyone. It was critical not to rely solely on scanning for active CIs to identify the prisoners. "Tear off breathing masks if you have to."

While the captured men were inspected, Morgan paced to calm his nerves. The importance of maintaining an air of cool confidence was paramount. Any sign of weakness on his part would only encourage plots to supplant him from within the ranks.

Until this moment, the possibility that the intelligence might be flawed, that his agent had been compromised and led them into a trap, had not entered his mind.

Looking up into the billowing dust, he could not see the raptor flying above that was assigned to lookout duty. Accessing his link, he gave instructions for it to extend its patrol radius, then after further consideration, he commanded the launch of a second ship to assist.

Turning his attention back to the prisoners, he slowly scanned them from his vantage point. Helmets obscured their features, so he resorted to interpreting body language. The ones his guards had interrogated appeared more relaxed, as if they believed they'd passed some test to prolong their own survival. Those yet to be questioned displayed an array of emotional tells, ranging from fear to outright defiance. Only one man tried to make himself look less conspicuous, though the fact that he was the only one not to wear a uniform created the opposite impression.

He ordered the man brought to him.

Hands bound behind him, the tall, well-muscled captive was forced to his knees before Morgan. One of the guards handed his commander the scanning device that had probed the prisoner's CI.

"Tyson Ross, is it?"

The man nodded but avoided eye contact, preferring to stare at the ground.

"Where is your uniform, soldier?"

The man did not look up. "It's in the laundry, sir."

"Only one uniform? I find that difficult to believe." Morgan paced around the prisoner. "Though if true, it might be a good indicator of how poorly financed your rebellion is."

He reached down and squeezed his shoulder. "You are a solid specimen."

"I'm from Terra."

"Oh, a mercenary? That is interesting." He surveyed the other prisoners. "You would seem to be the only one of your kind present. Did no one else from Earth see fit to join you in your noble cause?"

"There's only me."

Morgan slowly circled him a second time. On returning to face him, he seized the mercenary's head and forced him to look up. Long seconds passed as he inspected every visible feature through the prisoner's visor, but his gaze lingered on the man's eyes.

"You know me."

"No, sir."

"Oh, that isn't true at all, is it? We've met. In fact, I know your eyes. You are Dylan Hodgson."

"No, sir."

Releasing him, Morgan stepped back a pace and nodded to the guards. One grabbed Dylan's shoulders while the other seized his head, and, after a brief struggle, removed his helmet.

Dylan held his breath and stared defiantly at him.

Squatting on his heels to stare Dylan in the eyes, he wished he could remove his own mask to confront his former superior, face to face.

"I expected you would be here with your little bitch. Do us both a favour, traitor, and tell me where she is."

Dylan struggled to maintain eye contact with his captor, his face growing redder with the passing seconds. After an inordinately long interval, his breath exploded from him and he reflexively inhaled. Gasping and coughing, he instinctively fought to inhale oxygen that was not present.

When he'd determined his prisoner had suffered enough, Morgan motioned for the guard to replace the headgear. Dylan continued to cough and struggle for air until his breathing settled into a rapid rhythm.

He grasped Dylan's helmet by the lower rim and tugged on it teasingly.

"We both know I can do this all day until you tell me where she is, Dylan."

"She's...dead. Has been for...ten years."

Shaking his head, he stood and waved to the guards to repeat the procedure.

Dylan took longer to recover the second time. His head was

bent, almost to the ground, as his broad shoulders rose and fell with his rapid breaths.

Once more, Morgan crouched before him. "I have it on reliable authority that she is quite well and has been travelling with this merry troupe. Now, please don't waste my time. Where is she?"

Panting, Dylan looked up at him and shook his head. "Sorry, I can't help you."

Rising, he ordered the torture be repeated for three more intervals. Each exposure to the deadly atmosphere was longer than the previous, and the times for recovery shortened equivalently.

His chest heaving after the third iteration, Dylan was forced to look up. He couldn't sustain eye contact with his tormentor, and the veins were prominent on his blue-tinged face.

"You know, I once looked up to you. I modelled my career on yours and fought hard to earn my position as your lieutenant. To train under the great son of Mars, Dylan Hodgson, was the single-minded goal of my young life. When I succeeded and began my work with you, I thought my feet solidly on the path to a bright future."

Dylan's head sagged as his consciousness wavered. Morgan jerked his helmet back up so he could peer into his face and ensure his attention.

"Do you know what happened?" He shook Dylan. "Do you?"

Dylan stared blankly up at him, his jaw slack.

"You betrayed us! You abandoned your position and vanished, along with your whore." Morgan's chest rose and fell as he awaited any kind of response to the insult. Receiving none, he said, "Every one of us who worked beneath you came under suspicion. Every single one of us was forced, time and again, to demonstrate our loyalty to Mars in the wake of your treason. I alone redeemed my honour and rose to heights of power you could never imagine."

Not certain if he was actually heard, he squatted and spoke softly. "I am second only to the most powerful man alive. I intend to succeed him, and in a way, I suppose I have you to thank for it all."

His link pinged. Frowning, Morgan stood and accepted the communication. As he listened to the report, a smile formed. He acknowledged the message and bent down to speak intimately to Dylan once more.

"I know you're not going to give me what I want. As it turns out, I can live with that. My men have found the girl and the other great traitor, Felix Altius. They should be a sufficient prize for my master to compensate for the loss of your woman."

He grasped the rim of Dylan's respirator and slowly pried it off. As he lay on the ground, exposed and struggling to breathe, Morgan leaned over him. "Your troublesome woman will not long survive you."

Standing, his shoulders shook involuntarily from the influx of stress hormones. Discarding the helmet, he watched as his victim convulsed until Dylan finally stopped moving.

He ordered the execution of the remaining prisoners and the destruction of all vehicles. If the spy died among them, it no longer mattered to him. If Destin hid nearby, she would not survive long out in the open. She had always been a consolation prize in the event her clone could not be recovered. Now, with both the child and Altius in custody, Regis Mundi had everything he needed to swiftly end the rebellion and consolidate his power on Mars before stepping out into the solar system and beyond. Morgan's position and destiny were now more than assured.

CHAPTER 33

Grains of blowing sand rattled off my faceplate. The full brunt of the storm had descended upon us and visibility was reduced to a couple of metres. Past the edge of the large rock we hid behind, I could see nothing of the camp, and the wind was the only thing I could hear. If not for our private comm link I doubted Chen, who huddled next to me, would have heard me.

"Can you see anything?"

He risked exposing himself for another peek. After a few moments, he sat beside me in the meagre shelter the boulder offered.

"The infrared is only detecting the heat from the raptor's engines. I can't tell what is going on."

I leaned back into the rough surface and shivered. The dropping temperatures prompted me to sidle closer to Chen for warmth.

"Do you think they'll come looking for us?"

"If we remain hidden here, they won't detect our heat signatures. It is unsafe for them to wander far from their ships in this weather. We should be safe."

His arm wrapped around my shoulder. I shamelessly huddled in to accept his body's warmth, not concerned if it gave him the wrong idea. My eye fell on the backpack lying at his feet, and I nudged it with my foot.

"What's in that?"

"It contains an emergency survival pack."

"What prompted you to bring it?"

"The same reason I brought this." He raised his snub-nosed assault rifle. "It's standard procedure."

"Hmph. In ten years of living on the surface, I've seen dozens of dusters but only ever been stupid enough to be caught out in the open twice...both times in the past month."

"I grew up on Mars. As a boy, my friends and I often spent weeks camping and waiting them out. It was part of our training."

"Training for what? Why would anyone put a child through that?"

He chuckled. "How much do you know about the first Chinese colony?"

"Very little, I'm afraid. Didn't they arrive with the second colonization attempt?"

"The third one, actually."

"There weren't three."

"China participated in the first failed effort in the twenty-first century but declined to join the next successful wave in the 2170s. Political and economic tensions were high on Earth at the time, and the government thought it better to expend resources on defence."

"That didn't exactly work out in everyone's best interest, did it?"

"No, it didn't. After the war, China's lunar colony was all that remained of the nation's scientific and cultural legacy. Even though, by treaty, the Moon was not militarized by any nation, the winning coalition was determined to remove any surviving pocket of potential resistance. When it became clear that the Chinese community on Luna would be relocated back to Terra, a small group of academics and engineers secretly organized a colonization mission to Mars."

"To preserve the culture?"

"Yes, but after the devastating war China had largely provoked, the existing Martian colonies did not welcome them. They were forced to settle apart and become self-contained. Isolated, a community grew which placed a premium on survival skills, among other things."

"So if your people are traditionally isolationist, why do you fight for the rebellion?"

"We see what Regis Mundi is doing. If he gains control of the planet, it won't be long before our way of life ceases to exist. Joining forces with the rebels is preferable to sitting quietly on the sidelines."

"You trust Talus Varr that much?"

"Varr speaks the right words to my elders."

"You don't agree?"

"I'm pragmatic; I know things will change, regardless of the victor. It's better to choose the side that gives you the best possible deal in the end."

I well understood what being a pragmatist meant. Being one had kept me alive for most of my life, though lately I wondered when a series of compromises would back me into a corner from which I couldn't escape.

"What do you think is happening back there?" I asked.

"All comm links with my troops are down, and there's been no recent gunfire. That won't last for long."

"What are you saying?"

"While we gave Mundi's soldiers the choice, his men will not do the same."

"They're going to execute the prisoners?"

"I'm sorry."

The distant rumble of what sounded like thunder rose above the din of the storm.

"What was that?"

As if in answer, two more booms followed.

"Those are explosions," said Chen. His voice was emotionless, and I couldn't see enough of his face to read it.

The realization hit me that Dylan and Dani were still in the camp. I flipped through the comm channels, listening for anything other than static that would suggest they still lived. Chen's hand grasped mine and pulled it away from the control at my neck.

"They've jammed everything and will be monitoring for

activity. You'll only lead them to us if you continue."

Dylan was resourceful. So was Dani. They had to have found a way to hide from Mundi's men as we had. They just couldn't be dead.

A faint, deep roar rode on top of the storm. Seeming to have heard it too, Chen risked a peek over the edge of our protection.

"They're leaving."

Every muscle in my body tensed as the sound of the engines traversed over our heads and faded into the distance. I sat with my back glued to the rock and strained to listen over the wind and the hiss of blowing sand.

"Stay close to me," said Chen while pulling the backpack on. He picked up his rifle and crept out from behind our cover.

I followed him, doing my best to imitate his moves as he made his way forward. I shivered uncontrollably, though not entirely from the cold. Every step increased my anxiety. I wanted to run ahead and call out for Dylan. I imagined him entering the camp from the other direction where he had been watching and waiting, equally concerned with my safety. I longed for his comforting embrace.

Barely able to see my hand in front of my face, I remained within arm's reach of Chen, whose helmet's thermal imaging was the only guide available.

I tripped over, rather than saw, the first corpse. Dropping to my knees, I dug to exhume the body, already partly buried by the blowing sand.

"It's not him," I said, not attempting to hide my relief. It never crossed my mind it was a person familiar to Chen until I looked up at him.

"I...I'm sorry—"

"There is a stronger thermal signature this way," he said, indicating the direction with his gun.

My comment had not seemed to affect him. He was a soldier and probably accustomed to the deaths of comrades, but his detachment still caught me off guard.

Blindly following his lead, I stayed close as he led us toward the only indicator of life he'd seen. My hope, not yet dashed, still hung by a slender thread. If I had not been forced to keep up with Chen, I would probably have dragged my feet. If I didn't know who still gave off heat, Dylan could still be alive to me. If I didn't discover his body, there was a chance he still lived.

A familiar figure kneeling in the sand coalesced in front of me.

"Dani!" I rushed to her, arms outstretched. Falling to my knees beside her, I embraced her. "I'm so glad you're safe."

It took a moment for me notice that Dani cradled something in her lap. Looking down, I gradually realized that it was a person. I stared at him as if from a great distance, not able to convince myself of his familiarity. The man wore no helmet. What kind of fool took off his breathing equipment? His skin was the blue one expected from asphyxiation, and his oddly familiar features were contorted in the final agony he must have experienced.

"Mel, I am so sorry," she said, weeping openly.

"What are you talking about? Who is...?"

With my heart pounding, I looked at him again. The shape of his nose. The dimple on his chin. The scar on his cheek from a struggle with our engine last year. All these and more were features that belonged to Dylan. It made no sense that this blue corpse wore his face.

Like a clearing fog, the truth slowly materialized in my brain. I could not breathe. It was Dylan lying in Dani's lap. He didn't move. Dylan lay where a dead man was supposed to be. This was not possible.

I heard somebody screaming, and was surprised to realize it was me. Grabbing Dylan by the shoulders, I pulled his head to my chest and cuddled him protectively. I stroked his head and rocked back and forth, wanting too late to comfort him.

When my cries of anguish turned to whimpers, gentle hands pried me away from my Dylan. One set helped me to my feet while another laid his head on the ground. I stared at his body. If it hadn't been for his colouring, he might have been asleep.

Someone embraced me.

"I'm so very sorry, Mel," said Dani.

"Is it really him, Dani? Is Dylan really dead?"

"Yes, Sugar. I'm afraid so."

"Why? What happened?"

She continued to hold me and told me everything she'd seen.

Dani was at the opposite side of the camp during the attack. Realizing what was happening, she dove under the nearest vehicle and hid.

"I didn't think of how stupid an idea that was until they blew one up right next to me. By the time I worked up the courage to move, I was too late. The attackers had landed and engaged the few of our boys who had weapons. It was a short fight. The survivors were herded together. I could only watch and hope they didn't find me."

All I could do was to nod, my head still buried in her shoulder.

"I saw them pull Dylan from the group of prisoners and take him to their leader."

"His name is Morgan," I said. "I saw him before the storm got too bad."

"Yeah, well, whoever he is, once he figured out who Dylan was, he sort of went ape-shit crazy on him. He started to torture him, wanting to know where you and Adrianna were. He protected you to the end, Mel. He never cracked. Never gave that bastard a thing he wanted." Dani's voice broke and she wept. "But it didn't do any good. They found her and Felix."

I pulled my friend close and clumsily tried to comfort her. The two of us must have looked pathetic, huddled together, crying our eyes out. I couldn't begin to imagine what Chen might have thought and didn't really give a shit.

Dani didn't need to say it. Everyone was in this mess because of me. She cried into my shoulder at the moment, but a time would come when her resentment for me would outgrow our shared grief. Dylan had given his life for us. Adrianna and Felix were prisoners, subject to whatever fate the dictator had prepared for them. We would probably die in the wilderness together, with her resenting me every minute we survived.

As far as I was concerned, I deserved a death like that. Alone and loathed. I had failed everyone. The child I was supposed to protect was captured. The friends I asked to get me off this rock were doomed. My beloved was dead.

I had fooled myself that my decision to get Adrianna under Varr's protection had been altruistic. The more difficult path would have been to pack us all up and depart with Dani and Felix while we had the chance to escape. Dylan would be alive and have the family he always had wanted. I might not have made a perfect mother to Adrianna, or even a passably good one, but I could have taken the trouble to try. I certainly couldn't have done worse by her than my own mother.

Instead I opted for the hero's role, deluded there were bigger stakes to consider than the lives of ordinary folk. Though I pretended to dislike the moniker everyone had saddled me with, part of me swelled with pride whenever I heard the name 'the Mother of Mars.' My foolishness had cost me everything. If I were the only one to suffer the consequences of my stupidity, I could have lived with that. But those dear to me had paid the ultimate price, while I survived to enjoy the luxury of self-pity.

For most of my life I had considered my mother to be a self-absorbed bitch who hated me and only saw my value in the profit I brought her as a commodity. Never in my wildest imaginings did want to be like her, and yet I saw very little difference between us in that moment. How could I forgive myself and not her? It was a relief that I wouldn't live long enough for that to become a problem.

The swirling dust-laden wind seemed to grow stronger. Drifting sand had begun to cover Dylan's legs, and I wanted the planet to bury me as well.

Someone shook me by the shoulder.

"We need to find some shelter," said Chen.

"Why?" His posture suggested that he didn't understand my

question. "Take Dani and get out of here."

He leaned in to speak to me, even though I could hear him perfectly well over our comm link. "The storm is intensifying. You both have to come with me. Our rescue will be here in the morning."

Dani released me and stood next to Chen. I fell to my knees and pulled Dylan to me. I probably looked like a ridiculous, dust-covered parody of a pietà and would have chuckled at the irony if I hadn't been hurting so much.

Dani's hand gently rested on my shoulder. "Mel, you have to let him go."

"I can't. If I do, I leave the best part of me behind with him. There will be nothing good left of me; nothing to live for. Everyone will be far better off if I join him."

"Sweetie, I know you don't want to hear this, but I'm going to say it anyway. People still depend on you. Felix and Adrianna need you. I do too."

"What good can I possibly be to anyone? Everything I touch turns to ashes."

"You're hurting, Sugar. I get it. But, dammit, Mel, Felix is in trouble and I can't help him by myself. You owe me."

Dani, bless her, was trying hard to shake me back to my senses. She was right. I was in debt to her and Felix. That alone was enough for me to consider getting off my sorry ass. Nor could I permit anything to happen to Adrianna if it was somehow in my power to prevent it. But another, darker purpose stirred in the back of my mind; another reason for me to move on. Morgan and his boss owed me a life, and I intended to collect from them.

CHAPTER 34

Felix's attention was riveted to the gangway of the raptor. Three of Mundi's soldiers entered, struggling to carry a resisting burden. A fourth man followed, his hands clamped over a wound at his throat. The flexible section that protected his neck appeared torn, and bloody skin showed beneath the damage.

Adrianna continued to kick and resist being handled like an unwieldy sack of wildcats. She was unceremoniously dropped at Felix's feet. Jumping up, she hungrily eyed the four soldiers, as if considering her next victim.

"No more out of you!" said the man with the injury. He brandished a charged riot baton and did not appear to be hesitant about its use. Adrianna tensed her muscles to spring at the man. Before she could attack, Felix stood and faced her.

"Please stand down, child. It is best for—" His eyes squeezed shut in agony, and he sank to his knees while the officer pressed the business end of the baton into his back.

The girl wasted no time and lunged at the preoccupied soldier. Felix intercepted her with his shackled hands and pulled her down with him. "Calm yourself, or they will hurt you."

As if to fulfill Felix's prophecy, the man thrust the stick into her side. She doubled up and screamed in rage and pain as it discharged.

Faster than anyone could react, Felix ripped the device away and plunged it through the front of the man's faceplate. Before his victim could hit the floor, he turned on the other men, frozen in place by the suddenness of his attack. Within a few seconds, two were dead, their necks snapped, and the third struggled in Felix's grip.

"Enough!"

Out of the corner of his eye, Felix spotted a different man holding Adrianna by the hair, his sidearm pressed into the girl's temple. Felix released the soldier and dropped to his knees, his handcuffed hands raised above his head.

"A wise choice, Altius," said Morgan. He waited for the men who had accompanied him into the ship to restrain Felix before he gave the girl into the care of two others. "Although I suspect you knew I would not kill her."

"I couldn't risk her life on the chance I was wrong," said Felix as he was forced to his feet.

Morgan nodded to one of his men for the ramp to be raised and the cabin pressurized. He pulled off his helmet, revealing a man in his thirties, his blond hair dishevelled and wet with perspiration. He waved his arm to indicate the breathing masks should be removed from his prisoners.

"The child is quite the little warrior, isn't she?"

Adrianna snarled at him but was held firmly in place by the soldiers.

"I don't suppose you or your comrades realized what you were dealing with when you took her on?"

"It would seem that your men did not either," said Felix, glancing at the dead man lying beside the discharged baton.

Morgan regarded the body. "Those particular tendencies had not yet manifested when she was abducted, but they were anticipated. You and your friends should be grateful I've apprehended her before she could murder you all in your sleep."

The floor shook, and Felix felt his body weight increase with the raptor's liftoff. Morgan strolled forward, seeming to study him.

"While capturing her was a foregone conclusion, I must

admit to my delight in you falling into my lap. Our Dominus will be most pleased with your return."

"Regis Mundi is no longer my master."

"I think he disagrees with you, but it doesn't matter. You won't be returning to your former position, anyway."

"What revenge has he planned?"

Morgan chuckled. "He has railed on about what he would like to do to you, but his plan is not wasteful vengeance. He has a more important use for you."

"As his bioreceptical?"

A satisfied smile spread across Morgan's face. "It would seem that the process of reproducing you is more complex than any of his useless scientists predicted. The old fool doesn't have the time to wait for them to figure things out. He's dying, you see."

"Interesting," said Felix. "Your irreverence suggests that even with my availability, you do not anticipate a successful transference."

"The whole thing is theoretical at the moment. It has a low probability of success."

"I see, perhaps no chance, then?"

A smile turned the corners of Morgan's mouth. "Quite likely none."

Felix didn't have to ask to know who Mundi's successor was. He glanced at Adrianna. "What is his interest in the girl?"

"Surely you already know she is Melanie Destin's clone?"

"Not an exact one, though."

"No, she's not." Morgan narrowed his eyes and scrutinized Felix. "I suppose there is no point keeping you in the dark, Altius. You might even have figured it all out on your own before your end."

"Your confidence in my abilities is flattering."

Morgan's smile faded. "She is a hybrid clone; a combination of human and synthetic DNA. They haven't managed to create a living artificial being yet." He directed his attention to Adrianna. "She, however, is something the eggheads got right, though it took them over six hundred attempts. Merging natural and manufactured cell structure is only possible because of Destin's mutation; the same one that allows her to manipulate the nanites Mundi has obsessed over for decades."

"You forget who wrote those reports."

"That's right, Altius, you are one of the few people who knows of the true origin and nature of them. Whoever can control them, like Melanie Destin, can manipulate them to any purpose, including terraforming a planet. But can you imagine the possibilities if the Ares nanites could be incorporated directly into human tissue?"

"A being like that would have the potential to morph into any form."

"A creature with such ability can build or destroy whole civilizations. It could be a harbinger for the evolution of humanity."

"Or the ultimate means of its destruction." Felix briefly regarded Adrianna before returning his attention to Morgan. "You have achieved this?"

"As I said, several hundred failed experiments have led to this child, but the three-way combination of human and synthetic biology and alien technology is complex, as you might well imagine. Until recently, we had a problem obtaining the nanites because of Destin's destruction of the stock."

"You've located the mothership, then?"

"Stumbled upon it, actually. We were looking for suitable asteroids to drop on top of any rebel outposts still active. We lost quite a few men before we recovered sample from it."

Felix realized the implications if Mundi's scientists succeeded. The entire alien ship would be controllable. Mundi would have the means to conquer Terra and rule the solar system.

He tested the strength of his restraints. "I presume we are being returned to the research facility Adrianna came from?"

The girl tensed. Morgan waved to the men holding her, and they placed shackles on her wrists and ankles. They then carried her to a small cage and pushed her inside.

"Is that necessary?" asked Felix.

"Sedatives don't affect her, and she's proven herself to be

bothersome. I think this is best for everyone. Would you like to join her?"

Felix replied by returning to the bench. Two guards approached and shackled his ankles together, then connected them to the floor.

"It won't be a long flight. We'll have you out of those things before you realize it," said Morgan.

He departed, leaving behind three men assigned to guard them. They all stood as far from both Felix and Adrianna as the space allowed, their weapons at the ready. Felix could tell at a glance that these particular mercenaries were better trained than most of Mundi's men and would not be easy to overpower if the situation presented itself. There was nothing to do but settle in for the duration of the trip.

He looked over to the cage confining the girl. He doubted this was the first time she'd been treated like a rabid animal.

"Are you all right?" he asked her.

"No," she replied while rubbing her lower back where she'd been shocked.

"You must not antagonize them. They are frightened by you."

"They're going to stick me back into the chair and put the tubes in me again."

"Why did they do that to you?"

"I don't know. They're mean. They made me hurt people. I didn't want to, but they made me do the thing to them."

"What thing?"

"I made the people fall down and go away."

Interesting. "How did you do that?"

"I had to think about them falling to the floor and bleeding; then they would do it and the hurting would go away."

"Can you do that any time you want?" asked Felix, glancing up at the guards. They appeared more nervous than a few minutes before.

"No, only when they stick the tubes in and make the blue stuff go inside me."

Curious. The researchers were attempting to trigger some

kind of response in her. Based on Morgan's comments, it was entirely possible they primed Adrianna's system with samples of the Ares virus, but how that enabled her to kill was a mystery to him at the moment.

Adrianna curled up and closed her eyes. Felix thought that was a good idea, given the possibilities that might lie ahead. Even though he didn't need to sleep as a human did, he still required an hour or two of rest every night.

With his back against the hull, he felt the ship's vibrations. One of their main engine turbine blades was warped and needed replacement. Considering that it had the potential to fail at any time with catastrophic consequences, he found himself hoping it endured long enough to get them to their destination.

On the basis of that desire, he decided his subconscious must know of a way out that it had not yet passed on to his conscious brain. Perhaps sleep would allow the two to share information. He leaned his head back and soon fell asleep.

CHAPTER 35

The survival kit Chen had the foresight to grab was designed for two. It contained enough provisions for two weeks, so stretching the emergency rations between the three of us over a few days was not an issue. Our immediate problem was shelter. The kit's tent was a tight squeeze for two but presented a physical impossibility for three.

Chen played the gentleman and gave it to us while he improvised a suitable substitution out of the wreckage of one of the surface transports.

"In my youth I endured far worse conditions than this," he said. "On one of my first survival tests, my tent blew away and I had to dig myself a hole to ride out the winds. This transport chassis is a luxury hotel by comparison."

As the worst of the weather front passed over us, there was nothing to do but to lie inside our respective shelters and wait it out. Dani and I ran out of distracting topics of conversation after the first day. With nothing left to talk about except the things closest to our hearts, we agreed silence was better. Sleep was the only respite available from the mind-numbing grief.

Rescue arrived as the last of the wind blew itself out. I panicked on first seeing our rescuers, so similar were their ships to the ones that had attacked us. One raptor set down nearby while its companion circled on guard overhead.

Our anxious rescuers wished for us to depart, but we insisted something important needed to be done first.

The storm had covered everything with fine dust and sand, so it took us some time to locate the exact location of Dylan's body. Together we constructed a small cairn over it, on top of which we set his helmet. Dani recited some prayers she recalled from her childhood, and the rebels all stood around it with us in a moment of silence. Chen followed with a stirring tribute to all the fallen, complete with partisan rhetoric and promises of vengeance.

His words hardly registered with the men, who shifted their feet, seeming eager to return to the ship and depart.

The gathering broke up and everyone proceeded up the ramp. I lingered, kneeling in front of the cairn. I wanted to kiss the stones, but my stupid respirator restricted me to laying my hand on them. I had not kissed Dylan for days because of our argument. I was grateful we made up, but a wound festered in my heart at the thought of the things that would never again happen.

"Mel? We should go."

I looked up at Dani. Her shoulders were stooped, and she sounded exhausted. I rose and spent a last moment memorizing the sight of the memorial and my final moment with my beloved. Reluctantly, I turned and followed Dani into the aircraft.

For six days after our rescue we cooled our heels at the rebel base. Talus Varr, if he was present at all, had not bothered to greet us. Nobody could tell me where he was, and my patience was running on fumes.

With the exception of a few high-security areas, we were given the run of the massive underground compound that served as the nerve centre for Talus Varr's insurrection. After taking the first two days to explore it, Dani and I spent our time hanging around in our shared room or in the common area where everyone took their meals.

"Where could he be, Mel? I don't understand why he's ignoring you."

"Maybe I misjudge my importance to him or his cause."

"Chen says Varr's been inspecting other rebel installations.

He claims to not know his whereabouts at the moment. What kind of bullshit is that? Who misplaces their fearless leader?"

"Something strikes me odd about this rebellion. They are more of an annoyance than an insurrection."

"Maybe this base and these men are all there is?" Her eyes were wide and her face pale. "What if there isn't anything he can do to help Felix?"

I didn't want to tell Dani that I believed Talus Varr's role as the rebel leader was incongruent. He always worked behind the scenes, influencing change using the subtle tools of diplomacy, espionage, and assassination. For him to become the face of open opposition to Regis Mundi struck me as a poorly considered public relations campaign. The dictator had spent decades promoting his eccentric, ruthless persona across the solar system as the almost mythical head of his corporation.

"I think the rebellion was real once, until Mundi dropped asteroids on the settlements that showed open support. There are more in orbit, waiting to plummet down on any pocket of dissension that emerges. Everyone is afraid."

"Including Varr? That sucks if true."

"Courage cannot exist without fear," a resonant voice replied. I turned around to see Talus Varr enter the room, wearing a broad smile that revealed perfect white teeth. He was thinner than I remembered him, and his face was drawn, betraying most of his sixty or seventy years. His rebel uniform was unadorned, showing no sign of his rank. It was, perhaps, his only concession to a desire for anonymity.

He enveloped me in a bear hug, which I did not resist. I relished being greeted by someone who wanted to be with me, even if only for his own, selfish reasons.

My relations with Dani had been cordial but strained. If she held any lingering resentment toward me for Felix's plight, she said nothing, but I still sensed it lurking behind every word and expression. I, on the other hand, was not myself around her either. I tiptoed about with my words and deeds, careful not to say or do anything that might give her the impression that the safety of Felix was not foremost on my mind. I missed my friendship with her. Varr's unexpected, enthusiastic greeting only reminded me of how much Dani and I had drifted.

He greeted her with equal enthusiasm then led us to his office. Once within, he sat behind his desk and offered a seat for each of us. Chen entered and stood beside him, a scowl on his brow.

"The commander brought me up to date on everything. I'm so terribly sorry about Dylan. He was a good man."

I swallowed the lump in my throat and muttered my thanks.

Dani rescued me. "We want to know when you plan to rescue Felix and Adrianna."

"Adrianna?" asked Varr.

"The clone liberated from installation sixteen," said Chen.

"Oh, yes." Talus returned his attention to me. "Carlos shouldn't have involved you in this, Mel. I suspect his options were exhausted if he went against my wishes like that."

"You didn't tell him to contact me?"

"I didn't want anything to disturb your anonymity. I was dismayed enough to learn of Mundi's hunt for you." He glanced at Chen for a moment. "My officer, on the other hand, believes you would be an excellent asset for our cause. 'Poster child' I believe was your expression, wasn't it Melanie?"

"I, er..."

"It's quite all right. I agree with the reasons for your reluctance and don't want to exploit you in such a manner."

"As much as a relief that is for us all to hear, I think there is a more pressing issue to discuss," said Dani, now perched on the edge of her chair.

"Yes, you mean the capture of the others. How did you two become involved in this, anyway?"

"I asked them for help," I said. "With all the resources Mundi threw at my apprehension, I wanted to leave Mars."

There was sadness in Varr's eyes. "It might have been better if you did."

A suffocating silence fell over the room. That was the last thing I expected from him. The fact that Dani sat next to me and believed the same thing made me feel like a flawed specimen under a microscope.

Dani broke the ice. "Well, we're still here and will gladly leave once Felix is rescued."

"I'm afraid that won't be possible," said Varr.

"What the hell are you talking about?" I said. "Mundi recaptured the girl you liberated. Recovering Felix along with her should be no additional burden for your men."

"If we planned a mission of that kind, his rescue would figure prominently. The unfortunate truth is that there will be no recovery operation."

"Why not?" shouted Dani, causing Varr to jump back in his seat.

"I'm sorry, Dani, but where they're held in is deep inside Mundi's territory. It's too well defended for the prolonged military assault it would take, and the chances are high they would die in the attempt anyway." His eyes pleaded with me. "Believe me, we've looked at every possible scenario. Even the most optimistic projection computes a ten percent success rate. I can't risk the lives of the men it would require on such a hopeless mission."

Dani was in tears and unable to say what I knew she wanted to.

"What about Adrianna?" I said. "She was important enough for you to spend Carlos's life to retrieve. Why can't you do it again? Don't you want to stop whatever Mundi is planning for her?"

"Of course I do."

"Then I don't understand why you're just going to sit back and do nothing."

He regarded me like I was still the teenaged girl he rescued so many years before, too naive to know how the world really worked. "Melanie, we are not sitting back and doing nothing. Carlos's original plan took almost a year of planning and only succeeded because he had a well-placed ally on the inside. Since then, Mundi replaced most of the staff and fortified the facility to withstand any attack. Our only hope lies in an agent

I have put in place."

"So your man can help get them out," I said.

"No, he can't. Carlos's asset had access to the clone and the element of surprise. Both Adrianna and Felix will be under the highest level of security with only the most trusted people having contact with them. Our agent enjoys no such clearance and is assigned one objective."

The penny dropped for me. "He's on a suicide mission! He's going to kill everyone in that facility, including our friends."

"Regis Mundi must not be allowed to complete any of his plans. If he succeeds, the consequences would be catastrophic for the solar system for the next thousand years. This is the only plan that guarantees success. I'm sorry, but I can't save Felix or the girl."

CHAPTER 36

Upon delivering Felix and Adrianna's death sentence, Varr was at a loss for words. Dani's weeping only compounded his unease. He finally departed with Chen, allowing us to remain for as long as we needed to.

"You're not just going to lie down and accept this?" said Dani, having gotten a grip on herself.

"Of course not."

"He's going to die, Mel. Varr is going to kill him along with everyone else."

"I won't let that happen."

As confident as my words sounded, we both knew they rang hollow. Mundi's facility lay halfway around the planet. There was a significant chance that Varr and his people didn't really know its location.

Dani wiped her cheeks. "We need a plan."

"I already have one."

"You do?" She sat on the edge of her seat, her red eyes wide with attention.

I took her hands in mine. "Sweetie, you know how much I love you both. It's my fault Felix is in danger, and I can't bear the distance between us because of that. I'm going to do whatever it takes to free him."

Her brow furrowed. "What the hell are you thinking?"

"I'm going to give Mundi what he wants."

"No, you can't do that!"

"Dani, there is nothing else I CAN do. If I offer myself in exchange for the others, Mundi will possess what he's looking for; someone who can control the Ares Weapon."

"You're making a really big assumption, Mel. Morgan stopped his search for you once he found Adrianna. I heard him. They've got her, and they don't need you." New tears pooled in her eyes. "Besides, you can't offer what they want Felix for."

She explained their theory that the dictator wanted to transfer himself into Felix's body. "He's got everything he needs without you. You'd be sacrificing yourself for nothing."

"Not everything."

"What are you talking about? What else does he want?"

My jaw shook as I considered further my rash plan. "He doesn't know how to find this base."

"What? Keep your voice down, for chrissake. Do you want them to shoot us both?"

"That's only bargaining chip remaining for me, Dani."

"You can't betray Varr. You'll go from being the Mother of Mars to its Judas in no time."

"Do you really believe I care what others think of me? The only opinion that matters to me is yours." The tears flowed down my cheeks.

"No! Don't sell out to Mundi for me. I'm sorry we argued, but sisters do that. It doesn't mean I love you any less, you silly bitch."

I smiled. "So I'm a silly bitch?"

She hugged me. "The silliest."

I pulled her tight, and we cried into each other's shoulder.

The door opened, and an embarrassed Yu Chen stood in the doorway.

"I'm sorry to interrupt. I came to offer my apology for Talus Varr's decision."

Separating from Dani, I wiped my eyes. "Thank you Chen. That's sweet, but unless you know of a way to change your boss's mind about a rescue op—"

"There may be a way," he said. "It is risky, but I believe it is our best chance to save your friend."

"I'll be happy for even ten percent odds," I said.

"This plan holds a higher probability of success than that."

"But Varr said..."

Chen blushed again. "He was not entirely truthful. There is an overriding reason that all other plans were rejected. Regis Mundi is due to arrive at the facility. The only way to ensure his death is to let our agent fulfill his suicide mission during the visit."

I slammed my hand on the desk. "That son of a bitch!"

"Please understand, Varr is motivated to shorten the rebellion and save thousands of lives. In the grander scheme, the sacrifice of your friends is an acceptable price to him if it means an immediate end to the dictatorship."

"You come from a family of super patriots. Why are you not enthusiastically supporting Varr's plan?"

"Talus Varr, for his own reasons, does not wish to impose any further burdens upon you. He fails to appreciate the longer-term benefits of retaining your support. It is a foregone conclusion that allowing your friend to die will result in your departure. Think of the consequences if anyone should discover what drove the Mother of Mars away."

"On the other hand," I said, "if you could persuade her to remain on the planet as some kind of figurehead..."

The corners of his mouth turned up slightly. "In gratitude, she would willingly serve as a unifying presence for both sides in the reconciliation that must happen if Mars is to survive."

It was my turn to smile. "She would become your poster girl?"

"In a manner of speaking, yes."

"There only remains the problem of persuading your boss of this."

"If you were to approach him voluntarily with the idea, as if it came from you with no coercion, I believe he would accept."

"Surely, though, the risk of Mundi escaping is greater with this plan? There is something else you want."

"Mel," said Dani, "what are you doing?"

"It's quite all right, Miss O'Hara," said Chen, "she is correct. The girl is worth much more than Talus Varr let on."

"Why? What is so special about her to everyone?"

"Mundi's scientists were attempting to build the ultimate biological weapon by merging the human and the synthetic. Since she is your clone, Adrianna would have inherited your mutation for self healing, and, more important, your mastery over the alien Ares nanites."

"We already guessed that about her."

"What you might not have realized, however, is the true motivation for merging your DNA with synthetic tissue. They wish to create a creature who not only controls the nanoparticles but hosts them, unaltered, in her system, ready to deploy on command. She would become a living weapon."

"Why would Varr want to control something like that?" asked Dani. "Hasn't he always been opposed to their use? Didn't he want you to destroy them all, Mel?"

"He fears what you discovered in the asteroid belt all those years ago. More specifically, he realizes it is only a matter of time before someone else comes across it and the Ares weapon proliferates throughout the system. It may take centuries to happen, but he believes it will."

"Is he talking about the alien seed ship?" said Dani. "That thing is damaged and dormant and no longer a problem. Isn't that right, Mel?"

"It might be crippled, but it is far from harmless," I said. "It spent almost four billion years repairing itself once. It is still doing so now, but it will need millions of years to become a threat to anyone."

"Talus Varr and others want to control it before it becomes a danger," said Chen. "They want someone more dependable than you, Melanie: a being who can take full command of the technology and bend it to their will. Someone who will be around generations from now as our protector. That is the interest in your synthetic clone."

"If all that is true, your boss is no different from Regis Mundi," I said.

"He is a pragmatist," he said. "When it seemed like Mundi was near success with his experiment, Varr arranged for the girl to be abducted, so that at the very least Mundi would not be the only one with such a weapon. When Mundi recovered it, the only remaining recourse became its destruction."

"And now what happens if I agree to become involved with your plan?"

"Felix Altius will be saved."

"And Adrianna?"

"It will either come under our control or be destroyed."

The way he spoke of her as a thing made my blood boil. I wanted to strike him.

"Please inform Talus Varr that I wish to speak with him."

"He will be pleased of your decision to help us." He bowed his head before exiting to tell his boss.

"Mel, you're not really going aid them under those conditions, are you?"

"What can I do? I can't think of any other way to rescue Felix."

"But Adrianna..."

"I'm not letting that poor girl become anyone's slave."

"What's on your mind, then?"

"I...don't know exactly. In case you can't tell, I'm making this up as I go along. At least I'll secure their commitment to save Felix. As for Adrianna, I'll think of something."

Dani nodded, but like me, she was far from satisfied with the situation. For my part, I didn't believe that Chen actually represented any official position on the matter. His attitude toward that innocent girl had caused me to doubt his motives, and what he just told me about Varr.

Talus Varr was a manipulative bastard, but he wasn't a cold-hearted asshole like Regis Mundi, either. Something didn't ring true about what Chen had said. I needed his support to rally Varr to our plan, but he required close watching. There was something about him that didn't sit well with me, and I intended to find out what it was.

CHAPTER 37

Talus Varr managed to put off meeting with me for another six hours. Believing it better to ask for forgiveness than permission, we worked on refining Chen's plan during the wait. He gave me the distinct impression he would not hesitate to go against his boss's wishes, but he was not forthcoming with his reasons.

Thankfully, his overt flirting with me had ceased with the death of Dylan. He remained focused on the technical details and scenarios for our assault on Mundi's fortified base and deliberately avoided eye contact with me. I thought it was pretty clear, though, that his determination to help rescue Felix was driven by his attraction to me, regardless of how much he tried to hide it.

I was glad for his newfound shyness. The last thing I wanted to do was alienate one of the few allies I had by rejecting his advances. Relationships and I were strangers.

Dylan was the one anomaly in my life. When we first met, I hated him, believing him to be an obnoxious, muscle-bound jarhead. Whether he intended for it to happen or not, I fell for him. I thought I was worldly and jaded enough to be above such a thing, but it turned out this ex-hooker had a heart after all.

And now he was gone.

My thoughts turned to Dani and how she suffered over the loss of Felix. I couldn't face the possibility of her enduring what I experienced. We had to rescue him.

In the back of my mind, though, I wondered how far we could go before our actions threatened our own lives. Our determination to plan an operation that had already been rejected by the rebel leader was tantamount to insubordination at best and treason at worst.

I suppose my anticipation of Varr's retribution arose out of the stories Dylan recalled over the years about his time working under the man. Though he never actually witnessed him issue a death warrant, we both knew it was well within the capability of Varr to subtly arrange for someone's demise without resorting to pesky legalities. His enemies always vanished or exhibited a profound change of heart on some matter important to him. Through it all, no hint of his involvement ever came back on him. He was far more subtle in exercising power than Regis Mundi, but in my opinion it made him no less odious. I was merely glad he considered me an ally, and I really didn't want to fuck that up.

The difference between Mundi and Varr lay in their respective goals and the extremes to which they would go to achieve them. Mundi did nothing if it did not serve himself. More than anything else, his lust for power was what had set the two men against each other decades before.

Varr, despite his methods, always had the greater good in mind. His dedication was to the betterment of the Martian populace. He had demonstrated as much in his willingness to see the Ares weapon destroyed ten years before rather than exploiting it as Mundi wished to. Talus Varr had limits to what he would do. I banked on whatever conscience guided him that I could persuade him there was another way to defeat Mundi other than letting Felix and Adrianna die.

When Varr finally was ready to meet, our group agreed that I alone would present our case. I sweated profusely as I rang at his door, hoping he wouldn't be in. To my disappointment, the door opened and I steeled myself to enter and end the whole matter as soon as possible.

"Thank you for agreeing to speak with me," I said as I took the offered chair. Varr's private office had no desk, and the walls were lined with antique books, making it more like an ancient library. He sat comfortably in an armchair as if awaiting his servant to bring him a post-dinner cigar and brandy.

"My door is always open to you, Melanie."

"I'm glad to hear that, especially if we are going to be working with each other in the future."

He tilted his head, brow furrowed. "What do you mean?"

I exhaled my held breath. "I want to bargain."

"Go on," he said as he leaned back in his chair.

"I want to offer myself in exchange for the lives of Felix and Adrianna."

"Melanie, I..."

"I realize you think this is an opportunity to cut off the head of the snake and win your rebellion in one decisive action, but we both know that won't end up happening. Even if you do succeed in killing Mundi in the suicide attack, you won't eliminate everyone. There are more than a few individuals sitting in the wings, ready to seize power the moment the opportunity arises."

"It isn't about ending the war, Mel. Mundi must be stopped before he becomes too powerful. If he succeeds in his plans, nobody in the solar system will be safe from his megalomania for a thousand years."

"Do you know yet if Adrianna can control the nanites?"

"No, Carlos believed he removed her from the facility before that happened."

"So she still needs to be exposed to them to activate her mutation. That means there is some of it at the lab."

"My spies tell me Mundi recovered a sample from the alien seed ship stranded in the asteroid belt. What are you proposing, exactly?"

"Put me inside that facility. I can manipulate those bugs like I did before; force them to change their form—neutralize them and make them useless."

"And while you're there, the team may as well liberate your friends. I see what you're doing, Mel, but it just won't work."

"Why the hell not?"

"The building is too fortified for a direct assault."

"Who's talking about attacking? We have a plan to sneak into it instead. Dani is the best hacker on Mars. She can disable the security net, and Chen knows of a poorly guarded access point."

"And what happens when you're all caught or killed?"

"Then your inside man can still fulfill his orders and kill everyone."

He sat back and stroked his chin as he considered my proposal, never taking his eyes from me.

"Talus, if we're successful—if we rescue them and return alive, I'll be your symbol. I will be the Mother of Mars for you."

Varr spent a long time rubbing his two-day-old beard and staring at me, which made me increasingly uncomfortable. It was as if he sized me up with his bullshit meter to determine what my con might be.

"I don't want you to become indentured, Melanie. I do admit, however, that having you on our side would be a tremendous boon—more than you can possibly imagine."

"Talus, there is nothing else for me. If I allow Felix and Adrianna to die by refusing to do what is in my power to attempt, then I may as well join them."

It sounded dramatic when I heard myself say those words, but they were true. If they died, my relationship with Dani would never be the same. I would lose my only friend. I couldn't endure the guilt knowing there was something I could offer that might save them.

Since Dylan's death, I imagined my life as a mother to Adrianna—tormented myself with the what-if scenario. In hindsight, I realized my opposition to adopting and raising her was because of selfishness and fear. If anyone could understand her, and maybe even steer her to a better life path, it was me.

Now I wanted to try to be for her the mother I never had. The sentiment was a tribute to what Dylan wanted, but also an attempt to redeem the rotten portion of my soul. Whether she would want anything to do with me was another question, but it would never be addressed unless she could be rescued.

"Did Yu Chen tell you why he is so determined to save your friends?"

"Umm, no, he didn't."

"Two years ago, Mundi's forces raided the Shen Kuo settlement and captured several of the its elders. Among them were his parents, sister, and his wife."

"What happened to them?"

"They were tortured by the dictator's lieutenant and killed. Morgan made a recording of their executions and arranged for us to find it when our task force arrived to rescue them."

"I had no idea."

"He did not use them as leverage over Chen, as one might expect. He wanted to make them an example; to instil fear. Ever since that day, Chen's been obsessed with vengeance."

"Why are you telling me this?"

"Only to warn you that while you believe he has put together a sound plan, it may well be a suicidal undertaking disguised as a rescue operation."

"If he only wants to avenge his family, why isn't he supporting the mission of your man on the inside?"

"Because it won't be personal enough. He wants to look their murderer in the eye when he kills him."

I sat in silence, reviewing the new information Varr had just dumped on me. Chen's desire for vengeance might well be clouding his judgement and placing anyone participating in grave danger. On the other hand, so far, he was the only person with the balls to come up with any plan at all. Like it or not, I was still all-in with him, though now with diminished enthusiasm.

"You know, Talus, both Chen and I are desperate enough that we'll mount this operation without your sanction. If it is a suicide mission for him, he obviously doesn't care about the consequences of disobeying you."

"You're telling me I'll lose a trusted officer as well as the woman I've watched over since her birth."

I was shocked that he thought of me that way. Maybe there was some hope I could persuade him. "Yes, that is what I am saying."

His eyes studied me as if trying to peer into my brain to pick over my thoughts.

"I think we've all suffered enough loss of loved ones, Melanie. I will not sanction the planned mission."

My heart, which had begun to soar with the hope of success, plummeted into the pit of my stomach.

"But..."

He held up his hand to stop me from interrupting.

"You are right. I cannot allow anything to happen to Felix or the girl—Adrianna?"

I nodded.

"Instead, I am authorizing a new plan of attack to be drawn up. We've nipped at Mundi's heels for far too long. It is time we took a coordinated lunge at his throat. Perhaps we can still achieve our goals without too many unnecessary deaths."

CHAPTER 38

The battle suit they gave me was surprisingly light, though a bit awkward to move in. The combat helmet sat in my lap as I recalled my last episode donning one. Images of Dylan's infectious smile drifted across my mind, and I tried to stem the flow of tears before anyone noticed.

A jolt of turbulence brought me back to the present. Dani's head rested on my shoulder, and I wondered how she managed to remain asleep on such an uncomfortable surface.

Chen sat across from me in the troop carrier, his eyes closed, either lost in thought or occupying himself with some entertainment his CI provided.

I looked down the line at the men and women in the other seats on the benches that ran along the walls. They all wore well-used combat armour of similar design to mine. They all appeared detached from the reality of what we were attempting.

The day before, Chen had scrounged up a brand new suit for me that almost fit my small body.

"I guessed at your measurements."

I eyed him warily. "You have a good eye for sizing up women. It fits almost perfectly."

"Almost?"

I smiled and ran my hands over the plasteel armour hugging my hips. "You were a little too complimentary about some of my dimensions."

Like most equipment used by the rebels, the airborne troop transport had seen better days. It shuddered so much during takeoff, I feared it would fly apart before we were airborne, but after its initial convulsions, everything smoothed out and we launched without incident. How Varr had managed to maintain the lengthy struggle against Mundi being so poorly equipped amazed me. It was no wonder their combat activity had been restricted to hit-and-run harassment along their indistinct border. Recollection of the sleek, powerful raptors that had attacked us during our journey made the outdated transport seem like a joke at our expense.

Our team had two missions critical to the success of the plan. The first, which was presently being carried out, was to drop a series of scrambler boxes on the surface. It necessitated that we take a random, weaving route, skimming the ground and depositing our packages at predetermined locations. The units were designed to temporarily interfere with remote satellite imaging, radar, and other long-range scanning that would identify and lead to us being shot out of the skies. They were supposed to provide four hours of cover for our advance and that of the larger rebel force scheduled to follow us.

When he initially explained the details to me in our briefings, I said, "Won't the presence of a null zone on the monitoring net be a giveaway that something is coming?"

"Not really," said Chen. "The equipment mimics the signals of an approaching dust storm, even for anyone monitoring from orbit. Unless somebody actually looks out a window, they won't know the difference."

He went on to explain that the tactic was intended to be used during an actual storm, which was the reason Mundi's forces had come up on our convoy undetected. To try using it on a clear Martian day would have been foolish, so we were attempting it in a night raid. In my mind, it was still risky, but our choices were severely restricted. Word had come that Mundi was expected to arrive at the base the next morning, meaning the captives had little time left.

Our second objective was far more nebulous. We were to

make a real-time assessment of the facility and its vulnerability and send a go or no-go signal. Varr's forces, using the cover screen just laid down, were to make a lightning attack to buy us the distraction we needed to break in and try to find our friends. Our escape was less well defined, but it involved blowing out a wall and running away with Felix and Adrianna during the battle.

I never liked the plan, if you could even call it one. It was more of a demonstration of how far wishful thinking could get us. It had a high probability of being called off based on what we observed on arrival. Varr probably counted on the job being aborted—the bastard could still look me in the eye and say he'd tried. It was the best deal I could make with him that would give us the equipment and transportation into Mundi's territory.

Dani and I had other ideas. Aborted or not, we planned on sneaking inside on our own using her hacking skills. Our most difficult task, besides not getting killed, would be leaving the group, unnoticed. The likelihood was that we would die before we got within a hundred metres of the place, but we were desperate.

The pilot set us down as close to the target as he dared, which still left us with a two-kilometre hike over rocky terrain in the dark. Seeing was not an issue because of the built-in IR imaging in our helmets. Though on their own, the helmet, rifle, survival pack, and armour were all as light as technologically possible, together they made for a cumbersome load to wear and carry across the surface.

Struggling to the top of a ridge, we crawled on our bellies the last few metres to join Chen. We overlooked the research facility snuggled at the base of a misshapen crater rim. My HUD provided me with an enhanced and detailed view of the complex, and what I saw confused me.

"I don't see anything other than the building. Isn't this place supposed to be fortified?"

"That is what our intelligence suggested," replied Chen, not attempting to hide his own astonishment.

"What else did they get wrong?" asked Dani.

"There isn't a guard or a vehicle of any kind. Is it even occupied?" I asked.

"There may be automated missile bays hidden beneath the surface."

He pointed out some areas devoid of the randomly distributed boulders and rocks strewn about the rest of the crater floor.

"So they are anticipating an air attack," said Dani. "What about a ground assault?"

"The facility is built like an ancient citadel; one, maybe two entrances besides the landing platform," said Chen. "They all will be defended by automated systems. Troops, while present, will be limited in number and are meant to supplement the AI defences. The access points will all have human attendants in addition to requiring the appropriate codes. The periphery is covered by a surveillance system, but it looks like they aren't expecting an organized attack." He addressed Dani. "Can you see a point of entry?"

"They'll still spot us coming from a kilometre away," I said.

Chen's eyes smiled behind his visor. He signalled for something to be brought forward. A burly soldier approached carrying a disk-shaped object, about half a metre in diameter and ten centimetres thick. He placed it on the ground between us and knelt behind it.

"What is that?" I asked.

"That," he said, "is one of the scrambler boxes. I held it back. Dani modified it, and it will provide us with cover under darkness from the surveillance net."

I turned to her. "You didn't tell me about this."

"I made the modifications last night. You were busy charming Varr, and, as I told Chen, I don't think it'll work." She shrugged.

"It will. Now tell me, can you locate a point of entry?"

"Oh, what the hell," she said. "Some areas must require surface access from inside. Maintenance zones accessing external facilities. How do they exchange air, for example?"

"Like the CO2 scrubber intake vents?" I asked.

"Exactly. Those things are constantly getting clogged up with sand and dust and need regular cleaning. There should be an access door near it."

We all focussed on the building below, comparing what we saw with the stolen schematics that were displayed on our HUDs.

"I see it," I said, highlighting the area on the diagram for the others to see in their displays.

"Yup, that's pretty much what it is," said Dani.

"Won't it be monitored by the security system?" I asked.

"The AI will be watching, but our friend here will keep it blind to us." Chen patted the scrambler box. "No human would be wasting his life guarding it unless the workers have gone outside for a shift. That is our point of entry."

He turned to Dani. "How long will you need?"

"How the hell should I know? I have to see what I'm up against first."

I glared at her through my visor, my stomach doing a somersault. "Didn't they give you specs on it?"

"Of course, but if that information is as reliable as their initial intelligence about this place. I don't trust it."

As Chen conferred with his team leaders and Dani checked her equipment, I scanned what appeared to be the main entrance of the facility, and what I saw froze my blood. A large X-shaped object stood starkly alone about twenty metres from the door. At first I dismissed it as some kind of sculpture, but something fluttered along its surface and caught my attention.

Magnifying the image with my helmet optics, I gasped and my fingers dug into the sand.

"Mel, what is it?" asked Dani.

"That cross by the front entrance. There's a body attached to it."

"Oh my good Christ, you're right. Who the hell was that poor bastard, I wonder?"

"Our reports say it was the previous facility director in charge when the girl was abducted," said Chen.

If I still harboured lingering doubts about any difference between Mundi and Varr, they evaporated in that moment. I always thought Mundi a kook for his pretence at being a Roman patrician, but this crucifixion took crazy to a new level. The sight of the corpse on the cross made me want Mundi to pay for every one of his excesses. The son-of-a-bitch had to die, and not quietly in his bed. I wanted to send him to hell by express delivery.

Single file, we made our way down the wall of the crater in silence. If we were spotted, our only protection was our armour, and I knew firsthand how ineffective it could be under enough firepower. The thought flashed by that what we wore was only a placebo to make soldiers feel protected so they could carry out orders without shitting themselves.

I recalled watching an ancient Terran vid with Dylan that showed hundreds of storm troopers in white armour, easily being mown down by raggedly dressed rebels with simple laser weapons. We laughed at the silliness of the whole thing, and I never imagined I would find myself in such a situation.

Arriving at the maintenance entry without any resistance, the troops distributed themselves in a defensive perimeter while Dani, Chen, and I approached the door.

"What if this is some kind of trap?" I blurted.

"Now is a hell of a time to think of that," said Dani while she worked at establishing a link with the access panel.

Chen said nothing, but the way he kept regripping his weapon made me believe he thought as I did.

A sharp ringing in my earpiece almost deafened me, and I fumbled to turn down the volume. After deactivating my comm, I looked toward the others. They had all experienced something similar. I worried that the scrambler had failed or Dani had somehow set off a jamming signal, but she appeared oblivious to the unfolding chaos as she focused on the task of hacking the security system.

The rebels moved closer to defend Dani, their guns raised in anticipation of an attack. I was more concerned with the scary-looking weapon turret above the door. It didn't show any sign of activating, but visions of us all being mown down like those soldiers in the vid played through my mind.

After a short interval that felt far too long, Dani stepped away from the entrance as the door opened. Two rebels, weapons raised, rushed in, with two more taking a position at the opening behind them.

As the seconds ticked by, I couldn't take my eyes from the still inactive turret. A tap on my shoulder startled me. Using hand signals, Chen indicated that I should follow him through the doorway. With one last glance at the automated weapon over the door, I entered the building, glad to be getting out of the open.

It took Dani less time to hack the controls for the inner airlock doors. Before long we were inside the complex, and I took off my headgear. I ignored Chen's frantic arm waving around his head. Eventually, he removed his own head covering.

"Put your bloody helmet back on!"

"My comm is shot. I can't hear a thing with it on."

Removing hers, Dani said, "What's going on with communications?"

"I thought you might have tripped the security system," he said.

She blew a raspberry. "As if..."

"Well, if it wasn't Dani, what's happened? Did our scrambler fail?"

Frowning, he called one of his team leaders to join us. Lieutenant Singh removed her helmet, and the two of them engaged in a muted conversation on which I strained to eavesdrop.

When the woman departed, Chen said, "It is likely a suppressor net inhibiting our comms. CIs are offline as well. It will make coordinating our operation more difficult."

My pulse raced. "Do they know we're here?" I asked.

"This is standard operating procedure in preparation for the arrival of somebody important. Mundi or his advance team must be arriving soon."

"If it's Mundi, he's way ahead of schedule."

"I can hack the comm logs to see what's been going on here for the last few hours," said Dani.

Before either Chen or I could reply, she advanced to another panel and pried off the cover. After a ridiculously short interval, she gained access and was poring over the information on her personal interface.

"Mundi arrived about ten minutes ago—probably while we were breaking in through the maintenance entry."

"We're not ready," I said. "We don't have communications with Varr. He won't arrive with our backup."

"We'll have to proceed alone," said Chen as he picked up his weapon. "Dani, what is Mundi's location?"

"According to this security log, he's only just arrived and is still in the hangar area."

"And the prisoners?"

She fiddled with the interface. "They're held in different locations in the laboratory wing. I'm putting them up on our schematics now."

"We will split into two teams. Lieutenant Singh will accompany you with five men," he told me. "You are to make your way toward the lab area. Free your friends, then make your exit as planned."

"Where the hell are you going?"

"I cannot allow the butcher Mundi to escape justice when he is so close."

"That's crazy," I said. "The plan calls for us to all rescue Felix and Adrianna. He'll be under heavy guard. By attacking him you'll set the entire place into lockdown. Don't be a fool."

"Nothing indicates we've been detected. We will strike simultaneously while we have the advantage," he said. "The bulk of his forces will rush to his defence, giving you less resistance for your mission."

"How will we manage that?" asked Dani. "Our comms are jammed, and we have no way to coordinate an attack."

Chen indicated the chronometer on my sleeve. "At 0600 hours you will make your move. That gives you twenty minutes to get into position."

"But what about Varr's team? Our escape plan depends on him."

"I will provide enough of a distraction for you to get away," he said as he signalled the remaining soldiers to his side. "We will attack Mundi and with any luck kill him. If we don't succeed, our man on the inside will still fulfill his original orders at 0630."

"What you're planning is suicide."

"There is no time to argue. With the exception of the comm suppression, the operation is proceeding as we foresaw. However, despite Dani's efforts, our presence will be discovered soon. We either continue as planned, or we abort the mission now and let everyone die when our man sets off the device."

"It's Felix's only chance," Dani said, her voice cracking.

Chen's assurances that everything was within expectations didn't sit well with me. I couldn't shake my discomfort over how easily we gained entry to the supposedly well-guarded facility. Our plan had always been based on hope and desperation, with a big allowance for luck, but things were unfolding faster than I could keep track of. If we turned back now, our tail tucked between our legs, I would never be able to face Dani again, or myself, for that matter.

I bit my lower lip as I returned her gaze. "We don't have a choice. We have to do it this way," I said.

Dani made no effort to hide her relief. In that instant, I knew that our friendship was on its way to being restored. Even if nobody survived this, we were reconciled and I felt a weight lifted from my shoulders. I knew that if we had aborted the mission, she would have gone on alone. Of course I'd have followed her, idiot that I am. I suspected she understood that.

Chen and his twelve handpicked soldiers left for the hangar. I pondered the folly of attacking Mundi in one of his facilities and would have preferred he accompany us to rescue the prisoners. But he had made up his mind, and, like Dani, intended to follow his own course. I hoped his desire for vengeance hadn't doomed us all.

CHAPTER 39

The extent of Regis Mundi's sprawling facility spoke to the number and variety of projects his scientists were engaged in. We passed multiple doorways with nameplates that hinted at what kind of work was being conducted behind them. While the specifics were unknown, it was clear the majority of the research was weapons-related.

Despite the nature of the place, we encountered not a single guard. The entire complex seemed abandoned. Dani had jacked into the security system and disabled the AI surveillance along our route, but the emptiness of the halls left me feeling more tense with every step.

"Where is everybody?" I said, keeping my voice to a whisper.

"I'm creeped out too," said Dani. "At least we're making good time."

I checked my chronometer to see that we had another fifteen minutes until all hell was going to bust out in the hangar deck. That was assuming Chen and his men hadn't been caught or killed already.

As we approached the final turn leading to where they held Felix, Lieutenant Singh raised a fist, signalling us to stop. As done at every other intersection, she poured a handful of sand-sized pellets on the floor in front of her. The tiny recon robots immediately dispersed and rolled around the corner.

We waited as the minuscule cameras compiled and fed back to our helmet HUDs a 3D visualization of what lay beyond our line of sight. As with all the others, the hallway was abandoned.

"Why aren't there any guards outside of his door?" said Dani. "Have they taken him somewhere else?"

As if eager to answer the question, the lieutenant advanced with half her squad, weapons levelled and ready.

With the balance of troops watching our backs, Dani and I followed and within seconds stood before what was supposed to be Felix's cell. Singh indicated the door mechanism. Dani pried off the cover and fiddled with something before the door slid open.

Before she or I could react, our team leader and two of her men passed through the opening, weapons raised. Not willing to await the all-clear signal, Dani followed them in, leaving me no other choice than to join her.

Felix sat on the bunk, which was the only piece of furniture in the small room. At the sight of Dani, his look of consternation was replaced by a broad smile. She rushed to him as he stood to greet her and they embraced.

"Thank God you're alive."

"There was no deity involved," he replied as he reluctantly disengaged from her and looked at me and the soldiers in the room. "I must say, however, I am perplexed as to how you came to be here."

We filled him in on the plan and the abandoned state of the facility.

"Something is wrong," he said. "Since my arrival, my door has been under heavy guard. You may have walked into a trap."

"That's been our fear all along," I said.

"Ma'am," interrupted Singh. "The lack of resistance warrants a reappraisal of our plan. If we suspect an ambush, we need to retreat and reevaluate the situation."

"She's right," said Felix. "It is tactically foolish to continue with the operation."

I regarded Felix and Dani, together again. If I only achieved their reunion, and nothing else, I might have been tempted to call the mission a success. If we left now, the rebel bomb would forever end the threat of Mundi and the ultimate weapon he would make of Adrianna. She was a clone; one of hundreds. Not even completely human.

Then I looked closely at Felix. We'd risked much to save him, and he was entirely synthetic; inhuman. He and the girl were much more than where they came from. If natural humanity was the gold standard for being rescued, they needed to leave me behind too. Varr's manipulation of my gene code before I was born made me equally unnatural.

"What about Adrianna?" I was more surprised than either of them that the question came from me. I informed him about the agent preparing to set off a neutron device in a few minutes.

Dani looked up at him. "We can't abandon her."

We all turned to Singh. Her face was unreadable. "My orders come from Talus Varr. I am to protect you with my life."

My shoulders slumped. I prepared myself to tell her to retreat without me when she added, "We have wasted precious time and need to hurry if we are to rescue the child."

I wanted to hug her but restricted my gratitude to a simple, "Thank you."

Felix asked for a weapon. Singh promptly supplied him with her sidearm.

"In all fairness, I must warn you that the probability of our success is minuscule," he said. "You would be wise to escape with the lieutenant while the opportunity exists and allow me to make this attempt."

"Fuck that noise," said Dani. "I'm going with you."

"I'm with Dani on this one," I said.

We all turned to the squad leader and the men standing behind her.

"We have our orders," she said, her voice emotionless. A couple of the soldiers nodded in agreement.

"Then this is settled," I said. "Let's get going before we waste any more time."

With Singh leading point, we made swift progress toward

Adrianna's location. As we continued down more abandoned corridors, the hackles on the back of my neck rose, and I worried that Felix's suggestion might have been a better idea.

Pausing at the final intersection, Singh once again performed her mini-robot scan routine. Anxious about what they saw, I pulled on my helmet and watched as the image formed on my HUD. Two armed guards stood attentively before the door to the lab.

Wordlessly, the squad leader made an assertive hand signal, and two of her men joined her. Pausing only for a second to coordinate their efforts, they dashed around the corner, firing their noise-suppressed weapons. The holo-image in my visor showed the two guards drop lifelessly to the floor. Moments later we received the all-clear, and the rest of us followed.

Before I could get to within five metres of the door, Singh signalled a halt and called up two more of our rear guard. They stepped over the fallen bodies, avoiding the growing pools of blood, and took up their positions. She then indicated for Dani to come forward to hack the locking mechanism .

Dani took a lingering look into Felix's eyes. After kissing him on the cheek, she advanced to the doorway to assist. Felix raised his weapon in readiness, and I glanced back to see the remaining rebels ready to defend our backs.

When Dani completed her task, she moved aside, out of the line of fire, and put on her own helmet. I looked at Felix, and though the gun in his hand was rock-steady, there was an unfamiliar expression on his face. I realized from his fixed gaze on Dani that he was afraid for her.

An unbidden swell of grief rose up at the thought of how heroic Dylan would have been in this moment; how he would have had equal concern for my safety. I struggled to push the feelings back so I could focus on the next unfolding seconds. I wished I had insisted on being given a weapon, like Dani. Chen seemed to think it was safer for everyone if I didn't carry one, and I resented his patronizing attitude.

Singh, after ensuring we were all in place, signalled Dani to open the door. It slid aside and the squad rushed through. I surged forward to follow, but Felix restrained me.

The seconds ticked by as I chewed my lower lip and awaited any sound from within. When I thought I might ignore Felix and jump through the opening to satisfy my curiosity, one of the rebel soldiers appeared and signalled for us to enter.

Nobody was in the lab.

The room was large and sterile, more like an operating theatre than a laboratory. Along the walls were various inactive computer stations and tables with strange instruments laid out on them, ready to be employed for some kind of experiment. In the centre was a clinical-looking chair with multiple translucent tubes wrapping around and connecting to tanks on the back of it. Restraints for arms, chest, and legs lay open, awaiting the next person to sit in it. It faced a thick transparent glass wall of what appeared to be an isolation chamber. Inside was a seat similarly outfitted, but without tubing. Next to it, about a metre tall, stood a small, organic-appearing pillar with a disturbing familiarity.

At the sight of it, my knees gave way. Felix caught me before I could fall.

"Mel, what's wrong?" asked Dani.

I pointed at the object. "Is that familiar to either of you?"

"It has a similar texture to the alien vessel you crashed into the planet," said Dani. "How is that possible? I thought it was destroyed."

"It was," I said, finally able to recover and stand. "This isn't from that. It's from the mother ship."

"The one in the asteroid belt? How do you know that?"

"I just know."

"How the hell did it get here?"

Felix said, "Mundi's people must have discovered the location and recovered this sample."

"Okay, I'm now officially creeped out," she said. "Where is Adrianna? The computer log said she was supposed to be in here."

"As I feared, we have been led into a trap," said Felix.

"Why did they wait until now?" she said. "If they knew we

were coming, they could have captured or killed us at any time."

"Because they wanted to get us all in the same room as that thing," I said, my eyes fixed on the alien structure.

"We need to get out of here." Dani's eyes were wide with fear.

As if in response, the deafening noise of automatic weapons fire came from the corridor, interspersed with a loud buzzing sound and the screams of the wounded.

"Oh, no!" said Dani. "The AI has been reactivated."

Two of Singh's men dashed to the doorway and were cut down in midstride by a bright red laser that shot from the ceiling. Before Singh could react, she too was felled by another volley from the security system.

The stench of burned flesh filled the room as Felix pushed both of us into a corner and protected us with his body. One by one, the remaining rebel soldiers were methodically killed by the automated defender, their body armour providing no protection. They died like those damned white armoured troops in that stupid vid.

When the last of the rebels had fallen, everything fell silent. Dani and I both quaked with fear, cowering behind Felix. We all crouched and waited for something to happen. When it became apparent the system didn't seem interested in us, I slowly rose to my full height, not confident that my theory was sound.

"Mel, what the hell are you doing?" asked Dani.

"If the AI wanted us dead, we would be."

"She is correct," said Felix. He tossed his weapon to the side and stood, extending a hand to help Dani to her feet.

Running footsteps echoed in the corridor, and within seconds several armed men rushed into the room and trained their weapons on us.

A figure in a black uniform strode confidently into the lab behind them. Morgan wore a self-satisfied smirk as he stood, arms akimbo, and surveyed the devastation around him. He then turned his attention to us and his smile broadened.

"Felix Altius, it is so good to see you again. I am sorry I couldn't pay you a visit when you arrived earlier, but as you are well aware, the call of duty never ceases."

Not waiting for a response from Felix, Morgan addressed me. "And Melanie Destin, I truly never imagined we would meet."

I ground my teeth. "How could we have met? You buggered off after killing my husband and left me to die in the storm."

"Oh, I was never worried about you dying. I knew you were in capable hands."

I frowned. "What the hell are you talking about?"

As if to answer my question, another group of men entered the lab. My mouth fell open at the sight of Yu Chen, flanked on either side by Mundi's soldiers. He looked different, and it took me a moment to notice he no longer wore his rebel armour but instead sported the black uniform of the government security service.

The son-of-a-bitch had betrayed us.

CHAPTER 40

"Oh really, Melanie, surely you realized something was off?" Morgan appeared thoroughly amused by my consternation. "No?"

Turning to our betrayer, he said, "I must give you credit, she is as bamboozled as Talus Varr."

Chen avoided looking me in the eye and was clearly uncomfortable with Morgan's attempt to humiliate me. If it hadn't been for the fact that he sold us all down the river, I might have sympathized with him.

"Why go through the charade?" I said to Chen. "You could have captured me during the attack."

"That would have only netted you. I needed you to help persuade Varr to come out of hiding."

"This costly rebellion will soon be ended," said Morgan, his chest puffed out with self-importance. "Talus Varr's force will be shot from the skies when they make their advance against this facility. After we drop an asteroid on their base, there should be little stomach for resistance."

"I don't get it, Chen," I said. "They killed your family, and now you're working for them?"

He straightened as if kicked in the ass, all signs of embarrassment gone. "They chose to support the wrong cause. I told you I am a pragmatist. I see no profit in supporting the losing side."

"So you became a sellout and turned your back on

everything your ancestors worked for."

Anger flashed in his eyes. "When this conflict ends, everyone can return to the work of terraforming the planet. The cost of this conflict is far too great already."

My lip curled. The thought of Regis Mundi winning the war and everything that would follow turned my stomach. "I hope you can afford the price of what you have done."

"As entertaining as this is for me," said Morgan, "there is some urgent business to attend to."

At his nod, guards rushed forward and took hold of us, clamped restraints on our wrists, and herded us into the centre of the room. With only their attention focused on us, everyone else turned to the entrance in anticipation. Soon a parade of soldiers entered, their uniforms brocaded with elaborate patterns of laurel branches. The fronts of their tunics were fashioned to appear like Roman military breastplates, and at each man's hip swung a short sword that I think was called a gladius. Their helmets had a subtle raised plume running along the top.

"Regis Mundi's Praetorian Guard," whispered Felix.

A dozen disciplined men marched impressively into the lab and formed a line. They stood at attention, their snub-nosed rifles held at the ready as they awaited the next party to enter.

Moving much slower than the previous group, four more elaborately uniformed men entered. I recognized their costumes from history books. They wore replica Roman armour, complete with classical sandals, greaves, and horsehair plumed helmets. They accompanied a servant wearing a simple tunic who pushed a wheelchair in which was seated the main attraction.

Regis Mundi was a bulbous old man with heavy jowls and a liver-spotted face. He was dressed in a purple toga trimmed with gold brocade. All that was missing to complete the pretence of an emperor was a laurel leaf crown. His jaundiced skin had the look of the terminally ill.

His attendant wheeled him ceremoniously in front of the line of soldiers, and the four anachronisms took position on either side of him. It was all so bloody pompous. A band playing an anthem would have completed the show.

When the parade was finally finished, everyone in the room bowed from the waist in homage to their dictator. Dani, Felix, and I all stood straight, and my gaze was riveted on the rheumy eyes of the fossil on his wheelchair throne. There was no spark behind them, the joys of life long having departed from his soul. Had he been a patient of mine, I might have given him a few weeks to live.

With some effort, he raised his right arm and summoned Morgan to approach. The young lieutenant dutifully advanced and bowed before his master. I strained unsuccessfully to eavesdrop on what the old geezer said but realized I wouldn't be kept in suspense for long.

At Morgan's direction, rough hands pushed the three of us forward to stand before Mundi. I wanted to do something irreverent and defiant; curtsy, stick out my tongue—anything to let the old lizard know what I thought of him. What did I have to lose, after all? Instead I stood like a passive prisoner awaiting sentencing. My lack of courage disgusted me.

In a raspy croak, Mundi said, "It has been far too long, Felix Altius."

Extending the courtesy of a slight inclination of the head, Felix said, "Perhaps not long enough."

"You well knew your betrayal of me could have no other outcome. I never wanted it to end this way."

"You'll forgive me if I harbour doubt about the truth of that statement."

The old man frowned. "Your time away has made you insolent, Felix."

"It has changed my perspective and my values."

"Hmmph. You've become weak. There was a time when you would not have been captured by your enemies."

"I never considered you my enemy."

Mundi's face grew florid, and he struggled to stand as he shouted, "Yet you have made yourself one to me!"

A coughing fit seized him, and his servant assisted him to sit again, urging him to calm himself.

"You see what your betrayal has done to me, Felix? It has aged me before my time."

"As a friend reminded me, nobody lives forever."

It was the closest thing to disrespect Felix could utter. For him to say it to the face of his former Dominus spoke volumes of how he'd changed over a decade.

Mundi shifted in his chair and fixed Felix with a wicked glare. "That is where you are wrong, old friend. We will both live for many lifetimes, although you will have no ability to experience it in a sentient state."

He waved dismissively to Felix and addressed Morgan. "Take him away and have him prepared for the transfer. We will conduct it when our business here is completed."

At Morgan's direction, two guards grabbed Felix by the shoulders. Dani, tears flowing down her face, struggled to move to him, but was restrained. With sadness in his eyes, Felix softly shook his head at her. His unspoken message somehow clear, she stopped struggling and watched helplessly as he was ushered from the room.

"Do not fear, my dear," said Mundi. "Soon he will never realize you existed and will not miss you when you are dead."

Dani tried to lunge from her guard. "You bastard! I hope you die a horrible, lingering death."

"Once I occupy his body, that outcome will be highly unlikely."

He turned to Morgan once more. "Take her to watch the procedure before she is executed. I want her to look in her lover's blank eyes and realize the moment when he no longer recognizes her."

Dani was dragged, kicking and screaming, from the lab, calling every curse imaginable down on Mundi's head. The old man merely laughed.

My cheeks were soaked with my own tears, and I wondered what heinous fate the old monster had in store for me. With guilt for the impending doom of both of my friends gripping me, I had no desire to go on and wanted to die swiftly. I doubted Mundi had anything so simple planned, however.

It took me a few moments to realize he had been staring at me, apparently sizing me up. I suppressed the sudden urge to take a bath.

"So you are Talus Varr's pet," he said. "I was wondering if we would ever meet since I learned of your survival."

I sneered. "I'm sure the pleasure is all yours."

He chuckled. "Your reputation for insolence is well deserved, I see."

"And I see yours as a corpulent, diseased old weirdo is not exaggerated." Maybe I could goad him into having me shot on the spot.

My insult appeared to hit home as his smile faded. He snapped at Morgan, "Bring in the others."

Casting the evil eye at me, Mundi's lieutenant hurried from the lab, and after a minute of tension filled silence, returned. In his wake followed a man wearing a Mundi uniform and young girl, both under heavy guard. They were shackled at the wrists, and the man limped badly. Beaten, his face was a mass of recently acquired cuts and welts. Adrianna seemed unharmed but looked exhausted and frightened as she was prodded forward by her armed escort. On seeing me, her face brightened for a brief interval until she spotted the restraints on my arms. A look of despair and resignation replaced her hope.

"I wanted you to witness the reason I've permitted you to live, Doctor Destin," said Mundi.

"You mean you don't need a fourth for bridge?"

His scowl deepened, and he motioned for Morgan to get on with things.

Adrianna was dragged to the central chair and roughly forced into it. Two guards held the struggling child down while two others wasted no time strapping her down. Even with four burly men keeping her in check, it was apparent they wished to spend as little time as necessary fighting against the enraged girl.

The male prisoner, more resigned to his fate, was escorted

without incident into the isolation chamber. When the door opened, I was filled with confusion, my thoughts bounding uncontrolled from one distraction to the next. My eyes fell on the pillar next to the chair they now strapped the man into. I recognized an unwelcome sensation like millions of ants burrowing into my brain, attempting to establish contact with me.

"You have a gift, Miss Destin," said Mundi.

"What?" It was hard focusing on him with the nanites fighting for my attention.

"When Talus Varr manipulated your genetic code all those years ago, he sought to use you to destroy my Ares weapon. He very nearly succeeded."

"What makes you think I won't finish the job now?"

"I sincerely doubt you have the ability," he said with a patronizing smile. "But you are welcome to try."

Determined to make a fool of him, I forced myself to concentrate on the object behind the glass. The doorway was still open, and the noise in my head had grown into an almost overwhelming hiss of randomness. As I tried to focus on them, I realized these particular nanites behaved like nothing in my experience. There was no organization to them; no cohesion. It was as if they screamed for attention at once but spoke different languages. They were trapped in their physical configuration and isolated from each other in the dimension where they communed. Chaos reigned among them, and I could do nothing to organize or affect them.

I thought my head would burst, and when I could endure the pain, no longer my hands flew to my head and I dropped to my knees, screaming.

I don't know how long I writhed on the floor in agony, but somehow, mercifully, it abruptly ended. I looked up to see that someone had closed the door. The maddening mayhem that had felled me was now but a whisper.

"My scientists designed a polymer that prevents the nanites from communicating at the quantum level. As long as they remain within the chamber, their cooperative interaction is hampered," said Mundi, amusement written all over his fat, ugly face. "It seems your power to influence them with your miraculous mutation is equally stymied."

"You neutered them," I said between gasps. "They are useless as a weapon in that form." I had no need to force a smile. I was genuinely happy the machines were now impotent.

"You certainly demonstrated that they are beyond your ability to manipulate." As Mundi continued to grin like an annoying Cheshire cat, my unease grew. "Without access to you for testing, my researchers were not confident their little discovery would work."

He turned to some of the men who had accompanied Adrianna into the lab. "Doctor M'Bana, you may now complete your demonstration."

A tall man moved toward her, two assistants accompanying him. One grasped her restrained left arm to steady it while another inserted an object with a three-centimetre needle on one end into the muscle. She screamed and fought against their practised efforts as they repeated the operation on both sides of her until six attachment devices were embedded into her arms and legs.

The hoses extruding from the back of the chair were then attached to the still-bleeding connection sites on Adrianna. The poor child whimpered and writhed in pain as the assistants completed the procedure. When finished, they stepped away and M'Bana fiddled with the control panel the tubes connected to. A pale blue fluid poured through them and into her body.

She tensed as the compound entered her system. Her complexion paled, and a sheen of perspiration appeared on her face. With her jaw clenched and her eyes squeezed tight, her entire body shook as the chemical cocktail flowed into her.

Except for the hum of the pumps driving the fluid and Adrianna's gasps in response to the torture she endured, the room was deathly quiet. M'Bana spoke near her ear.

"You know what to do."

Her eyes screwed shut, she jerked her head from side to side in defiance. The scientist remained unperturbed and coaxed her. "You know the pain will not go away until you look at him."

She continued to defy him, her eyes closed and tears mixing with the perspiration that now ran down her face.

"Stop it, you bastard!" I shouted. "You're killing her!"

A sharp blow to my hamstrings from one of my guards dropped me to my knees and silenced my protest.

Adrianna's eyes met mine. There was no trace of the animosity or resentment with which she once regarded me. I saw in her an ancient soul that had witnessed far more suffering and horror than anyone deserved to experience in a single lifetime.

But I also sensed something else. It was both similar and unlike my contact with the nanite collective minutes before. Where they were chaotic, this presence, though frightened, was coherent enough to be familiar to me. Looking into her eyes, I realized I was somehow inside Adrianna's mind, and she in mine.

Thoughts, deeper than words could articulate, were exchanged, and in an instant I experienced all the horror and torture she had endured at the hands of these bastards during her short life. Nothing was hidden between us, yet I held no embarrassment about anything she now knew of my chequered past. There were no more secrets, only shared experience and understanding.

Together we pushed down her pain, and through her eyes I saw the man behind the glass. Inside her memories I witnessed what they had made her do dozens of times before. The physical agony compelled her to do it once more. I fought to maintain our connection as the suffering she experienced manifested in my body.

We focussed on the pillar. Time slowed, and one by one, Adrianna connected with the individual nanites as they were released from their captivity. Though invisible to the naked eye, through the mental link I was aware of every one of them. The construct melted away as the microscopic particles dispersed throughout the chamber. My chaotic connection with them was now more coherent, but feeble, as if I were but an observer.

Suppressing my panic, I struggled to exert my own influence on the nanites to force them back into an inert state, but nothing I did affected them. Helpless, I looked on as Adrianna was compelled by the pain to continue liberating the tiny machines from their torpor.

They identified the organic molecules of the man, and I recognized their primitive compulsion to consume them.

To everyone in the room, the man screamed for no apparent reason. Futilely, he struggled against the restraints, crying out in fear as blood dripped from his nose and ears. The bleeding fingernails of his flailing hands grew crimson as his body was broken down from within. Soon, the gaping, bloody holes where his eyes had once been signalled the final stage of his ordeal.

These nanites were more aggressive than my prior experience with them. It seemed as though they were driven by the same chemical whip that forced Adrianna to release them.

When the man was nothing more than a bloody stain in the chair, the scientists rushed to adjust the controls that drove the blue fluid through the tubes.

Still connected with the girl, I experienced her relax as the pain abated. Simultaneously, the presence of the nanites grew less distinct, until I could no longer sense them. The organic pillar construct reformed within the chamber. Without the whip of Adrianna's chemically enhanced contact driving them, they reverted to their inert hibernation state.

Mundi's gravelly voice jerked my attention back, and my connection with Adrianna was severed.

"That was an impressive demonstration, gentlemen. When will this weapon be ready to deploy?"

Beaming, M'Bana replied, "It is too early to tell, Dominus. More tests are required to refine the formula. Currently the range of influence is restricted to a few metres, and the fragility of the girl's physiology limits the time she can endure the fluid."

"How far can you push her?"

"This was the longest this particular subject has been exposed. As you can see, she is near physical exhaustion, and there are the unfortunate violent side effects we need to sort out. Until we can produce additional clones, we dare not proceed too aggressively."

Adrianna slumped in the chair, her eyes rolled to the top of her head. She was conscious, but only barely.

"Well, it is fortunate that we have acquired the source," said Mundi as he directed his attention to me. In his eyes I saw my entire future laid out before me.

I would be treated as seed stock and put into suspended animation to provide cells for Mundi's mad scientists. Adrianna would die as they continued to drive her past the limit of her endurance, only to be repeatedly replaced by duplicates until the perfect weapon was created. After that, nothing would prevent Mundi from expanding his empire throughout the solar system. Residing within Felix's body, the despot would rule unopposed for generations.

"Dominus, forgive my interruption, but we must consider what to do about Talus Varr," said Chen.

"What about him?"

"By now he is on his way here with a major force. He will attack in less than an hour."

"This facility is well defended, sire," said Morgan. "While there is no need for concern about the rebels penetrating the perimeter defences, it would be wise to spirit you away to a safer location as soon as possible."

"Transfer Felix Altius to my personal ship, as well as the females," said Mundi. He glanced at the bloody husk in the isolation chamber. "Where is the neutron device this traitor was to have used?"

"Secured in the armoury."

"Bring it here."

"Dominus?"

"The weapon will destroy every living thing inside a

hundred-kilometre radius but leave the equipment intact for later retrieval. We will evacuate, and when Talus Varr arrives at this undefended facility, curiosity will compel him to search it. When we trigger the device, as he would have in his attempt to assassinate me, it is he who shall die, along with his pathetic rebellion."

CHAPTER 41

Even though our plan had been flipped on its head by Chen's betrayal, that was only the final insult in the debacle I was responsible for. If we had left Mars when we had the chance, Dylan would still be alive, my friends would be safe, and none of this would be happening. Mundi would have died of one of his multiple ailments, and everyone would be able to muddle through an ordinary life.

But now I was destined to become a human Popsicle and seed stock for thousands of weaponized clones as they marched out to conquer everything. No matter how much I played the wishing card in my head, nothing altered the fact that I'd pretty much fucked up the universe.

Mundi and his cortege left to prepare for the evacuation, leaving three guards to escort us to his ship in the hangar. Two of them removed the restraints from Adrianna's limp body and lifted her from the chair. The third guard poked me in the back with his weapon, prompting me down the corridor.

Fear gripped me as my options were reduced with every step. My choice was simple. I could meekly allow myself to be herded to my fate, or I could fight. I had no illusion that I could escape; I was manacled and under armed guard. The best outcome I could hope for was to be killed by them if I put up a big enough struggle. The reality was they could smack me around and drag my unconscious body to Mundi's ship. Nothing I could do would change my future.

Adrianna had regained her senses and stumbled unassisted as we approached the door to a lift. When it opened a cramped space, barely large enough for three adults, was revealed. One of her guards grabbed her by the upper arm and led her inside. The soldier escorting me nudged me in the back to follow, and soon the four of us were standing in the crowded car as the door closed.

My escort, a head taller than I, faced me and exhaled his garlic-laced breath in my face. Adrianna's remaining guard stood behind her as the car lurched into motion. His stance was casual, his weapon slung over his shoulder, and he seemed distracted. Maybe he was annoyed at the trivial nature of his assignment, but his attention was not on his charge, and he began a conversation with his companion.

Adrianna's eyes caught mine. While she appeared weak and resigned to her fate, a familiar fire was in her eye. Seeming much older than her apparent age, her glance communicated the message that I should get ready.

Without warning, a feral scream of rage erupted from the diminutive girl, and before anyone could react, she leapt on the back of my guard. Her nails raked across his eyes as she buried her teeth into the side of his neck. A spray of blood from his punctured artery painted the interior of the lift and splashed in the face of his stunned companion.

The other soldier tried to pry the wildcat from his companion's back, exposing his own to me. Reacting at the opportunity, I lunged at him from behind and dropped my manacled hands around his exposed neck. Burying both of my knees into the small of his back, I pulled with all my weight against the chain of my restraints.

Panicked and choking, my victim threw himself backward to drive me into the wall and dislodge me, but I held tight and maintained my pressure on his throat. I felt the cartilage collapse, and moments later, he fell to the blood-soaked floor under my unrelenting stranglehold.

The man Adrianna attacked had fallen and desperately attempted to stop the bloody flow spurting from the savage wound she had dealt him. As the man lay dying, she patted his body down until she found the key to my manacles.

While I freed myself, she picked up the man's dropped weapon, incongruously large in her small hands. She looked at me for the first time since the attack, and I could still see the rage behind her eyes. Images of her shooting me or ripping my throat out flashed in my mind, and I pressed to the side of the car.

Her entire body shook as she handed me the gun.

"The blue stuff makes me angry," she said, as if in apology.

I examined the carnage around us and noted that the elevator was almost at the hangar level.

"Do you think you can stay that way a bit longer?"

A frown creased her forehead. "I want to hurt them all."

I smiled. "Let's see how many we can get then."

I didn't want to fill her with any false hope. The best we could expect to accomplish would be to take some of them out before they gunned us down. Adrianna, with the element of surprise, might be able to fell one or two. Despite my deplorable marksmanship skills, I would attempt to match her. The weapon I held was a different design than the one Chen trained me on. It had no targeting computer to assist me, meaning I had to rely on what little skill I possessed. I basically planned on spraying and praying. Perhaps I might get lucky and hit somebody.

The simplest course of action would be to hide somewhere in the facility until they departed without us. We could then try to run as far from the place as possible and hope we didn't die in the neutron blast. By the look on Adrianna's face, I didn't think I had any chance of persuading her of that hopeless plan.

Our only real opportunity to survive, if we even had one, stood in delaying their departure until Talus Varr arrived. That was a long shot. If we got ourselves killed too soon, they'd have time to recover cells from our bodies before their escape. They'd begin the cloning process again, and our effort might accomplish very little in the end.

The car jerked to a halt, and the door opened to the hangar. We caught a break in there being a stack of crates between us and the open space where Mundi's ship stood, fuelled and ready for his departure. Hiding behind them, I surveyed the interior while formulating our next step.

Aside from a few technicians readying the aircraft, there were no other people in sight. I worried that Mundi was already aboard when another set of lift doors closer to the ship opened. A stretcher was wheeled out, on which was strapped Felix. Dani walked behind, accompanied by one guard. Chen, Morgan, and Mundi in his wheelchair followed with his four historically costumed bodyguards bringing up the rear. Perhaps the capacity of the lift kept their numbers low, but in all, there were few armed people. Morgan and Chen both sported sidearms, and the Praetorians had replaced their ceremonial short swords with conventional weapons.

Seeing Felix changed my priorities. Killing Mundi became my first and best choice, but since I was such a lousy shot, I would probably only get one opportunity before they spirited him to safety. Felix, on the other hand, was restrained and relatively unguarded. Without him, Mundi would soon be dead of natural causes. Our suicide mission now stood a chance of achieving more than I first envisioned, but it meant I now had to kill my friend.

CHAPTER 42

Being completely out of my depth as a military tactician, I took a moment to try to think the problem through logically. Common sense screamed at me to empty the clip in the direction of the unprotected Felix. With his body unavailable to Mundi, it would mean an early end to the dictatorship and perhaps the war. I might accomplish the same goal by opening fire at Mundi and his escort, possibly saving the lives of my friends in the process. The likelihood was that I wouldn't hit anything before I got myself shot.

I needed to make a decision, but as the window of opportunity closed, I was frozen and uncertain of what to do. It was in that moment that I realized Adrianna was no longer at my side.

Fearful, I scanned the areas of the hangar that were visible from my hiding place. My eyes fell on a movement in the shadow of the aircraft. The girl, not willing to wait for me to act, had decided on her own course of action. By circling around the nose of the ship, she closed in on Dani and Felix.

Suddenly her apparent rashness made sense. Dani was the one she was the most protective of. She already had demonstrated the lengths she would take to defend her. There was no reason to doubt her intentions now.

Adrianna's decision changed everything. I pointed my gun at Mundi. A short hesitation later, my finger squeezed the trigger, and the staccato report of automatic weapon's fire rang in my ears.

Two of Mundi's guards staggered backward, their chests exploding in a spray of blood. The rest of my first volley ricocheted uselessly off walls and support pillars. It didn't take very long for the remaining men to locate my position and start shooting back. I ducked low to the ground as bullets sliced through the transport containers that were my protection, showering me with splinters.

My element of surprise now spent, I peeked through a crack between the crates to see Mundi being rushed back to the elevator under the cover fire of Chen, Morgan, and the remaining Praetorians. I despaired that my one opportunity to kill the old bastard was gone. My only accomplishment was to frighten him and hasten my own death.

I looked toward Felix and Dani, wondering if I should risk going with my first plan when my jaw fell open. Adrianna clung to the back of Dani's guard, scratching at his face and trying to bite him. He dropped his weapon and tried to reach up to pull the snarling harpy from his back. The two of them tumbled to the floor, the man landing heavily, sending the girl sprawling two metres away.

As he rolled to his knees and struggled to stand, Dani, grabbed up the gun, aimed, and shot him four times in the chest.

At the sound of the report, my attackers' attention turned toward her. Both of them directed their fire in Dani's direction. Adrianna was hit and fell to the ground. Another projectile struck Dani and sent her hurtling backward. She impacted and knocked over the stretcher with Felix still restrained to it.

With a scream of rage I raised myself above my cover and unleashed my automatic weapon once more. One of my bullets dropped another guard in his tracks. Morgan dashed behind a support pillar, leaving Chen and the remaining Praetorian to engage me from the elevator alcove.

Recognition crossed Chen's face. All signs of desperation or anxiety evaporated from him. Incredibly, he stepped out into the open, a satisfied smirk on his face. He defied me to shoot him, knowing full well what a terrible shot I was.

Determined to prove him wrong, I popped up to level my weapon at him and was rewarded with a hammer blow to my shoulder. The momentum sent me flying backward into the wall, knocking the wind out of me, and the gun out of my hand. I couldn't feel my left arm, and burning pain emanated from the bleeding wound.

Morgan advanced on me, pistol raised. He noticed my glance at the fallen weapon, just out of my reach. "Ah-ah-ah! Just keep your hands where I can see them."

I considered going for it in the hope that he would kill me, but something I saw made me reevaluate that tactic.

Both Chen and the remaining guard emerged from their cover and slowly moved to join Morgan. They paid no attention to where Dani and Adrianna had fallen.

The Praetorian guard's head exploded in a spray of blood, bone, and brains.

Everyone turned to see what had happened.

Felix wasted no time firing a second round, catching Chen squarely between the eyes.

As Morgan redirected his firearm at Felix, I grabbed my weapon from the floor. Without thought, I raised it and pulled hard on the trigger. One of the bullets found Morgan's back and dropped him to his knees.

Not waiting for him to recover, I fired again, hitting him two more times. He teetered, then fell face first to the floor.

I struggled to stand, then limped to his prone form. Tears filled my eyes as I pressed the muzzle of the gun into the back of Morgan's skull. With every ringing shot I saw Dylan lying in the sand, gasping for breath. I repeatedly fired rounds into Morgan until only the impotent click of the emptied firearm could be heard. I stared through watery eyes at the bloody smear that had once been his head, and I felt numb.

A hand on my shoulder startled me, and with my heart racing, I turned on my assailant. Felix redirected the empty gun away from his head with a gentle grip on my wrist.

"Dani! Adrianna..."

"Their wounds are not life-threatening." He looked to the remains of Morgan then returned his attention to me. "We have to leave before the bomb goes off."

I pulled my arm from his grasp and stooped to pick up Morgan's discarded weapon. When I stood, Felix produced a wad of cloth and pressed it against my wounded shoulder. I put the pistol into my belt and applied pressure to the wound myself.

"Time for you to go, Felix. Take Dani and Adrianna to safety. I have unfinished business here."

"This aircraft is the only means of escape. By now all remaining ground vehicles will have evacuated. If you don't come, you will die. Mundi cannot get away from the blast. He is doomed."

"Maybe, but his survival is nothing I intend leaving to chance."

Felix gazed at me with those milky blue eyes and his expression softened.

I said, "You've come a long way, friend. I wish you and Dani all the happiness you two deserve. Please take care of Adrianna and remember me kindly?"

A sad smile tugged at the corners of his mouth. "Of course we will, friend." He embraced me, careful not to aggravate my wounded shoulder, then returned to the others waiting near the aircraft.

CHAPTER 43

Regis Mundi was no fool. I doubted he or his servant had the technical knowledge to disable the neutron bomb, so I suspected he had a backup plan for how to survive the blast. The only variable I didn't know was how much time remained before it went off. There was a good chance I might not reach him in time, but if there was any way I could put an end to the cancer that was Mundi, I needed to try or die in the attempt.

The doors to the lift opened, and I tentatively poked my head out to survey the empty corridor. Felix's assessment that everyone had evacuated the facility seemed correct. Still, I proceeded with caution, my pistol raised. I no longer worried about my poor marksmanship. The weapon was set to automatic, and the spray and pray technique had worked well for me so far. As it turned out, I had nothing to concern myself with as the place was, indeed, abandoned.

At the open laboratory door I heard voices from within. I paused and lowered the gun to briefly rest my good arm. My shoulder hurt like hell. The wound still bled through the improvised dressing, but it would suffice for the time I had left.

Creeping around the corner, I peered into the lab. Just outside the opened door of the isolation chamber, Mundi and his servant were hunched over a cylindrical device replete with lights and a control panel. It was apparent neither of them had a clue of how to disarm the bomb. With their backs to me, I saw my chance and raised my gun for what I hoped would be the final victory.

Something alerted Mundi's servant to my presence. He looked up, surprise on his face, then pushed his master into the chamber. Cursing my bad luck, I jerked on the trigger and sent a spray of fire in their direction. Blood erupted from the servant's back, and he fell to the floor. With panic in his rheumy eyes, Mundi pulled the door closed and shut his eyes to prompt his CI to lock it.

"Shit! Fuck! Goddamit!" I advanced toward the transparent cage and unleashed my remaining bullets against the impenetrable glass. In a rage I hurled the useless, emptied weapon at it.

Overcoming his shock, the old man stood straighter and grinned in satisfaction. I pressed my face to the wall and glared at him through it as he limped to a panel and turned on the intercom. Before he could gloat, I unleashed a stream of curses that would have made even my mother blush.

"The standard tongue seems to be only fit for profanity," said Mundi, a smug smile plastered on his fat face.

"You fucking son of a bitch!" I screamed, pounding on the glass.

"Vent all you want, you little whore. Within a few minutes I will be the only one of us to survive." He admiringly surveyed the walls that protected him. "I am quite safe in here."

My energy spent, I wanted to collapse to the floor and cry. I trudged to the bomb and checked the interface. Any hopes I might have entertained of it possessing a simple "off" button were dispelled. I had no clue how to disarm the thing. The countdown timer showed about fifteen minutes remained. After that, I would be dead and Mundi free to continue his reign of terror.

Still not willing to give up, I scanned the room for anything that might prove helpful. My eyes fell on the seat that had been used to torture Adrianna. Looking back to the isolation chamber, I saw the organic-looking structure of dormant nanites and smiled.

My injured shoulder hampering me, I struggled to drag the

dead body of the servant to the door Mundi hid behind.

"The door is locked from this side."

I propped the corpse against it. Standing, I took a closer look at the nanite pillar.

Noticing what attracted my attention, Mundi said, "You have no influence on the Ares nanites while they are in this chamber."

"Uh-huh," I said while I walked back to the chair.

"These walls inhibit quantum connectivity and shield me from all forms of radiation. There is nothing you can do."

"Yup, I know that." I picked up one of the hoses and noted the needle was still present.

"What are you doing?" he asked.

"I'm thinking of testing a theory." I examined the control interface, gratified it was a simple and common design.

"You cannot harm me," he said, his voice now shaking with uncertainty.

"Maybe not, but I just want to see how this thing works. Call it professional curiosity."

Turning on the device, the pump pushed fluid through the tubes. Holding up the free end, I watched the blue liquid spray from the opening.

Sitting in the chair, I poised the needle over my leg and muttered to myself, "I bet this is going to hurt like shit."

"What did you say?"

Looking up at Mundi, I replied, "I said, get ready to kiss your fat ass goodbye."

Before I could lose my nerve, I jammed it into my thigh. The muscle burned like I had just stuck it with a hot poker, and I slammed my head into the back of the seat and ground my teeth. The pain spread through my body. I wanted to peel my skin off and dive into a pool of icy water. How Adrianna had endured this torture on a regular basis was beyond my ability to imagine.

Forcing my eyes open, I focussed on the pillar behind the protective glass. Time seemed to slow down. One by one the nanites replied to my call, each seemingly grateful to be no longer isolated. At my urging, they released themselves from their stasis form and flowed from the melting structure.

Realizing what was happening, Mundi flew into a panic. Squealing like a frightened child, he rushed to the door, but the body of his dead servant blocked it from opening. He pounded on it until his hands left bloody streaks on the glass as his flesh broke down. Blood dripped from his nose, ears, eyes, and mouth.

Overwhelmed, his corpulent form fell to the floor and began to dissolve before my eyes, even as he continued to cry out for mercy. Eventually his voice became a gurgle before it halted entirely. Within minutes the microscopic machines had fulfilled their base program and consumed every molecule of organic matter inside the chamber. By the time they were finished, not even a bloodstain remained on the toga that the old dictator had worn.

With some regret, I mustered the strength to urge them back into their dormant state. As I felt my connection with the last of them ebb, I reached down and yanked the needle from my leg.

Mundi was gone. Dylan was avenged and my friends were safe. Though still in pain, I allowed my mind to dwell on all the happy memories my loved ones had blessed me with over the years. A tear flowed down my cheek as I said my goodbyes to them. Maybe the blue toxin flowing through my body would kill me before the neutron bomb did. I didn't care how I would die. I accepted my fate.

As my eyes dimmed and the room darkened, I saw Dylan standing before me, grinning with pride. We would be together forever, and I couldn't have been happier.

CHAPTER 44

A distant ringing in my ears grew louder as I regained consciousness.

"Easy, Sugar," said Dani. "You're safe now."

"Dani? Are you dead? What happened?"

"No one died, hon, at least nobody worth anything. You're on the ship. Felix fetched you."

"Indeed," said Felix from the pilot seat, "my passengers would not permit me to launch without you."

"Adrianna sort of growled at him." A broad smile graced her cherub cheeks.

"Really?" I asked, looking at the dishevelled waif sitting next to Dani. She smiled shyly, reached down, and squeezed my hand.

Felix, the only one of us not shot and bleeding all over the expensive upholstery, piloted Mundi's personal shuttle. Once airborne, and not a moment too soon, he sent the coded signal to Talus Varr telling him to abort the attack. We barely had enough time to get out of the blast zone of the neutron bomb that Mundi had intended for the rebels.

Dani sat back in her seat. "With Mundi gone—he is dead, isn't he?"

It hurt to nod. "Yes."

Dani smiled in satisfaction. "With the old goat finished, what will happen next?"

I shrugged and winced in pain. "Hopefully Varr can quickly

end the conflict and form a new government."

"I don't trust him."

"Neither do I, but he has the best chance of pulling the planet together."

"Well, we won't be sticking around to see how this shit show ends. I have a business and a fleet to run."

"You only have two ships, darling," said Felix.

"It's 'Admiral darling' to you, mister."

After the laughter died down, she turned to me. "How about you, Mel? You're coming with us, right?"

"I don't know yet."

The smile faded from her face. I grasped her hand.

"I need to tie up a few loose ends. Give me time."

She nodded and wiped away a tear.

CHAPTER 45

With the death of Mundi, Talus Varr reactivated his dormant network of spies and contacts and began the long process of eliminating the last of Mundi's sycophants who still held out hope they could assume power. Within a few days, the rebels confidently declared victory.

We all spent the next couple of weeks recovering from our wounds in a rebel medical facility and watching history unfold. When the transition was completed, the new government eased travel restrictions, and it became time for Felix and Dani to leave Mars.

"You're sure I can't change your mind?"

"Dani, I promised to be Varr's poster girl, and I keep my word."

"Well, just remember your promise to join us when your term is ended."

"I will."

"Talus Varr deserves credit for being a clever son of a bitch. Turning the Mother of Mars into a titled office for the new government was a stroke of evil genius to get you to stick around."

"It's for four years, then somebody else gets to use the honorific, and I get my freedom."

Dani hugged me and whispered into my ear. "Don't trust him, Sugar. Do your time and then get the hell out of here."

I laughed. "You make it sound like a prison sentence."

"Do I?" She didn't smile.

The awkward moment was soon broken by Adrianna approaching with Felix. She broke away from him and ran up to hug me.

"I'm going to miss you, little sister," I said. It had taken the two of us a few days to work out a comfortable compromise on how to describe our relationship. Technically she was my clone, which made her a twin, so the sibling epitaph seemed appropriate. We certainly fought like sisters.

"I'll miss you too. When you join us, I'll teach you how to fight."

"I'm sure you will," I said as I tousled her hair.

Our bond is kind of creepy and sort of metaphysical, what with the brief sharing of consciousness. Only the two of us can possibly understand it. I call her little sis in front of the others, but alone with each other, we both knew we are the result of what happens when the other path is taken in a lifetime. I could only hope she would learn from my mistakes. I was confident Dani would make sure she did.

Felix embraced me warmly. "Remember the protocols I taught you. You only need call should you require our help."

"Thanks, Felix. I think I'll be safe, but I'm glad you've still got my back, even if I am a better marksman than you." I grinned.

There was a friendly disagreement between us over who actually killed Morgan. Felix contended that he fired the killing shot to the head while I reached for my gun. Since nothing remained of his skull to perform an autopsy on, neither of us could prove our claim.

I didn't mind sharing the victory with him. He had no idea what I considered doing to him to stop Mundi. Normally, I would allow him to declare Morgan's death as his, but I simply couldn't permit that. Dylan needed to be avenged. I had to be the one to avenge him. It didn't make his absence from my life any less painful, but it perhaps let his soul rest more peacefully.

We all wept when it was finally time for the three of them to depart; well, everyone except Felix, though he did look a bit sad too. Going with them sounded like a really good idea, but in the end, aside from my promise to Varr, I couldn't bring myself to leave for reasons I didn't share.

My official reason was that I felt obliged to keep my word to Talus Varr. Mars was in a critical political vacuum with the death of Regis Mundi. Many Martians were not prepared to cede power to the rebel faction; Varr had too many old ties to the former dictator and the previous government for the majority to learn to trust him. The new parliament had to test their wings and needed the Mother of Mars as a rallying point for the people's support. I would do my part.

My secret reasons for remaining revolved around what I experienced while killing Mundi. While I was connected to the nanites, masked behind the blinding pain dwelt a familiar presence. Somehow, during that connection I also touched the larger remnant of the alien collective consciousness still marooned in the asteroid belt. More frightening, I got the distinct sense that it was surprised I still lived. It definitely didn't seem happy about it.

Of course, the intensity of the moment has faded, and my certainty that it was real sometimes falters. Maybe the drug flowing through me at the time made me hallucinate the whole thing, like the vision of Dylan before I passed out. If there is even a remote chance that the Continuum remains a threat, Mars will become the final battleground, and I might be the only one to stand in their way.

Despite my promise to Dani, I expected to be on Mars for a long time yet.

CHAPTER 46

Dancing dust devils and drifting sand were the only moving things in the ancient valley. All life and hope had abandoned the place, leaving behind only shattered machinery and a single marked grave. Night fell with the temperature hours before and the two moons, Phobos and Deimos, rose high in the clear, star-strewn sky.

Gradually, a solitary pinpoint of light traced a rising path from the horizon. It grew as it approached in silence, until an observer would have seen a multifaceted object reflecting the starshine as it slowed and halted over the valley.

More gracefully than its size would belie, the enormous ellipsoid floated a hundred metres above the ground for several seconds before it descended to hover centimetres from the cairn.

Millions of microscopic machines sloughed invisibly from the vessel's crystalline surface and burrowed into the sand. Within moments, the earth heaved and once carefully laid stones tumbled from the object being exhumed.

An organic sarcophagus rose from the grasp of the parting soil and passed through the bottom of the floating crystal.

As silently as it approached, the vessel departed, vanishing among the billions of stars.

The dust devils continued their dance, and the incessant breeze began to refill the emptied grave with drifting sand.

Continue to follow the story of Mel Destin in the first two books of the *Mars Ascendant* series:

The Ares Weapon, *Book 1 in the Mars Ascendant Series*. Available at Amazon http://myBook.to/AresWeapon

Melanie Destin's life is a mess. In a desperate attempt to start over, she accepts an interplanetary salvage job that will pay her enough to rebuild a new life on Mars. When she learns the real purpose of the mission is to recover an apocalyptic virus, everything begins to unravel...

Planetary governments compete to control the pathogen which the expedition leader plans to steal. Meanwhile the corporation that hired her wants to eliminate anyone involved...

With her life in danger and not knowing who to trust, Mel must find a way to keep the virus out of the wrong hands. If she fails, billions will die...

Get your copy at http://myBook.to/AresWeapon

Mother of Mars   *Book 2 of the Mars Ascendant Series*. Available at Amazon http://mybook.to/Mother-of-Mars

All life in the solar system is about to be wiped out...

Dr. Melanie Destin thought she'd started a new life on Mars. While searching for answers to her mysterious past, she becomes embroiled in political intrigue and is falsely accused of assassinating the Martian High Chancellor...

On the run, with a price on her head and the authorities in close pursuit, Mel must evade capture long enough to accomplish the one task that can save her life; destroy the source of the deadly Ares nano-virus...

Little does she realize the pathogen is not what it seems, and her meddling will make her the catalyst for the destruction of all life in the solar system.

Pick up your copy today at this Amazon link http://mybook.to/Mother-of-Mars

Did you like this book?

Why not share the good news? Go to http://myBook.to/ChildofMars and add your review on Amazon and you are done. The link will take you to the book page. At the top, under the title, you can click and add your review.

I appreciate your support. Reviews are extremely important for marketing in the competitive ebook marketplace. Reviews give social proof to potential customers and make them more inclined to take a chance on a new author such as myself.

Do you want to read more?

If you liked this book, I am humbly gratified. If you liked this book enough to want to read more of my work, I am thrilled. Fortunately, there is a way for this to happen by joining my reader list. By signing up to my list you will also receive a **free ebook** containing a short story about one of Mel's early life exploits on Terra and a collection of other short stories, not available anywhere else. You will also receive advance notice of all future books, well in advance of publication, have opportunities to sign on as a member of my Advanced Review Team and receive a prepublication copy of the book for review purposes on Amazon.

Claim your free ebook by going to www.prudenauthor.com

Acknowledgements

Just as it takes a village to raise a child, writing a book requires a community of supporters. This work would not have been possible without the support, encouragement and critical eye of my wife, Colleen. Thanks to Allister Thompson for his meticulous proofreading. I also want to give a special thanks to my dedicated and enthusiastic street team who all suffered through the beta reading of my work and offered helpful insights in how to make it better. To all my supportive family and friends on Facebook, your encouragement helped me along when I thought this project would never end. Finally, to all my readers, my most humble thanks. I hope this book was worth the time you made to read it.

About the Author

D.M.(Doug) Pruden worked as a professional geophysicist for 35 years in the petroleum industry. For most of his life he has been plagued with stories banging around inside his head that demanded to be let out into the world. He currently spends his time as an empty nester in Calgary, Alberta, Canada with his long suffering wife of 35 years, Colleen. When he isn't writing science fiction stories, he likes to spend his time playing with his granddaughters and working on improving his golf handicap.

Go to www.prudenauthor.com and sign up to the email list. You will receive a free, never before published ebook about Mel Destin's early life on Terra as well as a collection of short stories. List members will receive early publication notice of upcoming books, blog posts and other goodies from time to time.

If you are social network inclined, Doug can be found on Facebook at https://www.facebook.com/prudenauthor/ and on Twitter at https://twitter.com/prudenauthor . Stop by and say hello.